Firefly in a Box

Susan Honeyman, Series Editor

Firefly in a Box

An Anthology of Soviet Kid Lit

Translated and edited by

Anna Krushelnitskaya and Dmitri Manin

University Press of Mississippi / Jackson

The University Press of Mississippi is the scholarly publishing agency of the Mississippi Institutions of Higher Learning: Alcorn State University, Delta State University, Jackson State University, Mississippi State University, Mississippi University for Women, Mississippi Valley State University, University of Mississippi, and University of Southern Mississippi.

www.upress.state.ms.us

The University Press of Mississippi is a member of the Association of University Presses.

Cover art by Sara Kendall
All interior images are from private collections unless otherwise noted.

Manufactured in the United States of America
∞

Publisher: University Press of Mississippi, Jackson, USA
Authorised GPSR Safety Representative: Easy Access System Europe - Mustamae tee 50, 10621 Tallinn, Estonia, *gpsr.requests@easproject.com*

Library of Congress Cataloging-in-Publication Data available

Print LCCN 2025013913
ISBN 9781496856579 (hardback)
ISBN 9781496856586 (trade paperback)
ISBN 9781496856593 (EPUB single)
ISBN 9781496856609 (EPUB institutional)
ISBN 9781496856616 (PDF single)
ISBN 9781496856623 (PDF institutional)

British Library Cataloging-in-Publication Data available

Contents

Firefly in a Box

Introduction

Anna Krushelnitskaya and Dmitri Manin

The idea for this anthology of Soviet children's rhyme and short prose initially came out of a desire for cultural brokerage. In 2020, we set out to compile, translate, and present an introductory selection of popular Russian-language Soviet children's texts, the cultural currency, potency, and valence of which are similar in scale to those of *Green Eggs and Ham* by Dr. Seuss, the *Curious George* books by Margret Rey and H. A. Rey, and *Make Way for Ducklings* by Robert McCloskey in US children's literature. In this, our original intent may have been humble; yet, as our work on the volume progressed, and both scholarly essays and a discussion of our translation practices were added, we found that the resultant book, in its hybridity, now meets several aims and serves various audiences.

The corpus of Soviet children's literature is voluminous, complex, and multifaceted. The selection of texts that we ultimately chose to translate for this anthology is by no means an exhaustive representation of popular Soviet children's literature, nor is it intended as such. To narrow and clarify the scope of the book, we opted not to include long fiction and nonfiction, focusing instead on short prose and rhyme. The offered texts vary in theme and didactic messaging, and they encompass reading difficulty levels from picture books to texts intended for middle school grades. The texts were chosen on the basis of how recognizable they are to the Soviet native and are organized by author and chronology. The selection contains works by Soviet writers who were, and remain, well known and much read in the (post)-Soviet space: Samuil Marshak, Kornei Chukovsky, Agniia Barto, Arkadii Gaidar, Vladimir Mayakovsky, Viktor Dragunskii, and more. Texts by these authors have been issued and reissued dozens of times by various publishing houses in different Soviet republics; they came illustrated by a plethora of excellent book artists and were adapted for the stage, for radio, EP (extended play) and LP (long play) recordings, film, filmstrips, and animated films—the last two often as artistic and striking as the respective book illustrations. The relative influence of these authors and their creative output on the history and shape of Soviet children's literature, the features and merits of their writing, and the literary and extraliterary factors of their enduring success vary, as they remain a subject of scholarly investigation and criticism in the Russophone sphere and beyond; one shared trait of all the included texts is that they are mainstays of Soviet kidlit.

During the Soviet years, many texts featured in this volume were published in English in the USSR by Progress, Raduga, and Malysh—publishing houses tasked with disseminating Soviet ideology and culture internationally. As a rule, text selections were made based on the ideas and goals of the Communist government, and the translations, varied in quality, were created by translators these publishers often employed: Dorian Rottenberg, Tom Botting, Avril Pyman, Lois Zellikoff, and a handful of others. Modest effort in popularizing Soviet kidlit was in evidence in the English-speaking world, as well, in particular during the détente; in the United States, for instance, an anthology of rather heterogeneous texts titled *A Harvest of Russian Children's Literature: A Treasury for All Ages* (ed. Miriam Morton, University of California Press/Cambridge University Press) was offered in four printings between 1967 and 1970. In it, poems by Marshak and Chukovsky appear in translations by Margaret Wettling and Miriam Morton, and children's prose by Kataev in Fainna Glagoleva's translation. In post-Soviet years, a handful of new translations of Soviet kidlit came out in English, including children's poems by Mayakovsky, Mandelstam, and Kharms translated by Eugene Ostashevsky (*The Fire Horse: Children's Poems by Vladimir Mayakovsky, Osip Mandelstam and Daniil Kharms*, NYRB Children's Collection, USA, 2017) and Jamie Gambrell's translations of Marshak's *Baggage* (Tate Publishing, 2013) and Chukovsky's *Telephone* (NorthSouth, 1996). While the available selection of Soviet kidlit in English is not negligible, it is far from plentiful, and finding older, out-of-print offerings often requires archival research. With this volume, we aim to supplement the existing corpus of English translations of quintessential Soviet children's texts. Finding comparisons between Soviet era translations (an inquiry into which would certainly, in our view, be timely and worthwhile both in translation studies and culture studies) and our new versions will prove useful to translation scholars and practitioners, especially if they focus on translating for the young. To assist scholarly search, we cite the names of certain Soviet authors in two English spellings in this volume: one standard for current publications, the other typical for earlier transliteration conventions.

In a departure from usual academic practice, the translations in this book are literary rather than literal. That is, because we don't treat them as mere material for scholarly studies, we aspire, first and foremost, to convey these little pieces of literature in their entirety: message, voice, and playfulness in a tightly wrapped package. We didn't want to leave the reader puzzled as to why these texts proved so central to the Soviet and post-Soviet culture—why they were so popular and so memorable—by providing a potentially dry, if technically "accurate" translation; that's why we set out to render in English the literary merits of the originals as best we could. To meet this goal, in addition to employing our professional skills, we relied on our own Soviet childhood memories and the insight our childhood experiences afforded us. As young children, we heard these stories and poems read and recited to us; we read them ourselves when we eventually learned to read; later, we read many of them to our own children. Such firsthand native encounters with these works of Soviet children's literature—particularly rhyme—informed our intent to produce translations that could themselves serve as children's texts in English in form and meaning. We address our translation process and outcomes in more detail in "Practitioners' Notes on Translating Soviet Children's Literature" to discuss how kidlit travels between languages from the instrumental point of view.

For centuries, illustrations have been essential to books for children. They help the child picture the plot and characters and bridge the gap between words and mental images. Children's book art carries the spirit and flavor of time and place and provides valuable insight into relevant contexts to adults and children alike, especially when the reading audience is removed from the historical moment at hand. Art depicting how children were dressed or what toy trucks and busy streets looked like back in the early—or late—Soviet times can enrich our perception of the respective texts. By studying and juxtaposing book art samples from different decades in, for instance, US and Soviet publishing, we may find that American and Soviet illustrations of the 1960s are similar, and both are significantly different from the visual style of the 1950s. In that way, we may begin to explore the evolution of Soviet children's book illustration and its place in the matrix of world children's book art. More scholarship and expertise in Soviet illustration is needed, and, while it is out of scope for this volume to provide an investigation of children's book art, we illustrate this anthology with images from Soviet books and filmstrips precisely to spur that investigation. We believe that the illustrations included—some done in signature styles by acclaimed artists, some by less-known book illustrators to the accepted standards of the day—complement the featured texts well and will help the reader understand and enjoy them.

For most of the twentieth century, Soviet literature, including works for children, was academically investigated through the lens of ideology. With these new translations, we invite exploration of Soviet kidlit as a children's literature proper, which is much more than just a vehicle for ideology. Soviet kidlit was forged under new social pressures at the time when, past the avant-garde years, children's lit was often the only venue available for writers to engage in literary experimentation and innovation. In cutting the language fabric in kidlit shape, we bring the texts in this book not only to Slavists—many of whom, indeed, are able to read the Russian originals—but to students of Russian language, literature, and culture; to children's lit scholars whose language expertise does not include Russian; and to lay audiences who may want to read these poems and short stories for their literary merits, whether by themselves or to kids.

As for the scholarly part of the book, we wanted to sample a broad range of approaches and methodologies applicable to our material. We thus invited scholars with different research interests to participate with articles on the topic of their own choosing, inspired by the selected works of Soviet children's prose and rhyme. The resulting contributions investigate much, but not all, of the offered literary material and cover many angles of inquiry without exhausting all possibilities for research.

The scholarly section of this volume opens with Svetlana Maslinskaya's discussion of the longevity of children's books in the framework of literary canon studies. The formation of the children's canon after the Bolshevik Revolution of 1917, its development during the Soviet era, and especially its evolution after the breakdown of the USSR are the main topics of her chapter, "To Keep and to Expand: The Canon of Soviet Children's Literature in Contemporary Publishing in Russia."

Serguei Oushakine's chapter, "In the Interlude: The Search for Form and Method in Early Soviet Children's Poetry," is devoted to investigating and outlining the process through which new Soviet children's literature was formed and defined in the 1920s and 1930s.

Marina Balina spotlights the poet Agniia Barto in an in-depth investigation of purposeful empathy building through the use of narrative imagination in Barto's verse in "Agniia Barto's Fun Rhymes:

Lost Toys, Torn Paws, and Emotional Maturation." She argues that Barto's poems skillfully incorporate pedagogical elements through literary devices without being overtly didactic.

Sibelan Forrester is interested in the interaction between literary texts for children and folklore. She explores echoes and connections between folkloric texts and the work of Arkadii Gaidar and Valentin Kataev in "People's Stories for the Kids: Folklore in Soviet Children's Literature." How folkloric elements are manifested in the work of these authors and what purposes they serve are the two main subjects of Forrester's essay.

Ainsley Morse and Dmitri Manin reflect on the interplay between Soviet and British children's poetry in "Baa-baa People's Sheep: On the Adventures of English Children's Poetry in Soviet Literature." They focus mostly on Marshak and Chukovsky, the two founding fathers of Soviet children's poetry, who were, at the same time, preeminent translators of rhyme from English.

The chapters by Balina, Maslinskaya, and Oushakine were translated by the editors from the original Russian in close collaboration with the authors.

More than half of this book was completed before Russia's full-scale war in Ukraine began in 2022. As we finalize the manuscript and write this introduction, we grapple with the incongruous but unavoidable task of reconciling our original intent with the inconceivable realities of Russia's barbaric aggression. During wartime, any study of the literatures of the aggressor state that is not overtly and unabashedly critical risks being taken as a tacit apologia of the actions and ideologies of the aggressor or, at a minimum, as an expression of indifference toward the harm inflicted by it. Being fully cognizant of the humanitarian and economic disaster that Russia's war has brought on Ukraine, we, the editors and translators of this anthology, couldn't but put our project on hold for the first six months of the war, and we seriously considered abandoning it altogether. We didn't foresee the events of 2022, and we don't know what awaits in the future. Now we can only hope that this peaceful investigation of Soviet children's literature—an investigation we once felt was robbed of meaning by the war—will again make sense to the readership as well as to the editorial team itself and to the contributing scholars who worked on this collection. If this book can help others to understand and interpret the Soviet roots of contemporary Russia's political climate and public sentiment, all the better; however, we hope that readers of this book will find value in it that goes beyond the Cold War standby of "learning the language of the enemy." We aspire to present this volume as an open-ended enterprise—a point from which many explorations can begin.

We would like to extend our sincere thanks to Marina Balina for her help in structuring the book, assistance with copyright issues, and unwavering championing of the study of children's literature in general; to Serguei Oushakine for his help in our work with Soviet book illustration reprints; to the anonymous reviewers of the manuscript for the necessary probing questions and constructive suggestions; and to the academic editor Elizabeth Stern, whose eagle eye and fundamental expertise in style formatting were much needed and much appreciated.

Part I

Poetry

Zinaida Aleksandrova

My Teddy Bear (1940)

I will make a shirt for Teddy.
I made shorts for him already,
With a pocket, nice and neat,
So he could bring a little treat.

Soup is bubbling, ready soon.
Let us get a nice big spoon!
Don't sit down to eat because
First we need to wash your paws.

Wear a bib, for goodness' sake!
Eat some steak, then eat some cake.
Drink your milk and do not pout.
Now, get dressed and let's go out!

These are duckies, these are chicks.
That's a puppy chewing sticks.
Do not call him, let him be.
We don't need him. Run with me!

Baby goat here, looking gruff,
Drinks his water from the trough.

Don't be scared, that's just a goose!
I'm scared when he is on the loose.

We will walk this narrow beam,
We will jump into the stream!
We will swim, we will have fun,
We'll dry our britches in the sun!

Teddy starts to stomp and play!
Then, the bridge begins to sway!
Ripples ripple in the eddy . . .
Puppy, puppy! Get my Teddy!

Now my Teddy's sopping wet!
His plush fur is not dry yet.
The puppy jumps around us.
I think my mom will ground us!

(Tr. Anna Krushelnitskaya)

Agniya Barto

Molly Made of Rubber (1930)

We saw her and we bought her,
A dolly made of rubber
Named Molly Made of Rubber.
We brought her from the shop.
She was a little flubber,
That Molly Made of Rubber,

Kept falling if we dropped her,
Kept plopping in the slop.
We'll rub with alcohol
That muddy rubber doll,
We'll scrub the doll with alcohol
And tell her she must stop
And not be such a flubber,
That Molly Made of Rubber,
Or else, or else we'll scrub her
And return her to the shop.

(Tr. Anna Krushelnitskaya)

Me and Tamara (1933)

Tanya brags: "We're managers,
We're managers of bandages!
Me and Tamara walk together,
Me and Tamara work together!
If you're hurt,
Come be our patient!
We're in charge of
Medication.

We have ice packs
To apply.
We're the Red Cross,
Tam and I.

Heat packs, too, and if you're worse,
We can make you herbal tea!
Tam and I are each a nurse.
Come see her or come see me."

But they're out of luck because
All their iodine and gauze,
All their splints,
They see no use:
Not a splinter,
Not a bruise . . .

Finally, our Red Cross crew
Has a nursing job to do.
Somebody got hurt, at last!
Nurses! Take your places fast.

But why is it that Tanya swayed,
Looking terribly afraid?
Why is it that Tanya swayed,
Dropping all of her first aid?

Tanya's hands grew weak: "Oh my!
Vova has a cut! There's blood!"
Our Red Cross began to cry.
Tears came running in a flood.

"We have bandages to use,
Pads,
And gauze,
And iodine.
Now, can I please be excused?
It's Tamara's turn to help,
Not mine."

Tanya brags: "We're managers,
We're managers of bandages!
Me and Tamara walk together,
Me and Tamara work together!

Illustration by Naum Tseitlin in *My s Tamaroi* by Agniia Barto (Moscow: Detskaia literatura, 1967)

We have potions for our patients,
We have heat packs to apply!
We are nurses,
Tam and I.
Tamara treats them.
I just cry."

(Tr. Anna Krushelnitskaya)

Chatterbox (1934)

Vovka says I like to talk!
I like to talk? Now, that's a crock!
How would I even find the time,
When in fact I got no time!

There's drama club, there's photo club,
There's choir, of which I'm also part,
And then I also have art club,
Which all the kids said we should start.

I was just sitting on the bleachers,
And there goes one of my old teachers:
"Both drama and photography—
It all seems like too much to me.
In the end, my little friend,
Just stick with one activity."

I pick the photo club, to start . . .
I also want to keep my part
In the choir, and there's art too,
Which all the kids said we should do.

Did Vovka say I like to talk?
Now that's a crock. When do I talk?
How would I even find the time,
When in fact I got no time!

I will be the class monitor
Till I'm old, or later.
But I really always wanted to
Become an aviator.
I would rise in a zeppelin . . .

And, by the way, what is that thing?
Could be a special zeppelin
For monitors to settle in!

I have tons of work this term in
Both my Russian class and German.

We got homework in reading
And a grammar exercise.
I sit there by the window—
Some kid pops before my eyes!
He says, "Come out here, chop-chop!
I'll give you a lollipop."
And I say, "Tons of work this term in
Both my Russian class and German!"
He says, "Come out here, chop-chop!
I'll give you a lollipop."

Did Vovka say I like to talk?
That's a crock. When do I talk?!
How would I even find the time,
When in fact I got no time!

(Tr. Anna Krushelnitskaya)

Toys (1936)

TEDDY BEAR

Teddy Bear left on the floor,
One paw missing, sad and sore.
I won't leave him lying there!
He's the best, my Teddy Bear.

LITTLE COW

The little cow walks carefully,
A sigh, a step, a sigh:
"The board is running out on me,
I'm gonna fall, oh my!"

BALL

Tanya cries and sobs and squeaks:
She dropped her ball into the creek.
Tanya, smile and wipe your cheek:
Bouncy balls don't sink in creeks.

TRUCK

It was silly that we tried
To give the cat a merry ride:
All he knew was fight and buck,
Run away and crash the truck.

BUNNY

In the garden little Bunny
Was left behind when it was sunny.
Then it rained and he got drenched:
He could not climb off the bench.

ELEPHANT

"Time for bed," the clock tick-tocks.
Cow sleeps in the cardboard box.
Bear is drowsy on his cot.
Only Elephant is not.
Softly nodding "all is well"
He sends hello to Mrs. El.

HORSE

I adore my horse, I do!
Riding, feeding, grooming too.

Illustration by Konstantin Kuznetsov in *Igrushki* by Agniia Barto (Moscow: Detskaia literatura, 1980)

I'll brush her tidy with a comb,
And ride her to my best friend's home.

BABY GOAT

Look: I have a baby goat
And I let him out to graze.
He is light enough to tote
To the green, and if he strays
In the tall grass in the garden,
I will always find and guard him.

AIRPLANE

We will build a motor plane
That can fly above the rain.
We will fly up there, and then
Come right back to mom again.

STICK FLAG

My flag burns brightly
As I run,
As if I hold
A little sun.

BOAT

A sailor's hat
And a Navy coat,
Down the swift river
I tow my boat.
Frogs leap behind me
And hop by my side
And ask me, "hey Captain,
Give us a ride!"

(Tr. Dmitri Manin)

Lovely Lyuba (1945)

Ribbons in her pretty curl,
Sweet and pretty clothes.
Lyuba is the pretty girl
Everybody knows.

At a party in the hall
Girls begin to dance.
Lyuba dances best of all!
No one stands a chance.

Lyuba twirls her pretty curl
And her pretty clothes.
Everyone admires the girl.
Everybody glows.

Illustration by Naum Tseitlin in *My s Tamaroi* by Agniia Barto (Moscow: Detskaia literatura, 1967)

But if you go back to her place,
You won't believe your eyes!
She puts on a different face
That's hard to recognize.

She drops her bags right on the floor.
She tells her mom right at the door:
"Don't send me out to buy you bread!
I need to do homework instead."

When she takes a bus somewhere,
She forgets to pay the fare.
Then, she pushes through the crowd,
Shoving everyone around.

Then, she grumbles, elbows spreading,
"Where are all these people heading?
You are in a children's seat!"
She tells a woman with a frown.
The old woman sighs, "Sit down."

Ribbons in her pretty curl,
Sweet and pretty clothes.
Lyuba is a pretty girl,
If that's how pretty goes.

A nasty girl is such a shame!
I see her quite a lot.
Sometimes, Lyuba is her name.
Other times, it's not.

(Tr. Anna Krushelnitskaya)

Valentin Berestov

Hide-and-Seek (1963)

When there's no one here, I wonder:
Where are those who are not here?
There just has to be that somewhere
Where they went to disappear.

(Tr. Dmitri Manin)

ИСКАЛОЧКА

Если где-то нет кого-то,
Значит, кто-то где-то есть.
Только где же этот кто-то
И куда он мог залезть?

Illustration by Lev Tokmakov in *Mishka, Mishka, lezheboka* by Valentin Berestov (Moscow: Detskaia literatura, 1983)

Sit-and-Read (1963)

I'm glad I taught myself to read!
I could ask Mom—but there's no need.
Now, I can let my Grandma be,
Not nagging her to read to me.
Big sister will not hear me whine:
"Just one more page, just one more line!"
No need to wait, no need to plead,
When I can simply sit and read.

(Tr. Anna Krushelnitskaya)

Illustrations by Erik Bulatov and Oleg Vasiliev in *Skuchno odnomu* by Valentin Berestov (Moscow: Malysh, 1989)

At Play (1966)

We played and argued, had a fight,
We pouted and shook hands,
And yet, we ended up alright:
We ended up best friends.

A game will end, get out of hand,
We'll change the way we play,
But friendship, it will never end.
Hooray! Hooray! Hooray!

(Tr. Dmitri Manin)

Петушки

Петушки распетушились,
Но подраться не решились,
Если очень петушиться,
Можно пёрышек лишиться.
Если пёрышек лишиться,
Нечем будет петушиться.

5

Illustrations by Erik Bulatov and Oleg Vasiliev in *Skuchno odnomu* by Valentin Berestov (Moscow: Malysh, 1989)

Roosters (1966)

Two young roosters huff and puff,
Looking tough with ruffled fluff.
They're not fighting; it's all bluff!
If they fight, they'll lose their fluff,
And without their ruffled fluff
They will never look so tough.

(Tr. Dmitri Manin and Anna Krushelnitskaya)

Sick Doll (1966)

Quiet. Hear the old clock tick.
See our doll in bed and sick.
See our doll in bed and sick,
Asking for some music, quick!
If you sing her favorite song,
She'll get better before long.

(Tr. Dmitri Manin)

Black Ice (1969)

Bad for driving, riding, striding,
Roads are covered in black ice!
Great for stalling,
falling, crawling—
Why does no one say,
"How nice!"

(Tr. Dmitri Manin)

Sparrows (1971)

Winter's almost ended.
Hear what sparrows sing?
"Cheer up, cheer up: we made it!
Chirp-chirp-hurray: it's spring!"

(Tr. Dmitri Manin)

Illustration by Viktor Konovalov in
Vot kakaia mama by Elena Blaginina
(Moscow: Detskaia literatura, 1970)

Yelena Blaginina

Let's Sit Still (1940)

Mommy's sleeping. She needs rest.
I was playing. Now I quit.
I put my spin tops in the chest.
I sat down. And now I sit.

Not a single toy is peeping,
And the empty room is still.
A golden ray of sun is creeping
To mommy from the windowsill.

So, I spoke to the ray.
I said, "I also want to play!
I also want to do it all:
To read aloud, to toss a ball,
To pick a song and start to sing,

To laugh at something funny!
I would do every single thing!
But I can't wake up my mommy."

The ray fled in a hurry.
It seemed to gently say
In my ear, "Don't worry.
Silence is okay."

(Tr. Anna Krushelnitskaya)

Kornei Chukovsky

Gottascrub (1923)

My sheets fled
From my own bed,
My blanket took off in a jog,
And the pillow,
Yes, the pillow,
Hopped away just like a frog.

My candle dove
Into the stove!
And my book, it went ahead,
And it took off
In a trot
To a hiding spot
Under my bed.

And my samovar took fright!
My fat old samovar took flight
Once it had a look at me,
And now I can't have any tea!

What's the deal?
What does this mean?
Can somebody please explain
Why things reel
And careen,
Totter, spin, and wheel away?

Boots and pies go,
Pies and boots go,
Irons, belts, and boots in flight.
They all canter,
They all scamper,
Up and down and left and right!

Then, out of my Mama's room
Walks a washstand! As he hobbles
On bowed legs, his big head wobbles,
And his voice is boom and doom:
"You are filthy, you are stinky,
You're a stinky dirty piggy!
Even chimney sweeps are cleaner!
You are quite a view!
There is shoe wax on your shirt,
And your neck is streaked with dirt.
You have such disgusting hands
That your pants, yes, your own pants,
Your own pants, yes, your own pants
Ran away from you.

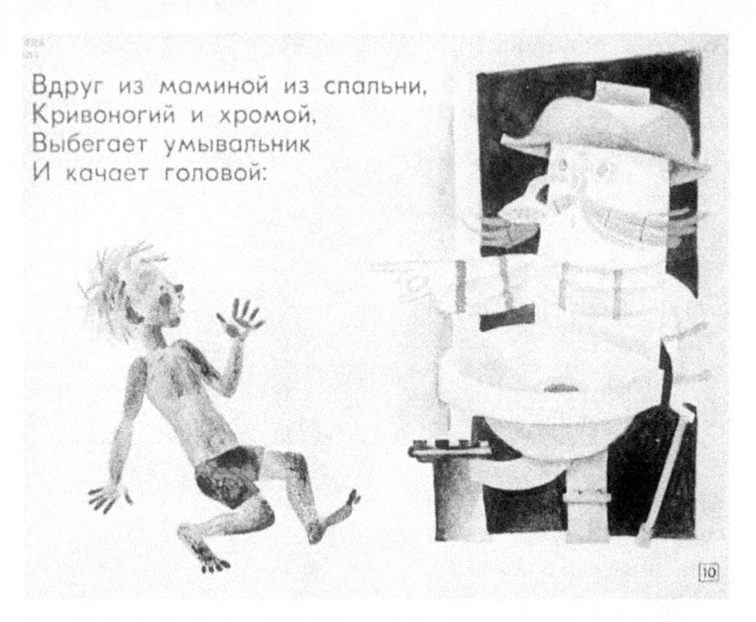

Illustrations by Yevgenii Monin and Vladimir Pertsov in filmstrip *Moidodyr* by Kornei Chukovsky (Moscow: Studia Diafilm, 1969)

Little mice and little duckies,
Little spiders, little buggies,
Little kitties all clean up
Every day when they wake up!

You're the only one who won't.
You're the only dirty slob!
And your boots and stockings don't
Want to stay to do their job.

I'm the Great and Mighty Washstand!
I'm the famous Gottascrub!
I rule over every washstand.
I'm the Commander-in-Tub!
If I choose to stomp my foot,

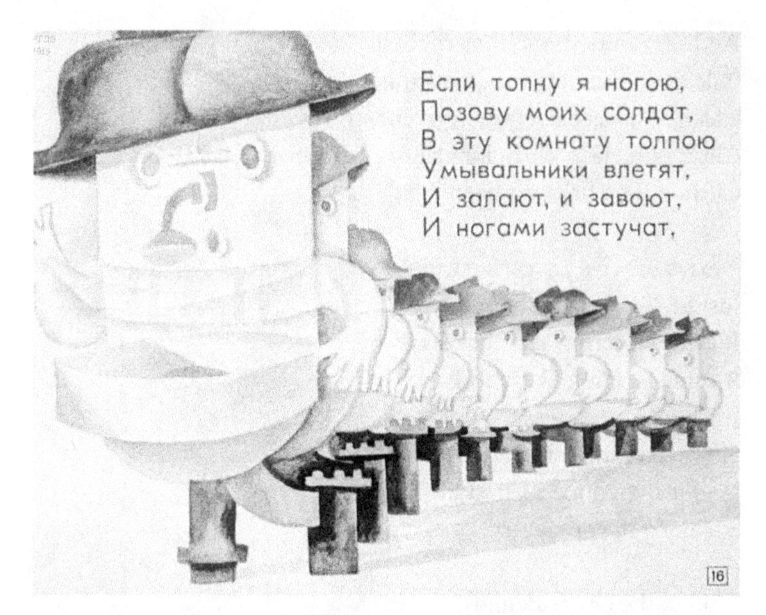

Illustrations by Yevgenii Monin and Vladimir Pertsov in filmstrip *Moidodyr* by Kornei Chukovsky (Moscow: Studia Diafilm, 1969)

If I choose to call my troops,
Sinks and tubs will howl and hoot,
And they will storm this filthy room!
They will scrub you, you old grub, you,
They will rub you till you squeak!
They will strip you,
They will flip you,
They will dip you in the creek!"

He banged a tin tub like a gong
And he yelled: "Barra-bah-bong!"

Brushes came down with a clatter
And began to scrub and chatter,
Scrub and chatter, scrub and chatter,

And they rattled, and they rubbed:
"Clean the stinker, clean the stinker,
Clean him cleaner, clean him pinker!
Clean him clean, clean him clean,
Cleaner than he's ever been!"

Next, a bar of soap came swinging
Just to fling itself at me!
It came lathering and clinging,
It came stinging like a bee!
And the sponge was looking feral,
So, I ran away from peril;
And it chased me, chased me hard
All along the boulevard!

I ran to the city park and
Jumped the fence and hid in trees;
And the sponge pursued me, barking,
Snarling, biting like a beast.

Luckily, I met my Croco
Dile, my friend, my dearest Croc,
With his kids Toto and Coco,
Who were out to take a walk,
And he gobbled up the sponge with all its bubbles, lock and stock.

Then, at once he started stomping at me,
And he almost started chomping at me:
"Get yourself back to your place!"
(So he said)
"Get yourself to wash your face!"
(So he said)
"Or I'll pounce, and I'll start beating you!
And I'll trounce you and start eating you!"

I ran faster than my eye could blink!
I ran back home to my trusty sink.
I was soaping, soaping, soaping
Up my face over the sink,
And I washed off, I was hoping,
All the grime and all the ink.

And my pants, my good old pants
Jumped at once into my hands!

Next, I heard a biscuit speak:
"Eat me, buddy, eat me quick!"

Next, a sandwich hops, and skips,
And shoves itself between my lips!
Next, my books and pens return,
They return so I can learn,
And my primer starts to dance,
And my math book starts to prance!

And the Great and Mighty Washstand,
The Distinguished Gottascrub,
The Grand Ruler of All Washstands,
The Chief Commander-in-Tub
Dances up to me, in bliss,
And with a kiss he tells me this:

"Now I praise you and embrace you!
With my love I shall now grace you!
Finally, Sir Dirtyface, you
Pleased the Mighty Gottascrub!"

Let's go washing at our sinks,
Night or morning, just the same!

And on every skunk that stinks—
Blame and shame!
Shame and blame!
Glory to soaps which are bubbly!
Glory to towels which are snuggly!
Glory to the fine-tooth comb
And the toothbrush in every home!
Come diving, come swimming and washing,
Come frolicking, splashing and sploshing,
In basins and buckets! Let's take
Baths in a sea or a lake,
In a bathtub or in a sauna—
Hosanna to water!
Hosanna!

(Tr. Anna Krushelnitskaya)

Squiggly Wiggly (1923)

Mura got a drawing pad today.
Mura started drawing right away.
"Here's a furry fir tree,
Here's a fuzzy buzz-bee,
A chimney smoking in the air,
A funny man with funny hair."
"Mura, what is this doodad
You drew in your drawing pad?
It looks so strange and weird:
Ten legs, ten horns, a beard?"
"She's a Squiggly Wiggly
With bitey teeth.
I made her up in my own head, myself."

"Your drawing pad is on the floor.
Why aren't you drawing anymore!"
"BECAUSE SHE'S SCARY!"

(Tr. Anna Krushelnitskaya)

Zizzy Lizzy the Fly (1924)

Meet a Fly named Zizzy Lizzy,
Shiny, snazzy, always busy!

Zizzy stepped out to the street.
She found a coin under her feet

And she bought, right then and there,
A copper kettle at the fair.
"Come on, Roaches, come right over!
I invite you all to tea!"

Thirsty Roaches came a-hopping.
They drained their glasses without stopping.
Baby Buggies
Drank from muggies.
They had cookies,
They had milk.
Zizzy Lizzy the Fly
Is a birthday Fly!

Zizzy greeted Little Fleas.
They brought her booties, if you please,
Which weren't worn, which weren't old,
Which had buckles made of gold!

Illustration by Vladimir Konashevich in *Mukha-tsokotukha* by Kornei Chukovsky (Moscow: Detskaia literatura, 1969)

Grandma Honeybee came flying,
But she brought no money.
Grandma Honeybee came flying,
And she brought her honey.
"Butterfly, milady!
Take a little jam!
Are you done already?
Are you full?"—"I am!"

All at once,
A Mean Old Spider
Saw the Fly and crept
Beside her—
Not to greet her, not to warn her—
To kill her in his spider corner!

Zizzy begged her guests as he tied her:
"Help me, friends! Please, stab the Mean Spider!
Did I not give you treats?
Did I not give you tea?
Don't leave me to die!
Come and fight for me!"

But the Beetles and Bugs
Were all scaredy bugs.
They all ran, they all hid
Under scatter rugs,
Every Louse
Quiet as a mouse,
Every Midge
Not moving a smidge,
And the Earwigs crawled under the bed,
Where they turned belly-up playing dead.

Under couches and chairs
They all lie.
Die, birthday Fly!
Die!

The Grasshopper, the Grasshopper
Hopped so fast you couldn't stop her!
Watch her bound, bound, bound!
Past the mound—
Not a sound—
Safe and sound!

Now, the Old Meanie keeps busy.
With his ropes, he binds the poor Lizzy.
He sinks his sharp fang into Lizzy's breast
And sips her blood from her chest.

Lizzy screams and screams
Hopelessly.
The Meanie just grins
With glee.
Suddenly, a Teeny Gnat
From a foreign land
Flies in carrying a torch
In his teeny hand.

"Where's the killer? Where is he?
His pincers are no match for me!"

He takes out his sword and makes
One quick dash!
He takes off the Spider's head
With one quick slash!

Now, he saved the Fly from harm.
Now, they come out arm-in-arm:
"I have killed the Deadly Beast!
You are saved! You are released!
Now, my darling, on my knee
I'm asking you to marry me!"

Now the Midges and the Bugs
Left their benches and their rugs:
"Glory, glory to the Gnat,
To the Hero Gnat!"

Lightning Bugs
Turned on the light—
What a twinkling!
What a sight!

Illustration by Vladimir Konashevich in *Mukha-tsokotukha* by Kornei Chukovsky (Moscow: Detskaia literatura, 1969)

Hey, Centipedes!
Go speeding through weeds!
Bring the Dancing Band Ants!
We're starting to dance!

Ants did not take long to come.
They came and they began to drum.
Boom! Boom! Boom! Boom!
The bride goes dancing with the groom.
The Centipede stomps all her feet
To the beat, the beat, the beat!

Worms and Weevils are wiggling.
Moths and Midges are jiggling.

Stag Beetles party, too.
They're very well-to-do.
They've put on fancy ties
To dance with Butterflies.

Womp-womp! Toot-toot!
Wasps and Skeeters swarm and scoot!
Bees dance, Ants play—
It's a wedding day!
Zizzy Lizzy's getting married
To the brave and handsome Gnat!

Leafhoppers dance in twos.
They might wear out their shoes!
Leafhopper gives his missus hugs,
Winking at the Ladybugs:
"Hey there, ladies,
Lovely ladies,
Lovely pretty spotty ladies!"

Heels clack,
Floors crack—
Dance, every Mite,
All day and all night!
Zizzy Lizzy the Fly
Is a birthday Fly!

(Tr. Anna Krushelnitskaya)

The Wondertree (1924)

My friend Miron—there he goes—
Keeps a magpie on his nose.

In a pine tree, crayfish rest
In a macaroni nest.

In the yard, a billy goat
Rides through brambles in a boat.

Brambles bear tasty crops
Of bonbons and lollipops,

And beside my porch, I see
A fantastic wondertree.

Wonder, wonder, wonder, wonder,
Oh-so-wondrous!

With no leaves at all,
With no blooms at all,
Only shoes, only socks,
Ripe and ready to fall!

The tree grows many shoes to choose.
Mama comes and picks her shoes:
Boots, galoshes, and a pair
Of pretty Sunday shoes to wear.

The tree grows many shoes to choose.
Papa picks some socks and shoes:
Slippers for Zina,
Stockings for Nina,
Sandals for Lina.
And for Little Baby Mura
Papa picks the best, for sure—
Teeny-weeny knitted booties
With blue bobbles, very cute!

Illustration by Vladimir Konashevich in *Murkina Kniga* by K. Chukovsky (Peterburg/Moscow: Raduga, 1924). Source: Cotsen Children's Library, Princeton Slavic Collections.

That's our wondertree!
Quite a wondertree!

If you have cold toes,
If your big toe shows,
If your boots got holes
Or old tattered soles,
If you need some shoes for free—
Quick! Run to the wondertree!

Pick new clogs—they're good to go!
Ripe shoelaces hanging low!
You're not picking—why?

No more standing shy!
Pick them, you unbooted kids!
Pick them, you barefooted kids!
Then, you'll never have to plod
Through the winter snows unshod,
Sporting holes in your hose,
Showing off your naked toes!

(Tr. Anna Krushelnitskaya)

Old Theodora's Trouble and Horror (1926)

Troughs come hopping through the alley!
Sieves come bopping through the valley!
Brooms, and rakes, and spades alike
Leave the house and take a hike!

Hatchet tumbling after hatchet,
Try to catch one—you can't catch it!
They keep dropping, they keep dropping
Past a goat whose eyes are popping:
"What is happening over there?
What a scare! What a scare!"

Look, a stoker black from fire and soot
Runs and jumps like a black iron foot,
And the street fills with escaping knives:
"We are running for our lives, lives, lives!"

And a pot shouts to the iron,
With a skip and with a hop:
"I am running, running, running
And I cannot, cannot stop!"

Illustration by Vladimir Suteev in *Fedorino gore* by Kornei Chukovsky (Moscow: Detskaia literatura, 1951)

And a teapot races swiftly, all a-clatter,
With a coffeepot behind it, pitter-patter,
And the heavy irons tumble
Over mud, and groan, and grumble.

And the tiniest plates—
Ding-dang-dong! Ding-dang-dong!—
Roll outside through the gates—
Ding-dang-dong! Ding-dang-dong!
Where they crash into tea glasses—bang!
And they smash all those tea glasses—dang!

And a frying pan is clanging like a gong:
"Where is everybody going-going-gone?"

Next go forks,
Spoons and corks,
Cups and bottles,
All full throttle.

A table fell out through the window with a thump:
Watch it bump and jump and bump and jump and bump!

And a huge samovar
Took the table for a ride!
It keeps shouting: "Run-run-run!
Run and hide! Save your hide!"
Its pipe is blaring at the top:
"Honk-honk-honk! Wop-wop-wop!"

And the poor old Theodora's out the door and giving chase:
"Back to where you were before, oh, please get back home to your place!"

"Theodora treats me rough!"
Said the angry feeding trough.

"Theodora treats me bad!"
Said the stoker, feeling mad.

Saucers laughed at Theodora:
"We will not be working for her!
We are leaving, leaving for
Ever-ever-evermore!"

Theodora's cats went chasing,
Puffy tails and eyes a-glare.
Fleet and fluffy, they went racing
To bring back the kitchenware.
"Hey you, plates! You think you're rabbits?

Drop your funny jumpy habits!
Must you run around in streaks
Like sparrows with their silly beaks?
You will slog
Through a bog!
You'll get stuck
In the muck!
Wait up, come back, wait up, come back,
Come back home, don't try your luck!"

But the plates kept slipping, ducking
Out of Theodora's hands:
"We would rather sink in muck than
Come back home to her again!"

A rooster, on his way somewhere,
Walked by all that kitchenware:
"Buck-buck! Cock-a-doodle-do!
Where'd you run from, and where to?"

And, in chorus, said the dishes:
"Theodora's bad and vicious!
She would never scrub or soak us!
And she dropped us! And she broke us!
We are slimy, grimy, cracked,
And our little lives are wrecked!"
"Cock-a-doodle-doo! Buck-buck!
Sounds like really rotten luck!"

"Right!" replied a copper tub.
"Look! We've never had a scrub.
We're all busted, we're defaced
And basted in disgusting waste!
See the filthy cockroach flock crawling in this pickle crock!
Think of all the frogs you'll face inside this dirty laundry basin!

That is why we left the woman.
That old woman, she is vermin!
Now, we wander out in fields,
And there are hills and dales we roam in.
But we won't come back to her,
Or her filthy home.
No Sir!"

So they ran through the woods, doing jumps
Over the stumps and the humps.

And the old woman sat down outside,
And she cried, and she cried, and she cried.

She can't sit at her table, no more!
The table walked out through the door.
She can't make any soup in a pot,
Because none of the pots could be caught!
All her cups had walked out in reproach!
All that's left is the common cockroach.
Oh, trouble befell Theodora!
The horror!

The dishes continued to stomp
Through the field, through the hedge, through the swamp.

And the teapot said to the iron,
"Oh, this journey is so very tiring!"

Then, saucers started to crack:
"Should we perhaps rather come back?"

And the trough had a sobbing fit:
"Oh goodness, I'm split! I quit!"

Illustration by Vladimir Suteev in *Fedorino gore* by Kornei Chukovsky (Moscow: Detskaia literatura, 1951)

Then, the serving platter said, "Gee!
Someone followed us! Who can that be?"

Theodora, wretched and weary,
Hobbled out of the woods dark and dreary
And, it seemed, through some magical switch,
Theodora was no more a witch!

She kept walking humbly along
And singing a humble song:

"Oh, my poor little orphan strays!
Oh, my poor little pans and trays!

Illustration by Vladimir Pertsov in *Fedorino gore* by Kornei Chukovsky (Moscow: Malysh, 1971)

My unwashed ones, turn back on your path.
I will give you a spring water bath!

I will scour you clean by hand,
With hot water and rough sand.
You will shine, my little ones!
You will shine like little suns!

All the icky cockroaches, I'll banish!
All the beetles and spiders will vanish!"

"Well, that struck a chord!"
Said a cutting board.

Illustration by Vladimir Pertsov in *Fedorino gore* by Kornei Chukovsky (Moscow: Malysh, 1971)

"Oh, she's a poor pup!"
Said a china cup.

"Guess we could come back!"
Said small plates in a stack.

"Theodora's a friend!"
Irons said at the end.

Theodora kissed them, hugged them,
Hugged them more, so nice and sweet!
Then, she washed them, and she scrubbed them!
Wash them, scrub them, rinse, repeat.

"I will never, I do swear,
Be so mean to kitchenware!

It will not get cracked or wrecked!
I will give it due respect."

Pans burst out laughing with a clink.
They gave the samovar a wink.
"Theodora! Do not cry.
We will give you one more try."

Jingling, jangling, shoving,
They flew into her oven!
They will fry and they will bake!
She'll have pie and she'll have cake.

And the broom, the happy broom
Went dancing all across the room!
Now it twists, now it trots, now it leaves no dusty spots!

And the tiny plates are giggling—
Ding-dang-dong! Ding-dang-dong!
They are jumping, they are jiggling—
Ding-dang-dong! Ding-dang-dong!

And the samovar,
Shining like a star,
Sits atop the white stool on a doily before her,
And it huffs: "Tea with jam!
I forgive you, Madame!
Pour yourself one more cup, Madame Theodora!"

(Tr. Anna Krushelnitskaya)

Daniil Kharms

Liar (1930)

Did you know?
Did you know?
Did you know?
Did you know?
But of course you do know!
Sure enough you do know!
  There's no doubt,
  There's no doubt,
There's no doubt you do know!

No! No! No! No!
No, we don't know anything,
Haven't seen it,
Haven't heard it,
So we don't know
Anything!

Bet you didn't know that MY?
Bet you didn't know that FA?
Bet you didn't know that THER?
Bet you didn't know my father
Had exactly forty sons?
Forty hulky bulky fellows:
Not just twenty,
Not just thirty,
But exactly forty sons!

Whoa, whoa, whoa, whoa!
Lies! Lies! Lies! Lies!
Maybe twenty,
Maybe thirty,
Hard to swallow, but okay,
But exactly
Forty sons—
Hogwash, gibberish, no way!

Bet you didn't know that BAR?
Bet you didn't know that KING?
Bet you didn't know that DOGS?
That our silly barking doggies
Took to flying in the sky?
That they learned to fly like eagles,
Not like crayfish,
Not like rabbits,
But like eagles in the sky!

Whoa, whoa, whoa, whoa!
Lies! Lies! Lies! Lies!
Say, like crayfish,
Say, like rabbits,
Hard to swallow, but okay,
But to fly like birds,
Like eagles—
Hogwash, gibberish, no way!

Bet you didn't know that A?
Bet you didn't know that CART?
Bet you didn't know that WHEEL?
That a cartwheel

Will go up there
To replace the shining sun?
To the sky it will go rolling—
Not a pancake
Not a platter,
But a giant golden wheel!

Whoa, whoa, whoa, whoa!
Lies! Lies! Lies! Lies!
Say, a pancake,
Say, a platter,
Hard to swallow, but okay,
But a giant golden cartwheel—
Hogwash, gibberish, no way!

Bet you didn't know that A?
Bet you didn't know that SOL?
Bet you didn't know that DIER?
There's a soldier with a rifle
Standing guard under the sea?

Whoa, whoa, whoa, whoa!
Lies! Lies! Lies! Lies!
With a broomstick,
With a duster,
Hard to swallow, but okay,
But to stand there with a rifle—
Hogwash, gibberish, no way!

Bet you didn't know that YOU?
Bet you didn't know that CAN?
Bet you didn't know that NOT?
That you cannot
Touch your nose

Illustration by Fedor Lemkul' in *Dvenadtsat' povarov* by Daniil Kharms (Moscow: Malysh, 1972)

With your fingers
Or your toes,
You can't touch it,
You can't reach it
Not by highway,
Not by railway,
There's just no way
You can ever
Touch your nose!

Illustration by Mai Miturich and Ivan Bruni in *Igra* by Daniil Kharms (Moscow: Detskii mir, 1962)

Whoa, whoa, whoa, whoa!!
Lies! Lies! Lies! Lies!
Say by highway,
Say by railway—
Hard to swallow, but okay,
But to touch it with your finger—
Hogwash!
Gibberish!
No way!

(Tr. Dmitri Manin)

Illustration by Mai Miturich and Ivan Bruni in *Igra* by Daniil Kharms (Moscow: Detskii mir, 1962)

What Was That? (1940)

Galoshes, glasses, hat and all,
I strolled along the winter brooks
And saw a stranger, swift and tall,
Swoosh by on shiny metal hooks.

I chased him down the snowy banks
And caught him doing something weird:
He fixed his feet to wooden planks,
Then squatted, jumped, and disappeared.

I wiped my glasses, watched the brooks
And wondered on the snowy banks:
"What were those curious metal hooks
And those peculiar wooden planks?"

(Tr. Dmitri Manin)

Samuil Marshak

The Tale of a Silly Mousie (1923)

Mama Mouse sang: "Night has come.
Hush, my baby, go to bed!
You will get a big cheese crumb
And a crust of dried-out bread."

The silly mousie, all tucked in,
Said, "Your voice is squeaky thin.
Stop your singing, do not bother,
Better get a nanny, Mother!"

Mama Mouse ran out to find
Auntie Duck: "If you don't mind,
Come and rockabye our baby,
Help me calm him, be so kind."

Duck came down and sang: "Quack! Quack!
Lie down, darling, on your back.
In the yard after the storm
We will find a tasty worm."

Illustration by Vladimir Lebedev in *O glupom myshenke* by Samuil Marshak (Moscow: Raduga, 1925)

"Auntie," said the silly mousie
All curled up in bed and drowsy,
"I don't like your lullaby,
It's too loud, you make me cry!"

Mama Mouse ran out to find
Auntie Toad: "If you don't mind,
Come and rockabye our baby,
Help me calm him, be so kind."

Toad came down and started croaking:
"Sleep, I say, I don't like joking!
And at dawn, if you don't cry,
We will catch a tasty fly."

"Auntie," said the silly mousie
All curled up in bed and drowsy,
"I don't like your lullaby,
It's too dull, you make me cry!"

Mama Mouse ran out to find
Auntie Horse: "I'm in a bind!
Come and rockabye our baby,
Help me calm him, be so kind."

Horse came down and sang: "Neigh, neigh!
Go to sleep, kid! Dream away!
Don't you cry, you'll get a treat:
A bale of hay, a sack of wheat."

"Auntie," said the silly mousie
All curled up in bed and drowsy,
"I don't like your lullaby,
It's so spooky I will cry!"

Mama Mouse ran out to find
Auntie Hen: "If you don't mind,
Come and rockabye our baby,
Help me calm him, be so kind."

Hen came down and sang: "Cluck-cluck,
Cheer up, baby, you're in luck!
Come and crawl under my wing,
You will sleep there like a king!"

"Auntie," said the silly mousie
All curled up in bed and drowsy,
"I don't like your lullaby,
I can't sleep, I want to cry!"

Illustration by Vladimir Lebedev in *O glupom myshenke* by Samuil Marshak (Moscow: Raduga, 1925)

Mama Mouse ran out to find
Auntie Pike: "If you don't mind,
Come and rockabye our baby,
Help me calm him, be so kind."

Pike came down and tried to sing,
But she couldn't say a thing.
Though she opened up her mouth,
Not a sound was coming out.

"Auntie," said the silly mousie
All curled up in bed and drowsy,
"I don't like your lullaby,
It's too soft, you make me cry!"

Mama Mouse ran out to find
Auntie Cat: "I'm in a bind,
Come and rockabye our baby,
Help me calm him, be so kind."

Cat came down and sang: "Meow, meow,
Hush my baby, do sleep now!
Here's a pillow for your head,
Let me tuck you in your bed."

"Auntie," said the silly mousie
All curled up in bed and drowsy,
"No one sang to me like that,
You're the sweetest, Auntie Cat!"

Mama Mouse came back around,
Saw no one and heard no sound.
Mama Mouse looked for her mousie,
But he was nowhere to be found . . .

(Tr. Dmitri Manin)

Who Is Who at the Zoo (1923)

BABY TIGER
Keep away, you, silly kiddie:
I'm a tiger, not a kitty!

ELEPHANT
We gave the elephant two shoes.
"These," he said, "I cannot use,
I would need a bigger shoe,
And four of them, for two won't do!"

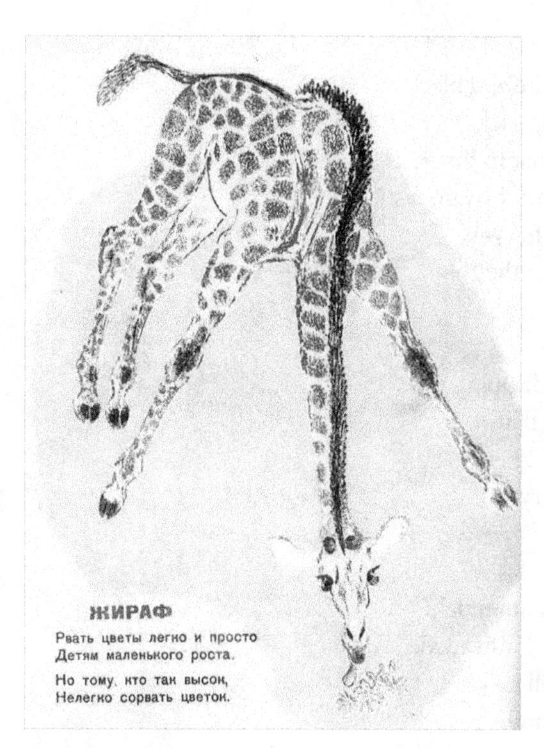

Illustration by Yevgenii Charushin in *Detki v kletke* by Samuil Marshak (Leningrad: TsK VLKSM Detizdat, 1937)

GIRAFFE

Picking flowers out in the wild
Isn't hard if you're a child,
But for someone very tall
It's not easy, not at all!

BABY OWLS

Baby owls sit on the bough
And they aren't sleeping now.
When not sleeping,
They are eating,
When they're eating,
They're not sleeping.

PENGUIN

I look great in white and black!
I am like a walking sack.
Can you believe that in the past
I chased speedboats, I swam fast?
But today I swim for you,
In the pond here at the zoo.

BABY SWAN

"Why's this baby dripping wet?"
"'Cause he swam, that's why.
Get the towel and I bet
We will get him dry!"

BABY OSTRICH

I'm baby ostrich, I am quick
On foot and quite hotheaded.
If I get angry, I will kick.
My foot is hard and heavy.
If I am scared, I'll run away
And flap my bony wings.
But I can't fly, try as I may,
And I can never sing.

MONKEY

A sailor came here, brave and strong,
From Africa by sea.
A baby monkey came along,
For all of us to see.

She keeps so quiet, sitting
With her head tucked in her hands.
She sings a little ditty
That no one understands:

"My southern land is far away,
Where palm leaves blow like sails
And all my sisters screech and sway,
Hanging by their long tails.

Bananas sweet and chunky
Enough for all to share—
My home's a land of monkeys.
There are no people there."

POLAR BEARS

Me and my brother have a pool.
It's deep enough to keep us cool.

Our keepers fill it to the brim
Each day, so we can play and swim.

We swim from wall to wall, we glide
Now on the back, now on the side.

Keep to the right and pass with care,
And tuck that foot in, brother bear!

ESKIMO DOG

My cage has signs that say:
"Stay back!" and "Keep away!"
But don't believe the signs:
I'm friendly, tame, and kind.

My friends, it makes no sense
That I'm behind a fence.

CAMEL

Baby camel is so sweet,
But he can't get enough to eat.

After breakfast he still drools:
He only ate two bucketfuls!

ZEBRAS

Little horses, quick and bright,
Hide and seek from dawn to night,
On the grass from dawn to night,
Running to and fro!

Like school notebooks, black and white,
Lined to help us read and write,
They are striped in black and white,
Painted head to toe.

(Tr. Dmitri Manin)

THE DINGO

I'm neither wolf nor fox, you see.
Come to our woods to visit me.
You might spot me behind a tree—
The snappy, scrappy dingo.

The kangaroo and I compete
For speed in the Australian heat.
He's fast, I'm faster on my feet—
The skinny, speedy dingo.

The kangaroo goes left—I chase;
The kangaroo goes right—I race;
He picks up pace—I match his pace,
The driven, dogged dingo.

His mind is quick—but I'm no snail.
All day I chased him on the trail,

And then I caught him by the tail—
The hardened hunter dingo.

But now, I live here in the zoo.
I run and dance around for you.
I jump for meat and catch it, too—
The spinning, swirling dingo.

(Tr. Anna Krushelnitskaya)

Scatterbrain (1930)

One scattered Mr. Scatterbrain
Lived in a house on Splatter Lane.

One day he rose, he put on his clothes,
As he got ready to leave,
And, like a charm, he shoved him arm
In his pant leg, not his sleeve.

That's our Mr. Scatterbrain,
Scatterbrain of Splatter Lane!

He picked a coat, a light one,
But it was not the right one!
He started trying on some belts:
Those belts belonged to someone else!

That's our Mr. Scatterbrain,
Scatterbrain of Splatter Lane!

For a hat, without much thought,
He put on a cooking pot,
And for boots, in a beat,
He put gloves on his feet.

That's our Mr. Scatterbrain,
Scatterbrain of Splatter Lane!

One time, Mr. Scatterbrain
Took a tram to catch a train.
By the doors, he begged the driver,
Trying to explain:
"My dear tram driver!
My dear drive trammer!
My driving tram dear!
My dear tramming Ma'am!
You see, I am impatient
To get off at the station,
So, can you train the station
To stop our driving tram?"
The driver's jaw dropped
And the tram stopped.

That's our Mr. Scatterbrain,
Scatterbrain of Splatter Lane!

He'd walk by a café and pick it
As a place to buy his ticket.
Then, to buy a soda, he'd go
Straight up to the ticket window!

That's our Mr. Scatterbrain,
Scatterbrain of Splatter Lane!

He rushed to make the trip he'd booked,
To a train car which was unhooked.
He took his travel bags and trunks
And stashed them underneath the bunks.
He settled in a window seat
And, as he slept, his dreams were sweet.

He peeked outside when he awoke.
He shouted: "What's this station, folks?"
The people on the platform said:
"It is a town called Leningrad."

He took another nap, and then
He woke up and peeked out again.
He saw the trains and platforms yonder,
Stuck out his head and said in wonder:
"What is this little whistle-stop?
Is this my stop? Did I miss my stop?"
The people on the platform said:
"It is a town called Leningrad."

He took another nap, and then
He woke up and peeked out again.
He saw big trains and tracks beyond.
He wondered, as he stretched and yawned:
"Please tell me how far I've gone!
Do I get off? Do I stay on?"
The people on the platform said:
"You're in a town called Leningrad!"

Then he shouted, brokenhearted:
"I came back to where I started!
I came back to Leningrad!

Which took two days! I'm mighty mad!"

That's our Mr. Scatterbrain,
Scatterbrain of Splatter Lane!

(Tr. Anna Krushelnitskaya)

Where the Sparrow Had Lunch (1934)

"Sparrow, where did you have lunch?"
"At the zoo, with all the bunch.

First, I visited the lion,
Tried a bit of what he dined on,

Tasted of the fox's meal,
Drank some water with the seal.

With the elephant I ate carrots,
Grabbed some bird seed from the parrots,

With the rhino in his pen
I had bran and drank again,

Saw the long-tailed kangaroo,
Got a bite on my way through,

Then, I visited the bear,
And he was very kind to share.

But the toothy crocodile
Nearly snatched me in his smile.

(Tr. Dmitri Manin)

Vladimir Mayakovsky

What Is Good and What Is Bad (1925)

A teeny boy
  came to his dad.
He came to ask his dad:
"Daddy! Tell me,
  what is good?
Tell me—
  what is bad?"
Listen,
Little kids,
  and look—
I got no things
  to hide!
Let me tell you
  in this book
What his dad
  replied.
"When roofs
  rattle
As wind blows,
As thunder
  bangs
And knocks,
That's when
  everybody knows:
It's bad
  for taking walks.
When rain drip-dropped
  and then it stopped,
The world is filled

with sun—
It's good
For all folks
big and small,
The father
and the son.
Let's say
the son
Has grime and soot
On his
kiddie chin—
Now, it's always
bad to put
Dirt
on kiddie skin.
This young boy is friends
with soap
And a box of dental powder.
This boy is good,
Acts like he should,
And I could not
be prouder.
A big bully
beats with glee
A kid who's weak and small—
I tell you,
I don't want to see
Him in my book
at all.
But here's a boy who shouts,
'Don't touch
The small kid!
Don't you bug him!'
He's good!

Illustration by Aleksei Laptev in *Chto takoe khorosho I chto takoe plokho?* by Vladimir Mayakovsky (Moscow: Gosizdat, 1930)

I like him
  very much.
He's so good
  I could hug him.
If you tore up
  your book today
And broke apart
  your toy,
Your October Troop will say:
'Here goes
  a baddish boy!'
When a boy
Sits down
  to read,

Illustration by Aleksei Laptev in *Chto takoe khorosho I chto takoe plokho?* by Vladimir Mayakovsky (Moscow: Gosizdat, 1930)

Tracing every line—
  he likes to work!
That's what we need.
He's good.
  He's doing fine.
This boy starts
  to whine and run
When he sees a crow.
This baby is
  a wimpy one!
It's very bad,
  you know.
This itsy-bitsy baby stood
  up to scary crows!

He's a brave boy,
Which is
  good.
It'll help him as he grows.
This boy
Drags his shirt
  through mud.
It's dirty and he's glad.
People say:
  you're yucky, bud!
Yucky equals
  bad.
This boy
Polishes
  his boots.
He keeps his booties
  shiny.
That means
  he is pretty good
For somebody
  so tiny.
Every boy and kid
  should know
Before they grow up
  big:
If you're a piglet
  as you grow,
You'll grow
  into a pig!"
The happy boy
Knew what he should
Do as he spoke
  to dad:
"I will forever

do what's good
And never
do what's bad!"

(Tr. Anna Krushelnitskaya)

What to Be? (1929)

My years have been growing up.
I'll be seventeen.
What kind of work should I take up?
What should I be?

Much needed jobs are carpentry
And, also, joinery!
Building furniture takes skill:
take a round
timber
to mill
Into planks,
Long and lank.
Planks go
in a clench,
Like so,
on a workbench.
All that
Work got
The saw
white-hot.
With each
New thrust
The saw makes
sawdust.

Next comes a job
For the hand plane:
To shave knots and knobs
Off the grain.
The yellow shavings
Are nice to play with.
Should we need
  a wood ball,
Very round and clean,
That job
Would call
For a lathe machine.
Bit by bit,
We make more and more.
First, a leg,
  next, a drawer.
We made a good share
Of tables and chairs!

Carpenters are good,
But
Engineers are great! Me,
I would build a house, I would.
Let them educate me.
I'll make
  a drawing
    and a chart
Of a house
  I like,
    to start.
The house I draw
Should look and feel
Nice
  and neat,

Illustration by Tatiana Solovieva in *Kem byt'?* by Vladimir Mayakovsky (Minsk: Yunatstva, 1987)

and like it's real.
This here is the front wall,
called
the facade.
Here's a garden,
bathroom, hall.
See? Not too hard.
Now the draft is ready
And
There's a hundred jobs
for a thousand
hands.
The scaffolding goes high.
It's stuck into the sky.

Where work is rough,
 the winch
  will whine
With beams, like toy sticks,
 up the line.
It is also willing
To hoist bricks dried in a kiln.
Next, the roof is laid with tin:
 the house is done,
  the roof is in.
The house is huge,
 the house is good,
Left, right, and floor to ceiling.
Now kids will live there like they should,
With a free and roomy feeling.

Engineers are good,
But
Doctors are great! Me,
I would treat sick kids, I would.
Let them educate me.
I would make a house call
To Petya and to Polya:
"Greetings, children! Morning, all!
Who is feeling poorly?
How's your tummy?
Not too crummy?"
I'll peer
 over my spectacles
At the dear young ones
 to check their tongues.
"Kids! This is a thermometer.
It's a fever monitor."
The kids are ready, and it's

    already
        In their armpits.
"You would really
    cheer up
If you took
    this syrup,
Bit by bit,
    spoon by spoon.
Swallow up this powder soon!
You could use a heat wrap,
And you
    could use
        a nice nap.
You should start
    to feel okay
        well before
Your wedding day."

Doctors are good,
But
Factories are great! Me,
I'd work at a plant, I would.
Let them educate me.
"Get up and go!"
The bell
    will call
Us to the factory,
    one and all.
We are
    A huge crew,
Twelve hundred to a man.
What one of us can't do,
All of us can.
We snip sheet metal

Illustration by Aleksei Pakhomov in *Kem byt'?* by Vladimir Mayakovsky (Moscow: Detgiz, 1947)

with shears,
with mettle.
We drag things
Without strain
With an overhead crane.
A jackhammer aids:
Rails bend like grass blades.
We smelt tin.
We rule the machine.
Work by every name,
We need it just the same.
I make bolts,
that's my bit.
You make nuts
to fit.

Everything we did,
 combined,
Goes straight to the assembly line.
Hey, bolts!
 Get driven
In holes,
 nice and even.
Take these parts and ram
 them together—
  Slam!
Things
 smoke,
Things
 bang.
Every-
 thing
Goes
 clang!
A new train engine
 coming through!
To drive
 and carry
  me
   and you.

Factories are good,
But
Streetcars are great! Me,
I'd sell tickets there, I would.
Let them educate me.
The ticket man,
 he rides all day,
Big satchel on his side.
He rides the streetcar

Illustration by Aleksei Pakhomov in *Kem byt'?* by Vladimir Mayakovsky (Moscow: Detgiz, 1947)

all the way.
He can always ride.
"People big and small!
Buy tickets, one and all.
I got many kinds for you!
I got green,
red
or blue.
Any ticket!
You can pick it."
The streetcar goes on tracks,
And at the end of tracks,
We get off by the woods and sit,
warm sun
on our backs.

Streetcars are good,
But
Taxicabs are great! Me,
I would drive a cab, I would.
Let them educate me.
The taxi purrs off in a blur,
It slides and flies around.
I'll show you a good chauffeur!
You cannot tie me down!
Just give me the address,
I'll drive you fast and best.
I will take you home with speed.
  No tracks,
    which I don't need.
Blast
  off!
We
  whoop:
"Get
  off!
Beep-
  boop!"

Taxicabs are good,
But
Airplanes are great! Me,
I would fly a plane, I would.
Let them educate me.
I pour in
Gasoline,
I make the propeller
Spin:
"Motor, take me higher still
Through the sky

Where birds trill."
It hailed,
It rained—
    I'm not
        afraid.
I fly around
A flying cloud.
Like a seagull, white and free,
I hover high above the sea.
I fly with ease
Above the trees.
"Motor, take us
    to the Moon,
        then, to any star,
Though the Moon and every star
    are
        very
            far."

Pilots are good,
But
Sailors are great! Me,
I would sail the seas, I would.
Let them educate me.
Ribbons in my sailor cap,
Anchors on
    my collar flap,
All summer I'm in motion,
Conquering
The ocean.
Waves may blast,
Waves may splat.
I climb the mast.
I'm like a cat.

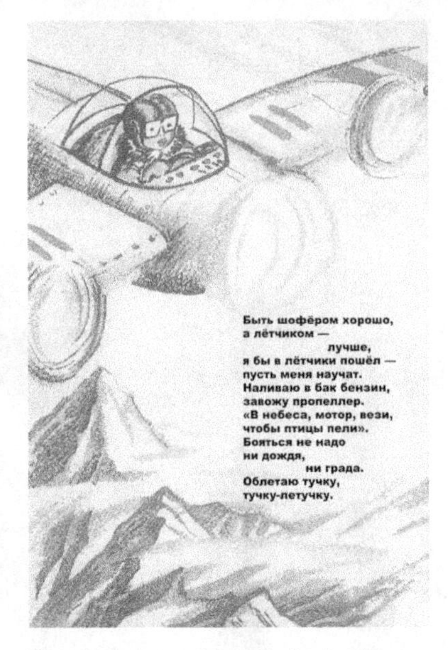

Illustration by Tatiana Solovieva in *Kem byt'?* by Vladimir Mayakovsky (Minsk: Yunatstva, 1987)

Surrender, winds that chill my soul!
Give in, squalls blowing forth!
I will
  discover
    the South Pole
And probably
  the North.

Now, when you've read the whole book straight
Through, and not in haste,
Take this in: all jobs are great!
Pick one
  that's to your taste.

(Tr. Anna Krushelnitskaya)

Sergei Mikhalkov

Mimosa (1935)

Who's this person lying down,
Piled with blankets stuffed with down?
Who's this, resting on three pillows
Near a table laid with food?
Who has left his bed a mess,
Who took centuries to dress,
Who washed his cheeks with tepid water
Just as gently as he could?

It's a grandpa, you must mean,
Aged one hundred and fourteen?
No.

Who grabs a cake and starts to chew,
Then says: "I want my juice now, too!
Bring me this!
No, gimme that!
That's not what you're supposed to do!"

Is this someone we heard speak
Sick and weak?
No.

So who is he?
And why is he
Given winter booties and
Thick woolen gloves to warm his hands,
So he won't catch any chills

Illustration by Genrikh Valk in *Pro mimozu* by Sergei Mikhalkov (Moscow: Detskaia literatura, 1963)

Or a deadly flu that kills,
Though it's sunny out and though
For six months we've had no snow?

Is he going to the North Pole,
To bears swimming in an ice hole?
No.

Take a better look and—wait!
It's just Vitya; he's a boy,
Mama's boy
And Papa's boy
From Apartment Number Eight.

He's the one who's lying down,
Piled with blankets stuffed with down!

Illustration by Genrikh Valk in *Pro mimozu* by Sergei Mikhalkov (Moscow: Detskaia literatura, 1963)

He's the one who will eat nothing
But his pastries and his cakes!

For what reason?
For the reason
That as soon as he's awake,
Someone will run up and take
His temperature; then someone goes
To fetch his booties and his clothes,
And he will always, day or night,
Get what he wants without a fight.

If he's sleepy in the morning,
He will stay in bed all day.
If a cloudy day is dawning,
He will wear rain boots all day.

For what reason?
For the reason
That he's treated like a king,
And that he lives in his new house,
Unprepared for anything.

Unprepared to pull a trailer,
Or be a courageous sailor,
Or to fly a plane, or step in
And learn how to fire a weapon!

He's raised warm like in a bathhouse,
With his Ma and Pa as wardens,
Like a mimosa in a glasshouse,
Which they have in botanic gardens.

(Tr. Anna Krushelnitskaya)

What's New with You? (1935)

Kids found a bench and took a seat.
They sat there staring at the street:
Tolya silent, Borya singing,
Kolya dangling his feet.

It was the evening of the day:
Not much to do, no games to play.

A magpie landed on the fence.
A stray cat sat and licked his paws.
Then, Borya went and told his friends,
Just because:
"In my coat, I keep a nail.
What you got?"

"We got postcards in the mail.
What you got?"
"Yesterday our cat had babies.
It was only just today!
They grew a little bigger, maybe,
But won't eat cat food anyway!"
"Our kitchen oven runs on gas.
Yes!"
"But we get water from the tap!
Yep."

"When we look outside our window,
We can see the whole Red Square!
What's outside your little window?
Just this boring street! So there!"

"We walked along the avenue
And by the boulevard at noon.
Our parents bought a blue, so blue,
Bright green
And very red balloon!"

"Our heat and lights went out today,
So that's A.
B, a truck brought firewood.
So that's good.
Number four, today our mommy
Will be flying in the skies.
And that is because our mommy,
She's a pilot, so she flies!"

"You got a pilot mom? Big deal!"
Said Vova, rocking on his heel.
"Kolya's mom, I'm told,
Keeps our streets patrolled.

Illustration by Grigorii Tseitlin in *A chto u vas?* by Sergei Mikhalkov (Moscow: Detskaia literatura, 1971)

Tolya's and Vera's
Moms are engineers.
Leva's mom cooks people's meals.
Pilot moms are no big deals!"

Nata said, "It's best for us
To have a mom who drives a bus.
My mom drives two about
On the circle route."

Nina said, "Do you suppose
We don't need moms making clothes?
Who has made your underwear?
Not a pilot! So, not fair!"

Illustration by Grigorii Tseitlin in *A chto u vas?* by Sergei Mikhalkov (Moscow: Detskaia literatura, 1971)

A pilot takes planes in the air,
Which is very, very good.
A chef will bake you an éclair,
Which is also very good.
Doctors treat us when we bleed.
Teachers teach us all to read.
We need all our moms combined!
We need moms of every kind.

It was the evening of the day.
There was nothing left to say.

(Tr. Anna Krushelnitskaya)

Part II
Prose

Arkadii Gaidar

Tale of a Great Military Secret and a Brave Boy Whose Word Was Firm (1933)

In the days long gone by, when war was just done thundering over our homeland, there lived a kid. His name was Braveboy.

In those days Red Army had chased the damn Tyranny Troops out and away, and so our broad fields found peace, as did our green meadows; rye grew tall, buckwheat bloomed white, and lush cherry orchards hid the small house in which Braveboy, a motherless kid, lived with his father and his older brother.

His father worked: he cut hay. His brother worked: he stacked hay. Braveboy helped his father sometimes, he helped his brother other times, and there were also times when he simply jumped around and played with boys.

Hop! Hop! Life is good! Bullets don't whizz, shells don't boom, villages don't burn. No need to fall to the floor to hide from the bullets, no need to go to the cellar to hide from the shells, no need to run to the woods to hide from the fires. No damn Tyranny Troops to fear. No boss to bow down to. Live and work! Things are good.

One time, late in the day, Braveboy came out on his porch. He looked at the sky: the sky was clear. The wind was warm, and the sun

* *(All prose translated by Anna Krushelnitskaya)*

beyond the Black Mountains was settling for the night. Everything seemed right, yet something felt wrong.

Braveboy heard knocking; or, maybe, it was banging he heard. Braveboy sniffed the air: the wind smelled not of orchard blossoms nor of meadow honey, but of smoke and fire, or explosions and gunpowder.

He told this to his father, who had come home very tired that day.

"Come on," said Braveboy's father. "The banging is just thunder from beyond the Black Mountains. The smoke is coming from the bonfires on which Blue River shepherds cook their supper as they mind their herds. Go to bed, Boy, and sleep tight."

Braveboy went to bed. He tried to sleep. He tried to sleep but he could not, he could not sleep no matter what.

Then, he heard stomping by his house. He heard rapping on the window. Braveboy looked out and saw a rider whose horse was black, whose blade was bright, whose hat was gray with a star that was red.

"Arise!" shouted the rider. "Trouble came where there was none! The damn Tyranny Troops attacked us from beyond the Black Mountains! Again, bullets whizz; again, shells boom. Again, our Troops must fight Tyranny, and messengers ride far and fast on horseback to call the whole Red Army to arms."

The rider made his alarming speech and off he galloped like lightning. Braveboy's father got up, took his rifle off the hook on the wall, threw his bag over his shoulder, and strapped on his ammunition belt.

"Son," he said to his oldest, "I sowed a lot of rye, and the harvesting now falls to you."

"Son," he said to Braveboy, "I saw a lot of trouble in my life and living well now falls to you."

That was how he spoke. Then, he gave Braveboy one big kiss good-bye and left. He had no time for more kisses and long partings: everyone could already see and hear blasts booming beyond the meadows and smoky fires giving red glow to the sky beyond the mountains.

A day passed, then another day passed. Braveboy came out on the porch to see if the Red Army was there—but it wasn't yet. Braveboy climbed on the roof. He kept watch all day—no Red Army yet. It got late and he went to bed.

Then, he heard stomping by his house. He heard rapping on the window. Braveboy looked out and saw it was the same rider as before, but his horse was now tired and gaunt, his blade was bent, his hat had a bullet hole in it, his red star was cut in half, and his head was bandaged.

"Arise!" the rider shouted. "We had some trouble before, but we have nothing but trouble now! The Tyranny Troops are many and our men are few. Bullets swarm thick over the battlefields and shells drop on our Troops by the thousand. Arise, arise, give help!"

Braveboy's big brother stood up and said to Braveboy:

"Farewell, Boy. It's just you now. You have soup in the pot, you have bread on the table, you have fresh water in the stream and a good head on your shoulders. Take care of yourself the best you can, and do not wait for my return."

A day passed, then another day passed. Braveboy was sitting on the roof by the chimney when he saw a new rider coming in on horseback from afar.

The rider made it to Braveboy's house, hopped off his horse and said:

"Good Boy, give me some water to drink. I've had no water for three days, no sleep for three nights, and I wore out three horses on my journey. The Red Army did hear about the trouble we are in. The buglers are playing all the bugles they have. The drummers are playing their loudest drums. The flag bearers have their battle flags up! Our whole Red Army is rushing to help! We just need to last till tomorrow night."

Braveboy got off the roof and brought water to the man. The rider drank his fill and off he went.

Night fell, and Braveboy went to bed. He tried to sleep, but he could not—sleep never came.

Then, he heard steps by his house. He heard rustling by his window. Braveboy looked out; there was the man he saw before. The

Illustration by Vladimir Konashevich in *Skazka o voennoĭ taĭne o mal'chishe-kibal'chishe i ego tverdom slove* by Arkadii Gaĭdar (Moscow/Leningrad: Ogiz-Molodaia gvardiia, 1933). Source: Cotsen Children's Library, Princeton Slavic Collections.

man was the same, yet not the same: his horse was now gone, his blade was broken, his hat had been lost in battle, and he himself kept swaying back and forth because he could barely stand.

"Arise!" he shouted, one last time. "We have shells to launch but our soldiers are down. We have rifles to shoot but our Troops are few. We have help coming, but no strength to hold on. Arise, arise whoever's left! We must last one more night and a day after that."

Braveboy looked outside. The street was empty. No shutters flapping, no gates screeching; no people left to arise. All fathers had gone, all brothers had gone. There was no one to spare.

The only man Braveboy saw come out of his gate was a hundred years old. The old man tried to get his rifle up, but he was so old that he couldn't. The old man tried to put his saber on, but he was so weak that he couldn't. The old man sat on the stoop by his house, and he hung his head, and he cried.

Braveboy's heart ached.

Braveboy rushed outside and he gave the loudest call:

"Hey you, Boys, hey you, Kids! Let's show we can do more than throw sticks and jump ropes! Our fathers have gone; our brothers have gone. We Kids should not be sitting here waiting

Illustration by Veniamin Losin in filmstrip *Skazka o voennoi taine* by Arkadii Gaïdar (Moscow: Studia Diafilm, 1968)

for the damn Tyranny Troops to round us up and take us to their damn Tyranny!"

All Boys and Kids heard his words, and they made such a ruckus! They shouted and clamored. They hopped out of windows, they jumped out of doors, and they leaped over fences, too.

They all wanted to help. There was only one Boy, named Bratboy, who wanted to live in Tyranny. Bratboy was so sly that he never said anything to anyone; he just pulled up his pants and ran together with the rest of the Boys, pretending to want to be helpful.

Boys battled as night fell dark and they battled as day dawned bright. Bratboy alone did no battle at all. He kept walking around and looking around, figuring out how to help the Tyranny Troops. At last, Bratboy saw a pile of boxes stacked behind a small hill. The boxes were full of black bombs, white shells, and yellow bullets. "Nice!" Bratboy thought. "This is exactly what I need."

At that time, Master of Tyranny asked his Generals of Tyranny:

"Well, my faithful Tyranny Generals, did you win a victory yet?"

"No, Master," the Generals replied. "We beat the fathers and we beat the brothers; victory was almost ours when Braveboy came rushing to give help, and we can't beat that Braveboy yet."

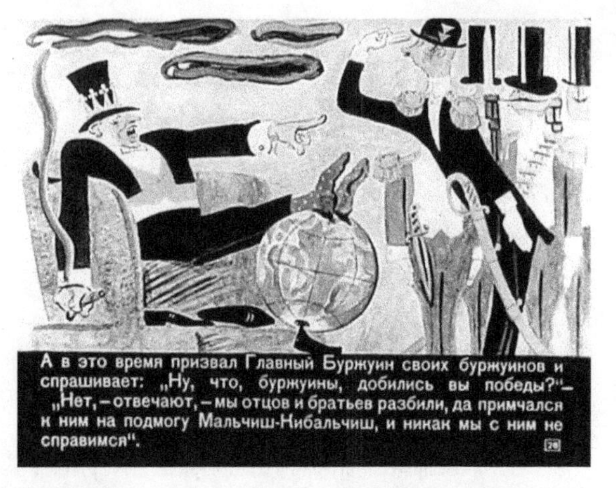

Illustration by Veniamin Losin in filmstrip *Skazka o voennoi taine* by Arkadii Gaidar (Moscow: Studia Diafilm, 1968)

Master of Tyranny was angry and stunned. He yelled in a booming voice:

"How could it be that Braveboy has not been beaten? You yellow-bellied Tyranny dupes, you! Why can't you beat him? He is so runty! Off you go! Don't come back till you win!"

The Generals sat down to think. What evil plan could they hatch?

Then, they saw Bratboy crawl out of the bushes and run straight toward them.

"Cheer up!" Bratboy shouted. "I did it! Me, Bratboy! It was all me! I chopped firewood, I spread hay, and I set fire to all the boxes with black bombs, white shells, and yellow bullets. Watch them go bang and ka-pow!"

The Generals of Tyranny got very excited. They quickly gave Bratboy his Tyranny papers, a big barrel of jam, and a big basket of cookies.

Bratboy sat there and gleefully stuffed his stupid face.

Then—boom!—went the boxes he had set on fire! The blast was as loud as a thousand thunders and as bright as a thousand lightnings coming from one big storm cloud.

Illustration by Vladimir Konashevich in *Skazka o voennoĭ taĭne o mal'chishe-kibal'chishe i ego tverdom slove* by Arkadii Gaĭdar (Moscow/ Leningrad: Ogiz-Molodaia͡ gvardii͡a, 1933). Source: Cotsen Children's Library, Princeton Slavic Collections.

"Treason!" Braveboy shouted.

"Treason!" shouted all his true Boys-in-Arms.

Out of smoke, out of flames Tyranny Troops came flying in droves; they seized Braveboy and tied him up.

They put Braveboy in heavy chains and locked him in a tall stone tower. Then, they sped off to ask their Master what plans he had for the captured Braveboy.

Master of Tyranny thought for a long time, and he thought up a plan. He said:

"Braveboy will be destroyed. But first, we will make him reveal their Great Military Secret. Go to him, my faithful Troops, and ask him these questions.

'Braveboy, why did Forty Kingdoms and Forty Empires go to war with the Red Army, yet they fought the fight just to lose the fight?'

'Braveboy, why are all our prisons, jails, and labor camps filled to the brim, all our police out in the street, all our troops up on their feet, yet we know no peace, not in the light of day nor in the dark of night?'

'Braveboy, damn your stupid bravery, why do the subjects of my High Tyranny, like the subjects of the Low Kingdom, the Snow

Tsardom and the Scorch Empire, sing the same songs, though not in the same language, but on the same days, in early spring and in late fall; and they carry the same banners, although not in the same hands; and they all speak the same, think the same, act the same?'

Then, ask him this, my faithful troops:

'Does or does not the Red Army have a Great Military Secret?'

He must tell you the Secret.

'Do or do not our workers receive outside aid?'

He must tell you where the aid comes from.

'Does or does not your Land, Braveboy, have a secret tunnel to other Lands? Do you call into the tunnel to make our subjects respond, do you sing into the tunnel to make our subjects sing back, do you say things into the tunnel that make our subjects think?'

The Tyranny Troops left, only to return very soon.

"No, Master of Tyranny, Braveboy did not reveal the Military Secret to us. He laughed in our faces!

He said, 'Yes, our strong Red Army does have a powerful Secret. Any time you attack, you will lose.'

'Yes, we do give endless aid. Throw people in prisons all you want; more will come in their place. You won't know peace in the light of day nor in the dark of night.'

'Yes, we do have deep secret tunnels. Search and search again; your search will come to nothing. And even if you find them, you won't ever fill, close, or block them. This is my last word to you, damn Tyranny Men, and I bet you won't figure out the answers on your own, not in a century or longer!'"

Master of Tyranny frowned and said:

"If that's how it's going to be, then put this Braveboy through the most unbearable Torture in the world, my faithful Troops, and make him give up the Military Secret, because we won't be able to live and breathe until this very important Secret is ours."

The Tyranny Troops left. This time, they took a long time to return.

They walked up, shaking their heads.

"No," they said, "no, Master. Braveboy stood pale but proud. He never gave up the Military Secret; his word was that firm. When we were leaving, he fell to the ground, put his ear against the hard stone of the cold floor, and would you believe it, Master? He smiled, and his smile made our Tyranny selves shudder, because we feared he might have heard our certain death marching forth to get us through the secret tunnels."

"I can't make sense of this Land!" exclaimed Master of Tyranny in wonder. "What is this impossible place where even runty Boys know the Military Secret and keep their firm word no matter what? Hurry now, my Tyranny Troops, and destroy this prideful Braveboy! Load your cannons, unsheathe your sabers, unfold your Tyranny Banners, for I can hear our buglers call an alarm and I can see our wavers wave their flags. This will be no small fight; this will be a deadly battle."

And Braveboy did perish.

But!

Have you ever seen a big rainstorm?

Like in a rainstorm, cannons went booming loud as thunder. Fiery explosions went flashing bright like lightning. Cavalry Troops blew in like the wind, and red banners flew by like storm clouds. The Red Army went on the attack.

Have you ever seen a heavy downpour during a hot dry summer?

Like streams running down dusty cliffs, joining to make fast-flowing foamy rivers, uprisings came to the High Tyranny at the first roll of war thunder to be joined by thousands of furious voices from the Low Kingdom, the Snow Tsardom and the Scorch Empire.

Then, the vanquished Master of Tyranny ran away in terror, loudly cursing the Land where the people were incredibly strong, the army undefeated, and the Great Military Secret forever kept a secret.

Braveboy was buried on a green hill by the Blue River. A big red banner waves over his grave.

When ships sail by, they greet Braveboy!

When planes fly by, they greet Braveboy!

When trains run by, they greet Braveboy!

When Young Pioneers go by, they salute Braveboy!

Viktor Dragunsky

What I Love (1960)

I love to lie belly-down in my Papa's lap, dangle my arms and legs, and just hang over his knee like I'm laundry drying on a fence. I also really like to play checkers, chess, and dominoes, but only if I win every time. If I don't win, then no-thank-you.

I love to listen to a beetle scramble inside a matchbox. And on Sundays, I love to climb into Papa's bed to talk to him about us getting a dog: how one day we'll have more living space, and then we'll get a puppy, and we'll take care of him, and feed him, and he'll be so funny and so smart, and he'll steal sugar cubes from the kitchen, and I'll mop up his puppy puddles, and he'll follow me around like a faithful dog.

I also like to watch TV. I don't care what's on. I'll even watch static.

I love to sniffle into Mama's ear. I especially love to sing, and I always sing very loudly.

I like to read stories about the Red Cavalry a whole lot, and I like for them to win every battle.

I like to stand in front of the mirror and pull faces like I'm Petrushka from the puppet show. And I also really like sardines.

I like to read stories about Sang Kancil. Sang Kancil is a small, clever and playful mouse-deer. He has bright little eyes, small horns, and tiny shiny pink hooves. When we have more living space, we'll buy a Sang Kancil and he'll live in the bathroom. Also, I love to swim where it's shallow, so I can walk with my hands on the sandy bottom.

At May Day parades, I like to wave my small red flag around and blow my loud balloon whistle.

I love talking on the phone.

I like whittling and sawing. I know how to make heads of ancient warriors and bison out of clay. I have sculpted a clay pheasant and the Tsar Cannon. I love to give those things as gifts.

When I sit down to read, I like to snack on something crunchy.

I love having guests over.

I also love garter snakes, lizards, and frogs. They are so quick! I carry them around in my pockets. I like to put a garter snake in front of me on the table when I eat dinner. I love it when Grandma sees a baby frog, screams, "Put this disgusting thing away!"—and runs out of the room.

I like to laugh. Sometimes I don't even feel like laughing at all, but I just force myself. I squeeze laughs out of my belly and then, hey, in five minutes things do start to seem funny!

When I'm in a good mood, I like to hop. Once, Papa and I went to the zoo, and I started hopping around him in the street. He asked, "Why are you hopping?" I said, "I'm hopping that you are my Papa!"

He understood!

I love going to the zoo! They have wonderful big elephants there. And one baby elephant. When we have more living space, we'll buy a baby elephant. I'll build a garage for him.

I really like to stand behind a purring automobile and smell the exhaust.

I like to go to the café to eat ice cream and drink soda water. The soda prickles inside my nose and makes my eyes run.

When I run up and down the hallway, I like to stomp my feet as hard as I can.

I love horses. They have such beautiful and kind faces.

I love so many things!

. . . And What I Hate! (1960)

What I really hate is going to the dentist. When I spy a dentist's chair, I want to run to the end of the earth right away. I also hate to be told to stand on a kitchen stool and recite poems for our guests.

I don't like it when Mama and Papa go to the theater without me.

I can't stand it when they feed me runny soft-boiled eggs mashed in a cup and mixed with bread chunks.

I also don't like it when Mama takes me for a walk and then suddenly runs into Auntie Roza!

Then, they only talk to each other, and I can't find anything to do with myself.

I hate wearing new suits. They make me feel wooden.

When we play Red Army and White Army, I hate being a White. Then, I just quit the game, and that's it! And when I'm a Red, I hate being captured. I run away all the same.

I hate it when I don't win a game.

I don't like it when people do the happy birthday dance around me: I'm not a baby.

I don't like kids who show off.

And I really hate it when I cut my finger and, to make things worse, I get iodine poured over the cut—it burns.

I don't like it that our hallway is so narrow and that grown-ups are always in the hallway, scurrying back and forth, first with a kettle, then with a pot, shouting, "Kids! Get out from underfoot! Watch out, this pot is hot!"

And when I go to bed, I hate it if the neighbors in the room next door start to sing in chorus, "Blooms of spring, blooms of spring . . ."

I really can't stand it that girls and boys in radio plays sound like old ladies.

I hate it that there's no fix for ink spills yet!

All Secrets Come to Light (1961)

Once, I overheard my Mama say to someone out in the hallway, "All secrets eventually come to light."

When she came into the room, I asked: "What does it mean, 'secrets come to light,' Mama?"

"It means, if someone does something dishonest, people will find out about it sooner or later, and the person will feel shame and be given some punishment," said Mama. "Get it? Now get yourself to bed."

I brushed my teeth and went to bed, but instead of sleeping I kept thinking: How does it work, all secrets coming to light? I could not fall asleep for a long time, and when I woke up, it was morning, Papa had left for work, and Mama and I were alone in the house. I brushed my teeth again and sat down to breakfast.

First, I ate an egg. The egg was not so bad, because I managed to eat just the yolk from the middle and to mince the white into the shells to hide it. But then Mama brought me a whole bowl of hot porridge.

"Eat!" said Mama. "And I don't want to hear anything about it."

I said, "I can't stomach hot porridge!"

Mama shouted at me: "Just look at what you have become! You're a walking skeleton! Eat. You need to fill out."

I said, "It makes me gag."

Mama sat down next to me, hugged me around the shoulders, and asked me sweetly, "Do you want me to take you to the Kremlin?"

Did I ever! I don't think there is anything more beautiful in the world than the Kremlin. I've been to the Palace of Facets and to the Armory, I stood by the Tsar Cannon, and I know where the throne of Ivan the Terrible used to be. There are many more interesting things there, as well, and that's why I gave Mama a very quick answer: "Of course, I want to go to the Kremlin! I very much want to!"

Mama smiled: "All right then. Eat all your porridge and then we'll go. Meanwhile, I'll be doing the dishes. Just make sure to eat all of it so I can see the bottom of the bowl!"

Then, Mama went to the kitchen.

I was left alone to face my porridge. I slapped it with the spoon. I sprinkled salt on it. I tried it, but it was inedible! Then, I thought that perhaps it needed sugar. I sprinkled sugar on the porridge and tried it again. It tasted even worse. I hate porridge, like I already told you.

To make things worse, it was very thick. If it were thin and runny, it would be different: I could just squeeze my eyes shut and drink it. With that thought, I poured some hot water in the porridge. It was slimy, sticky, and nasty all the same. The hardest thing was, when I tried to swallow it, my throat closed on its own and pushed the porridge back out. It was terribly frustrating! I really wanted to go to the Kremlin! Then, I remembered we had horseradish sauce. I think horseradish sauce can help anything go down. So, I took the jar and poured most sauce out of it in the porridge and, when I put a little bit of that mix in my mouth, my eyes popped out of my head, and I stopped breathing. I must have lost consciousness for a moment because I grabbed the bowl, ran up to the window very fast, and tossed the porridge out in the street. Then, I ran right back and sat down at the table.

The same minute, Mama came in. She saw the bowl and said, very pleased: "Hey, Deniska, you're a champion today! You ate all the porridge, and the bottom of the bowl shows. Okay, rise up, brave citizens, get dressed, and let's go see the Kremlin!" And then she kissed me.

In that instant, our door opened, and a policeman entered the room. He said, "Good morning!" Then, he went to the window, looked down, and said, "I can't believe they call themselves cultured people."

"What do you need?" asked Mama sternly.

"Shame on you!" The policeman stood at attention. "The government provides you with a new residence, which has all modern conveniences and a garbage chute, by the way, and you choose to toss all kinds of slime out the window!"

"That's a bald-faced lie! I don't toss anything out."

"Oh, is that right? You don't toss anything?" The policeman gave a mocking laugh. "Let's see the victim!"

A strange man walked into our room.

The second I laid my eyes on him I realized I was not going to the Kremlin.

The strange man wore a hat on top of his head. On top of the hat, there was our porridge. The porridge sat neatly in the middle of the hat, in the dip, and around the edges next to the band; there was porridge inside his collar, on his shoulders and on his left pant leg. The man came in and began to stutter:

"But the thing is, I was going to get my picture taken. And then this happens.... This puh-puh-porridge.... This huh-huh-hot puh-porridge, it even burned me through the huh-hat. . . . How am I going to mail my fuh-fuh-photo now that I am covered in porridge?"

Mama looked at me and her eyes turned gooseberry-green, which is always a certain sign that Mama is terribly angry.

"Please forgive us," she said quietly. "Please allow me to clean you up. Just come through here."

All three of them went out in the hallway.

When Mama returned, I was too scared to even lift my eyes at her. But I forced myself to, and I came up to her and said:

"You were right yesterday, Mama. All secrets eventually come to light!"

Mama looked me in the eyes. She kept looking for a long, long time. Then, she asked, "Are you going to remember this for the rest of your life?"

I answered, "Yes."

He's Alive and He Glows (1964)

One evening, I was sitting by a pile of sand in our yard, waiting for my Mama. She must have been held up at the Institute or at the store, or, maybe, she was simply waiting for her bus. I'm not sure. All I knew was, the parents of all other neighborhood kids had come and taken their children home; they were probably all cozy now, having tea with salty cheese and crackers, and my Mama was still out somewhere.

Lights went on in the windows, one by one; radio music began playing and dark clouds started across the sky. The clouds looked like beardy old men.

I was getting hungry, but Mama was still not coming. I thought that if I had found out my Mama was waiting for me somewhere on the edge of the world, all hungry, I would run to her right away, instead of being late and making her sit on a pile of sand and miss me.

And then, my friend Mishka came out.

He said, "Hey."

I said, "Hey."

Mishka sat down next to me and picked up my dump truck.

"Neat!" Mishka said. "Where'd you get it? Does it scoop sand? No? Does it dump sand? Yeah? What's this handle? What's it for? Does it spin? Yeah? Wow! Can I borrow it?"

I said:

"No, you can't. It's a gift. Papa gave it to me before he left town."

Mishka got all huffy and moved a little bit away from me. The evening became even darker than before.

I kept looking at the gate, making sure I would not miss the moment Mama came. But Mama kept not coming. She probably ran into Auntie Roza and chose to stand there and chat with her, not thinking about me at all.

I lay down on the sand.

Then, Mishka said:

"So, can I have your dump truck?"

"Get lost, Mishka."

Mishka said:

"I'll trade it for stamps! One Guatemala and two Barbadoses!"

I said:

"Your Barbadoses are no match for my truck."

Mishka went:

"Wanna take my swim ring?"

I said:

"It's bursted."

Mishka went:

"You'll fix it up!"

That made me a little angry.

"Where would I swim? In the communal bathtub? On Tuesdays, when it's our turn to use it?"

Illustration by Veniamin Losin in *On zhivoi i svetitsia* by Viktor Dragunsky (Moscow: Detskaia literatura, 1987)

Mishka got huffy again. After a while, he said:

"Oh, whatever. Remember my kindhood! Here, take this!"

He offered me a matchbox. I took it.

"Open it!" Mishka said. "You'll see!"

I opened the box and saw nothing at first. Then, I saw a little pale-green flicker; it looked like a tiny star burning far, far away from me, and at the same time sitting in a box, in my hands.

"What is this, Mishka," I whispered. "What is this?"

"It's a firefly," Mishka said. "Isn't he nice? Don't worry, he's alive."

"Mishka!" I said. "Take my dump truck if you want to, okay? Take it for keeps! Just let me have this star. I'll take it home with me. . . ."

Mishka grabbed my dump truck and ran to his house. I stayed where I was, holding my firefly, looking at him, looking at him again and again; I could not get enough of how green he was, a fairy-tale green, and how faraway his light was, though he was so close, right

Illustration by Veniamin Losin in *On zhivoi i svetitsia* by Viktor Dragunsky (Moscow: Detskaia literatura, 1987)

there in my palm. I couldn't catch a breath, I heard my heart hammer in my chest, and a funny prickly feeling inside my nose made me think I was about to cry.

I sat like that for a long, long time. There was no one else anywhere around. I forgot about everyone living in the whole wide world.

But then my Mama came, and I was very happy. We walked home together. When we sat down to have tea with salty cheese and crackers, Mama asked me:

"How's your new dump truck?"

I said:

"I traded it, Mama."

Mama said:

"How curious! What did you trade it for?"

I said:

"I traded it for a firefly who lives in this box. Turn off the lights!"

Mama turned off the lights, the room went dark, and we both sat down to look at the tiny magical pale-green star.

After a while, Mama turned the lights back on.

"Yes," she said, "this is magic, of course. But still! What made you want to trade your precious dump truck for this little bug?"

"You were taking such a long time," I said. "I was so lonely, and then this firefly, he turned out to be better than all the dump trucks in the world."

Mama looked at me thoughtfully and asked:

"Why? What's making it better?"

I said:

"Don't you understand? He is alive! And he glows."

Valentin Katayev

The Seven-Petal Flower (1940)

There once was a little girl whose name was Zhenya. One day, her Mama sent her to the bakery to buy treats for tea. Zhenya bought seven cookies: two spice cookies for her Papa, two poppyseed cookies for her Mama, two sugar cookies for herself, and one small pink-glazed cookie for her baby brother Pavlik. Each cookie was shaped like a ring and strung on a string. Zhenya took the bundle and headed home. She walked home in no hurry, without a worry, dragging her toes, and counting crows. Little did she know that a stray dog was walking right behind her, eating the cookies one after another: first her Papa's spice cookies, then her Mama's poppyseed cookies, and then Zhenya's sugar cookies. Zhenya felt the cookie bundle getting too light. She turned around, but it was too late. The string dangled bare, and the dog was eating the last crumbs of Pavlik's pink-glazed baby cookie, licking his chops.

"Bad doggie!" shouted Zhenya and chased after the dog.

She ran and ran, she chased and chased, but she never caught up with the dog. Instead, she got lost. She looked around: the place was unfamiliar. There were no tall houses she was used to seeing, just a few small ones. Zhenya got scared and began to cry. Suddenly, a little old lady popped out of nowhere:

"Little girl, little girl, why are you crying?"

Zhenya told the old lady what had happened.

The old lady felt sorry for Zhenya. She took Zhenya to the little garden by her house and said:

"No need to worry, no need to cry. I will help you out. Truth be told, I have no cookies and I have no money, but I do have a special flower in my garden. I call it my Seven-Petal Flower, and it has magic powers. I can see that you are a good girl, even though you like to count crows. I will give you the Seven-Petal Flower to keep and it will help you whenever you need help."

With those words, the old lady plucked a very pretty blossom from her flowerbed. The flower looked like a daisy, and its seven petals were see-through. Each petal was a different color: one yellow, one red, one green, one indigo, one orange, one violet, and one blue.

"This is not just any old flower," the old lady said. "This flower will grant any wish. You only need to pull off one petal, throw it to the wind and say,

'Fly, my petal, fly, my petal,
East through west, and never settle,
Fly south after you fly north,
Fly back after you fly forth,
Fly until you land,
Follow my command!
I command you to do this, or that!'
At once, your wish will be granted."

Zhenya thanked the old lady politely, walked out of the garden gate, and only then remembered that she did not know the way back home. She wanted to return to the little garden and ask the old lady to walk her to the nearest police officer on traffic duty, but both the garden and the old lady had vanished into thin air. What was the girl to do? Zhenya was about to start crying, as was her habit, and she even scrunched up her nose, so it looked like a little accordion, when she remembered that she had a magic flower.

"Let's see what this Seven-Petal Flower can do!"

Zhenya tore off the yellow petal in a hurry, tossed it to the wind and said,

"Fly, my petal, fly, my petal,
East through west, and never settle,
Fly south after you fly north,
Fly back after you fly forth,
Fly until you land,
Follow my command!
I command you to take me to my house and give me all my cookies back!"

Hardly had she said it when she was back home, holding a bundle of cookies on a string!

Zhenya gave the cookies to her Mama and thought to herself, "This flower is truly fantastic! I must put it in the prettiest vase we have."

Zhenya was not a tall girl at all; that's why she had to get up on a chair to reach for her Mama's favorite vase which was kept on the highest shelf. Right then, as luck would have it, she saw crows flying past her window. Of course, she had to count the crows to find out how many they were exactly: seven or eight. She opened her mouth and started counting on her fingers. Meanwhile, the vase fell with a crash and smashed into a hundred tiny pieces.

"Did you break something again, Miss Loosey Goosey?" her mother yelled from the kitchen. "Was it my favorite vase, by any chance?"

"No, no, Mama darling, I broke nothing. You are just hearing things!" Zhenya shouted back. She quickly tore the red petal off her flower, tossed it up and whispered:

"Fly, my petal, fly, my petal,

East through west, and never settle,
Fly south after you fly north,
Fly back after you fly forth,
Fly until you land,
Follow my command!
I command you to make Mama's favorite vase whole!"

Hardly had she said it when the shards crawled across the floor and began to stick back together.

When Mama came running from the kitchen, she saw her favorite vase up on the shelf, looking like it had never been moved. Mama shook her finger at Zhenya, just in case, and sent her outside to play.

Zhenya went outside and saw boys playing in the yard, pretending to be Arctic explorers adrift in the ocean. The boys sat on some old wooden boards around a stick pushed in the sand.

"Boys, boys, can I come play with you?"

"No, you can't! Don't you see we're on the North Pole? Girls are not invited to go to the North Pole."

"What kind of North Pole is that? It's just some old wood!"

"It's not old wood; it's an ice floe! Stop bugging us and go away! We're badly squeezed between icebergs just now."

"I guess you won't let me play!"

"We won't. Get lost!"

"Big deal! I don't need you. I can get to the real North Pole by myself right now, and it will be much better than your stupid little made-up pole! I get to go to the North Pole, and you get nothing but a dead cat's tail!"

Zhenya stepped aside, closer to the gate, took out her secret Seven-Petal Flower, tore off the indigo petal, tossed it to the wind and said:

"Fly, my petal, fly, my petal,
East through west, and never settle,
Fly south after you fly north,
Fly back after you fly forth,
Fly until you land,

Illustration by Villi Trubkovich in *Tsvetik-semitsvetik* by Valentin Kataev (Moscow: Malysh, 1985)

Follow my command!

I command you to take me to the North Pole right this second!"

Hardly had she said it when a windstorm came out of nowhere, the sun vanished, the day turned to wicked night, and the earth spun under her feet like a wheel.

Zhenya, still in her sleeveless summer dress, her legs bare, found herself on the North Pole, alone as alone can be, in the negative one hundred degree cold!

"Oh, no, no, no! I'm freezing!" Zhenya cried and began to weep. Her tears froze at once. They dangled off her nose like icicles off a rain pipe.

Seven polar bears came from behind an iceberg and headed straight for the girl, each bear scarier than the next: the first bear with his fangs bare, the second bear with an angry glare, then the third, shaggy-furred, then the fourth, the beast of the north, then the fifth who wore a beret, then the sixth who had spots of gray, and then the last, the seventh bear, the biggest, the tallest, with the shaggiest hair.

Terrified out of her wits, Zhenya grabbed the flower with her icy-cold fingers, yanked out the green petal, threw it to the wind and shouted as loudly as she could:

"Fly, my petal, fly, my petal,
East through west, and never settle,
Fly south after you fly north,
Fly back after you fly forth,
Fly until you land,
Follow my command!
I command that you carry me to my yard back home, right now!"

In an instant, she was back home in her yard. The boys were still there. They looked at her and laughed:

"How was the North Pole?"

"I did go there! I did!"

"We saw nothing. Where's the proof?"

"Look, I still have an icicle on my nose!

"That's not an icicle! That's a dead cat's tail! Gotcha!"

Zhenya was offended. She decided not to bother playing with boys ever again and crossed the yard to play with girls. The girls, she discovered, had all kinds of toys with them. One girl had a toy stroller, another had a ball; one had a jump rope, another had a tricycle; one girl even had a big talking baby doll dressed in a straw baby doll hat and tiny baby doll rain boots. Zhenya was overcome by envy. Her jealous eyes turned yellowish green, like a goat's.

"You know what? I'll show you who has the best toys around here!" she thought to herself.

She took out the Seven-Petal Flower, pulled the orange petal off, threw it to the wind, and said:

"Fly, my petal, fly, my petal,
East through west, and never settle,
Fly south after you fly north,
Fly back after you fly forth,

Fly until you land,
Follow my command!
I command that you make all the toys in the world mine!"

In a blink of an eye, droves of toys came running to Zhenya from every direction. Dolls toddled over first, of course, batting their eyelashes and tirelessly squeaking 'mam-ma, mam-ma, mam-ma!' They made Zhenya very happy for a minute, but so many dolls kept coming that they quickly filled the yard, the lane, two streets, and half the neighborhood square. She couldn't take a step without stepping on a doll. Can you imagine the racket made by five million talking dolls? There were no fewer than five million. Besides, those were just the Moscow dolls. Dolls from Leningrad, Kharkov, Kiev, Lvov, and other Soviet cities were still on the way, running and screeching like parrots along every road in the USSR. Zhenya felt a little uneasy.

But that was just the beginning. Balls, balloons, scooters, tricycles, tractors, cars, tanks, tankettes, and wheeled cannons came rolling in behind the dolls on their own. Jump ropes slithered on the ground like snakes, getting tangled underfoot and making the nervous dolls squeak louder than ever. Millions of toy planes, gliders, and blimps were coming in by air. Tiny stuffed paratroopers were dropping from the sky with their parachutes looking like upside-down tulips; they got caught in trees and telephone wires. The city traffic was at a dead stop. Traffic policemen climbed on streetlight poles and sat there perched, at a loss for what to do.

"Enough, enough!" shouted Zhenya in terror, clutching her head. "Enough already! What are you doing? I don't need this many toys. I was joking! I'm scared!"

But did she stop them? No such luck! Toys kept pouring in. After Soviet toys had all arrived, American toys began to show. The whole city was up to its roofs in toys. Zhenya walked up the stairs, and so did the toys. Zhenya ran out to her balcony, and so did the toys. Zhenya raced to the attic, and so did the toys. Zhenya climbed on the roof, tore the purple petal off the flower as fast as she could, threw it to the wind, and said:

"Fly, my petal, fly, my petal,
East through west, and never settle,
Fly south after you fly north,
Fly back after you fly forth,
Fly until you land,
Follow my command!

I command that you send all the toys back to the shops right this second!"

The toys were gone in a whiff.

Zhenya looked at her flower and saw that it had but one petal left.

"Will you look at that! Turns out I wasted six petals, and I am not any happier! Oh well. I'll be smarter from now on."

She went for a walk along her street. She walked and she thought:

"Now, what's my next command going to be? How about I command two kilograms of chocolate candy for myself, or maybe. . . . No, two kilograms of bonbons. Or, better yet, here's what I'll order: half a kilo of chocolates, half a kilo of bonbons, a hundred grams of honey sweets, a hundred grams of sugared nuts, and, as long as I'm being generous and kind, one pink-glazed cookie for my brother Pavlik. Although, what good would it do? Let's say I command and eat all of that. I'll be left with nothing! No, I better command a tricycle. Although, what would I do with it? I'd ride it a couple of times and then those mean boys would probably take it from me! They might even beat me up. No, I better command a movie ticket or a circus ticket instead. At least I would have fun. Or should I command a new pair of sandals? New sandals are as good as the circus! Although, truth be told, what's so great about new sandals anyway? I could command something a lot better! I just have to make sure to take my time."

Walking and reasoning with herself, Zhenya stopped when she saw a most excellent boy sitting on the bench by the gate. His big blue eyes were full of humor and calm. He looked like a very good-natured boy, and he was clearly not a bully. Zhenya thought she wanted to be friends with him. With no fear in her heart the girl came so close to the boy that she saw reflections of her own face and her own pigtails draped over her shoulders, one in each of his pupils.

"Hello, boy! What's your name?"

"Vitya. What's yours?"

"Zhenya. Want to play tag?"

"I can't. I have a bad foot."

Zhenya looked at his foot. It was dressed in an ugly shoe with a very thick sole.

"That's too bad!" Zhenya said. "I really like you, and I think I'd really enjoy running around with you."

"I really like you, too. I'd also like to run around with you but, unfortunately, it is impossible for me. There's nothing to be done. I'll always have this bad foot."

"Oh, what silly, silly things you are saying!" Zhenya exclaimed as she took her secret Seven-Petal Flower out of her pocket. "Look!"

With those words, the girl carefully pulled off the last petal, the blue one, pressed it to her eyelids for a split second, then let her fingers fall open and began singing in a high, quivering, happy voice:

"Fly, my petal, fly, my petal,
East through west, and never settle,
Fly south after you fly north,
Fly back after you fly forth,
Fly until you land,
Follow my command!
I command that you make Vitya healthy!"

At once, the boy leapt off the bench and off he was to play tag with Zhenya! He ran so fast that she could not catch him, hard as she tried.

The Pipe and the Jug (1940)

Wild strawberries grew ripe in the summer forest.

Zhenya took a small jug, her Papa took a big mug, her Mama took a pretty cup, and Pavlik the baby got the saucer.

The family walked to the forest and began picking berries. They set a bet on who would pick the most. Mama chose a nice clearing in the trees and said:

"This is a great little spot for you, Zhenya! A lot of berries here. All you have to do is pick them."

Zhenya cleaned her jug with a large fuzzy leaf and began walking around the clearing.

She walked around once, then twice. She looked around once, then twice. She found nothing and returned with her little jug empty.

She saw that everyone had gathered some strawberries. Her Papa's mug was a quarter full. Her Mama's cup was half-full. Even Pavlik the baby had two berries in his saucer.

"Mama, why do all of you have berries and I have none? I think you gave me the worst spot!"

"Did you look around carefully?"

"Very carefully. There were no berries at all, just leaves."

"Did you peek under the leaves?"

"No."

"Well, there you go! You need to peek under the leaves."

"Why is Pavlik not peeking?"

"Pavlik is little. He is no taller than a strawberry plant, so he does not need to stoop. You, on the other hand, are quite a tall girl now."

Papa said:

"Berries are sly. Berries hide from us. There is a trick to getting them. Look at what I do!"

Papa squatted, stooped low to the ground, lifted the leaves, and began searching for berries leaf by leaf, chanting:

"One berry isn't hard to find, the second one is close behind, and then I have a third in sight, and then a fourth one on my mind!"

"Very good, Papa," said Zhenya. "Thank you! I'll do what you did."

Zhenya returned to her spot, squatted, stooped low to the ground, and peeked under the leaves. There were more berries under the leaves than the eye could see or the mind could count! Zhenya did not even know where to look first. She began to pull berries off the stalks and toss them in her little jug. She kept picking and chanting:

"One berry isn't hard to find, the second one is close behind, and then I have a third in sight, and then a fourth one on my mind!"

Soon, however, Zhenya grew tired of squatting.

"I've done enough," she thought. "I probably have a whole bunch picked already."

Zhenya stood up and looked inside the jug. There were just four berries in it.

That was too few! She had no choice but to squat down again.

Zhenya squatted and plucked at the strawberry plants, chanting: "One berry isn't hard to find, the second one is close behind, and then I have a third in sight, and then a fourth one on my mind!"

Zhenya peered into the jug and saw only eight berries in it; the bottom of the jug was still showing!

"You know," she thought, "I don't much like this kind of berry picking. All this stooping, all this squatting. I might even tire myself out trying to fill this jug! I better go look for a different spot."

Off she went to look for a spot in the forest where strawberries did not hide under leaves but jumped out at her begging to be picked and tossed in the jug.

Zhenya walked and walked, but there was no such spot to be seen. She got tired and sat down on a tree stump to catch a breath. Because she had nothing else to do, she took the strawberries out of the jug and put them in her mouth, one by one. Soon, she swallowed all eight, peered inside the empty jug and thought, "Well, now what do I do? I wish I had some help out here!"

As soon as she thought that, moss wiggled under her feet, tufts of grass spread apart, and a short burly old man crawled out from under the tree stump. He had a white jacket, a smoky-gray beard, and a velvet hat with dry straw stuck to it.

"Good afternoon, little girl," he said.

"Good afternoon, sir."

"Don't call me sir, call me Grandpa. Don't you know who I am? I'm Old Mushroom White the Forest Sprite, who is in charge of mushrooms and berries small and large. Now, why do you sigh so hard? Did anyone hurt you?"

"Berries hurt me, Grandpa Mushroom."

"That's something I never heard before! They are usually quite tame. What did they do to hurt you?"

"They won't show themselves to me. They hide under leaves. They make it so I can't see them! That's why I keep bending down, and I wouldn't want to tire myself out trying to fill this jug, thank you very much!"

Old Mushroom White the Forest Sprite smoothed his stringy gray beard, smiled into his whiskers, and said:

"Ah! This won't take me long to fix. You see, I have a special little pipe. When it plays, all berries pop above the leaves to show themselves at once."

Old Mushroom White the Forest Sprite took a small pipe out of his pocket and said:

"Play, pipe, play!"

The pipe began playing all by itself, and when it did, berries popped out from under leaves here and there.

"Stop, pipe, stop!"

The pipe stopped playing and the berries hid again.

Zhenya was excited:

"Grandpa Mushroom, Grandpa Mushroom, give me your pipe to keep!"

"I can't just give it to you. Let us trade: I give you the pipe and you give me this little jug, which I like very much."

"Yes, let's! I'll be very pleased."

Zhenya gave Old Mushroom White the Forest Sprite her little jug, took the pipe, and ran back to her first picking spot at once.

She ran out to the middle of the clearing, stood still, and said:

"Play, pipe, play!"

The pipe began to play and, right then, all the leaves around her wiggled and turned up as if stirred by wind.

The first berries to peek out were the newest, youngest ones, green-tipped and curious. Next, the berries which were a tad older showed their faces, one cheek pink and the other white. Next, the ripe berries glowed big and red. The last ones to show were the elderly berries, wet, fragrant, almost black, covered with bright yellow seeds.

Soon the entire clearing around Zhenya was richly studded with berries glowing bright in the sun and straining toward the pipe.

"Play, pipe, play!" Zhenya cried out. "Play faster!"

The pipe played faster, and even more berries popped up; there were so many berries that she could no longer see the leaves underneath.

Nevertheless, Zhenya was not content.

"Play, pipe, play, pipe! Faster! Faster!"

The pipe played faster still, and the forest filled with such sweet whirlwind chiming that it seemed it was no longer a forest but a music box. Bees stopped pushing a butterfly off a flower; the butterfly clapped her wings shut like a book; young robins poked their heads out of their lightweight nest swinging in the elderberry branches, their yellow mouths agape with delight; mushrooms stood on tiptoes, striving not to miss a single sound, and even the old bulgy-eyed dragonfly, famous for her nasty disposition, froze midflight, seized with awe over the marvelous music.

"Now, I'm ready to start picking!" thought Zhenya but, as soon as she reached out for the biggest reddest berry, she remembered she had traded her jug for the pipe, and now she had nowhere to put the berries.

"You, dumb old pipe!" Zhenya shouted angrily. "Playing your dumb happy tunes when I have nowhere to put my berries! Pipe down at once!"

Zhenya rushed back to see Old Mushroom White the Forest Sprite.

"Grandpa Mushroom, Grandpa Mushroom! Please let me have my jug back! I have nowhere to put my berries."

"Sure," said Old Mushroom White the Forest Sprite. "You can have your jug back if you give me my pipe."

Zhenya gave the pipe back to Old Mushroom White the Forest Sprite, took her jug, and ran back fast to the spot she came from.

When she got there, not a single berry was to be seen; there were only leaves. What rotten luck! She had the jug but not the pipe. What was she to do?

Zhenya thought awhile and decided to go see Old Mushroom White one more time, to get the pipe back.

So, she went to him and said:

"Grandpa Mushroom, Grandpa Mushroom, give me your pipe again, please!"

"Sure, as long as you give me the jug."

"I won't give you the jug. I need the jug for my berries."

"I won't give you the pipe then."

Zhenya begged and pleaded:

"Grandpa Mushroom, Grandpa Mushroom! How do I put berries in my jug if they just stay under the leaves and won't even show themselves to me without your pipe? I need both the pipe and the jug for everything to work!"

"What a sly little girl you are! Both the jug and the pipe? Will you look at that! No, you will have to work it out with just the jug. No pipe for you."

"But I can't work it out, Grandpa Mushroom!"

"Oh? How do other people work it out?"

"Other people stoop low to the ground, peek under the leaves from the side and pick one berry at a time. One berry isn't hard to find, the second one is close behind, and then they have a third in sight, and then a fourth one on their mind! I don't like that kind of berry picking at all. All that bending, all that stooping! I wouldn't want to tire myself out trying to fill this jug, thank you very much!"

"Is that right?" said Old Mushroom White the Forest Sprite, and so angry were his words that his beard turned from gray to pitch-black. "Is that right? Well, now I see that you are just very lazy! Take your jug and go! I'll never let you borrow my pipe again."

With those words, Old Mushroom White the Forest Sprite stomped his foot and vanished under the tree stump with a pop.

Zhenya looked at her empty jug, remembered that her Papa, Mama, and baby brother Pavlik were waiting for her, ran back to her clearing, squatted, peeked under the leaves, and began picking berries quickly, one by one. The first one wasn't hard to find, the second one was close behind, then she had a third in sight, and then the fourth one on her mind.

Soon, Zhenya gathered a whole jug full of strawberries and returned to her Papa, Mama, and baby brother Pavlik.

"Good girl!" said Papa. "That's a very full jug! You must be very tired."

"Not very, Papa. The jug helped me."

Then, the whole family went home: Zhenya's Papa with a full mug, Zhenya with a full jug, her Mama with a full cup, and baby Pavlik with a full saucer.

As for the pipe, Zhenya never told anyone about it.

L. Panteleev

Honest Word (1941)

It is a great pity that I can't tell you the name of this little person, or where he lives, or who his Mama and Papa are. In the dark, I didn't even get the chance to see his face properly. I only remember that his nose was covered in freckles, and that his short pants were held up not with a belt but with those straps that go over the shoulders and get buttoned down somewhere on the stomach.

One time, last summer, I walked into a little park. I do not know what the park is called; it's the one on Vasilevskiy Island, near the white church. I brought a good book with me, and so I stayed late. I lost track of time reading and did not notice it was already evening.

When the print before my eyes became blurry and difficult to read, I clapped the book shut, got up, and walked toward the exit.

The park had emptied out, lights flickered in the street, and the bell of the custodian trilled out somewhere in the trees.

I was afraid that the park entrance would close, and so I walked very fast. Then, I stopped abruptly. I thought I heard someone crying in the bushes.

I turned into a side alley. A small stone building stood white in the dark; it was the kind they have in all city parks, perhaps a shed or a gatehouse. Next to its wall, a small boy of about seven or eight stood with his head hung low, crying loudly and inconsolably.

I came up and called out to him:

"Hey, what's the matter, boy?"

He stopped crying immediately, as if on command, then raised his head, looked at me and said:

"Nothing."

"What do you mean, nothing? Someone hurt you?"

"No one."

"So why are you crying?"

He found it hard to talk, as he hadn't swallowed all his tears yet. He was still sobbing, hiccuping, and sniffling.

"Come on, let's go!" I said. "Look, it's late. They are closing up the park."

I wanted to take the boy by the hand, but he hastily drew his hand away and said:

"I can't."

"You can't what?"

"Can't go."

"How come? Why? What's up with you?"

"Nothing," said the boy.

"Are you unwell or something?"

"No," he said. "I am well."

"So why can't you go?"

"I am a guard," he said.

"What kind of guard? What do you mean, you're a guard?"

"Don't you understand? We are playing."

"And who are you playing with?"

The boy went silent for a while, then he sighed and said:

"I don't know."

Then, I must admit, I thought that the boy must have been truly unwell and that something was wrong with his head.

"Listen," I said to him, "What are you talking about? How does this work? You are playing, but you don't know with whom?"

"No," said the boy. "I don't. There I was, sitting on the bench, and then some big boys came up to me and said, 'Do you want to play war?' I go, 'I do.' We started to play, and they said, 'You be a sergeant.' One big boy—he was a general—he takes me over here and he says, 'Our ammunition stockpile is here in this shed. You'll be the guard. Stand here until I take you off.' I say, 'Okay.' And he says, 'Give me your honest word you won't leave.'"

"Then what?"

"Then I said, 'You have my honest word that I won't leave.'"

"And then what?"

"And then this! I keep standing and standing here, and they keep not coming back."

"Right," I smiled. "And did they put you here a long time ago?"

"It was still light out."

"So where are they now?"

The boy sighed heavily again and said:

"I think they left."

"What do you mean, they left?"

"They forgot."

"Then why are you standing here?"

"I gave them my honest word."

I nearly laughed, but then I caught myself and thought that there was nothing funny about it and that the boy was perfectly right.

Once you give anyone your honest word, you must keep standing there whatever may happen, even if it blows you apart. It doesn't matter if it's a game or not.

"Quite a story!" I said to him. "What are you going to do?"

"I don't know," said the boy and started crying again.

I really wanted to find a way to help him. But what could I do? Would I go looking for those silly boys who had left him to stand guard, asked for his honest word and then run home? Where would I find them at that hour, those boys?

They each had probably already had supper, gone to bed, and were now enjoying their tenth dream of the night.

Meanwhile, here was this person, standing guard. In the dark. He was probably hungry, too.

"I guess you need to eat something," I said to him.

"Yes," he said, "I do."

"OK, listen here," I said, upon some thought. "You run along home and eat your supper, and I'll stand guard for you here."

"OK," said the boy. "Is it even allowed?"

"Why would it be forbidden?"

"You are not in the army."

I scratched the back of my head and said:

"Right. That won't work. I can't even take you off guard duty. Only a military man, only an officer can do that. . . ."

Suddenly, I had a lucky thought. I thought that if only an army man could release the boy from his honest promise and take him off guard duty, then that was the solution! I had to go look for an army man.

The only thing I told the boy was to wait a minute; then, I ran to the gate with no time to waste.

The gate was not yet locked, and the custodian was still out walking in the farthest reaches of the park, his bell ringing out the last rings of the day.

I stood by the gate and patiently waited for some lieutenant or even a Red Army private to walk by. But, as if to spite me, not a single military man was to be seen outside. I saw a glimpse of black overcoats on the other side of the street; I cheered up, thinking they were Navy, and ran across the street only to realize they were not sailors but kids in tech school uniform. A tall railroad worker walked by, wearing a very handsome overcoat with green insignia. However, I had no use for the tall railroad man with his fabulous overcoat at that moment. I was about to go back to the park empty-handed, when suddenly I saw a khaki officer's cap with a blue cavalry band at the streetcar stop around the corner. It seemed I had never felt happier in my life! I ran for the streetcar stop at breakneck speed. I was not even there yet when I saw that the streetcar had arrived at the stop and that the officer, a young cavalry major, was pushing forward to squeeze into the car together with the rest of the passengers.

Out of breath, I ran up to him, grabbed him by the arm and shouted:

"Comrade Major! A minute of your time! Wait! Comrade Major!"

He turned around, looked at me in bewilderment and said:

"What's going on?"

"You see, here is the problem," said I. "Right here, in this park, next to the stone shed, there is a boy standing guard. . . . He can't leave; he gave his honest word. He is very small. He is crying. . . ." The officer blinked a few times and gave me a frightened look. He, too, must have thought that I was unwell and that something was wrong with my head.

"What does that have to do with me?" he said.

His streetcar had left, and he was looking at me very angrily.

But when I explained everything to him in more detail, he did not think twice. Right away, he said:

"Let's go, let's go. Of course. Why didn't you tell me this in the first place?"

When we came to the park, the custodian was just putting the padlock on the gates. I asked him to wait a few minutes, saying that I had left a small boy in there, and then the major and I went running deep into the park.

It was not easy to find the white shed in the dark. The boy was standing in the same place I had left him. He was weeping again, this time very quietly. I called to him. He cheered up and even gave a small cry of joy, and I said:

"Well, here we go. I brought a superior."

Seeing the officer, the boy straightened up; somehow, he extended his entire body and became several centimeters taller.

"Comrade Guard," said the officer. "What is your rank?"

"I am a sergeant," said the boy.

"Comrade Sergeant, your orders are to leave the post of duty."

The boy sniffled in silence and then said:

"What is your rank? I can't see how many stars you have on your uniform."

"I am a major," said the officer.

Then, the boy raised his hand to the wide bill of his gray cap and said:

"Yes sir, Comrade Major! My orders are to leave the post."

His words were so clear and so neat that neither of us could keep from laughing out loud. The boy laughed too, happy and relieved.

Barely had we three come out of the park when the gates behind us swung shut and the custodian gave the key in the lock a few turns.

The major offered his hand to the boy.

"Well done, Comrade Sergeant," he said. "You will grow up to be a real warrior. Good-bye."

The boy mumbled something and then said, "Good-bye."

The major saluted us both and, seeing that a streetcar was approaching, ran back to the stop.

I also said good-bye to the boy and shook his hand.

"Should I walk you home?" I asked him.

"No, I live nearby. I am not scared," said the boy.

I looked at his small freckled nose and thought that he, indeed, had nothing to fear. A boy with a will that strong and a word that firm would not be afraid of the dark, he would not be afraid of bullies, and he would not be afraid of more frightening things either.

And when he grows up. . . . It is yet uncertain what he will become when he grows up, but, whatever he chooses to be, I bet he will be a real man.

That thought made me glad that I had a chance to meet the boy.

I shook the boy's hand once again, firmly and with pleasure.

Part III

Practitioners' Notes on Translating Soviet Children's Literature

Kid Lit Not Split by a Colon

Anna Krushelnitskaya

When we set out to compile this anthology of Soviet children's rhyme and short prose in translation, we did not begin with scholarship in mind. As a binational—and not a scholar, at that—I tend to be particularly drawn to translator's tasks that bridge or fill existing cultural gaps, rather than provide literary material for minute and sophisticated investigation by experts in the field. To that end, in consultation with my cotranslator and coeditor Dmitri Manin, we selected texts that many native informants told us were an indispensable part of their childhoods and that they remembered as having been widely read and memorized; issued in print; produced in recordings, film, and theater; and included in elementary and secondary school curricula. The selected poems and short prose, we reasoned, could serve as a starter pack of sorts for a US reader seeking exposure to Soviet children's literature, its didactic aims, and aesthetic pathways—if only conditionally.

However, there is no escaping the fact that translated Soviet children's literature published in the United States is more likely to be read by scholars in the English-speaking world than by the general public. This fact compels the translator to contend with the issue of multiple addressees, where one addressee of the text is a child; the second is the adult responsible for raising, or reading to, the child; and the third is a scholar seeing the text for its appurtenant topics and investigative tangents. The triple address turns quadruple with the possibility of having fellow practitioners expertly evaluate said text as a product of translation; if we factor in the editor's and publisher's opinions of the suitability of the translation, the address becomes quintuple.

The translator, then, is endowed with several responsibilities that may conflict with one another. The purpose of this chapter is to provide a glimpse into the practical process through which such responsibilities are met and such conflicts are resolved (to the extent that they are).

Early on, I decided to make the child the main addressee of my translations. The central task of children's literature is, after all, the edification, instruction, and, post-Rousseau, entertainment of young humans. The fact that the poems and stories included in this anthology lasted in Soviet culture across generations at least in part confirms that the texts met that central task: the young audience was addressed successfully. When I picked my tools from the kit of translator's strategies and tactics, my choices were driven by utility rather than creed; ultimately, I set out to create effective children's texts in English, even if on occasion, by necessity, the process made them less authentic Soviet artifacts.

One complicated aspect of translating for the young reader is the treatment of the realia—that is, the material elements of a given culture—in our case, Soviet. Had my translations been created with scholarship in mind, I would have elected to render all Soviet cultural specifics undisturbed, even at the expense of form. The characters in the stories would eat the same Soviet foods in translation as they do in the originals, all Moscow and Leningrad street names would be transliterated, and the doll from Agniia Barto's 1935 poem would retain the name Zina, a name popular in the USSR in the 1930s. However, we decided that the translations included in this collection should be intended for the contemporary young English-speaking audience. How do we bring distant, obsolete, and foreign content to such an audience? Let's look at a few examples of how this practical task is approached within this volume.

In Viktor Dragunskii's short story "Tainoe stanovitsia iavnym" (All secrets come to light), a mother tries to persuade her son to eat his breakfast, insisting that the boy is underweight. In her words, the child is a *vylityi Koshchei*—an exact look-alike of the gaunt Russian folk villain Koschei the Deathless. Most Russian-speaking children will have a ready visual idea of Koschei; in US culture, this evil character enjoys niche popularity at best. Having resolved to keep the translation child-friendly and footnote-free, I chose the general over the specific in the portrayal of Koschei. Thinking in terms of categorial meanings helps the translator to make hierarchical or lateral vocabulary switches within a category—to substitute the genus for the species, so to speak, or vice versa, or to replace the species with a similar species when warranted. I substituted the expression "a walking skeleton" for "Koschei"—an ambulatory skeleton by any other name, which, importantly, would not be out of place in Soviet culture either.

In Valentin Kataev's "Tsvetik-semitsvetik" (The seven-petal flower), a child is sent to the bakery to buy some *baranki* for tea. *Baranki* are traditional Russian bread rings. They are a widely sold teatime snack; for Russians, they are nothing exotic. In the translation, I chose a lateral vocabulary substitution, so *baranki* became *cookies*: cookies can also be a teatime treat in Russia, and they do not come with the exoticism tag or a need for a footnote in English. Similarly, in "A chto u vas?" (What's new with you), by Sergei Mikhalkov, *kompoty*—sweet drinks made by boiling fruit in water—were laterally replaced by *an éclair* in the category of sweets made by professional chefs. Eclairs would not be out of place on a Soviet dessert table and are more familiar to American children than hot fruit drinks are. In Zinaida Aleksandrova's "Moi mishka" (My teddy bear) "esh' kotletku, esh' konfetku" became "eat your steak, then eat your cake." Here, the parent-approved progression of dinner dishes is preserved—eat your meat, then eat your sweet—while the culture-specific meat and sweet—a big flattened meatball and a piece of hard or soft candy—are replaced with staples that the American preschool set are more used to. As a variation on this maneuver, in Dragunskii's short story "On zhivoi i svetitsia" (He's alive and he glows), *brynza*, the pungent salty cheese made from sheep's milk, moved up within its category of fermented dairy and became *salty cheese*. No lateral substitute would work since feta, *brynza*'s closest relative, was not available in Moscow at the time described in the story.

Toponyms, like other culturally specific units, can be challenging for the translator. In "Vot kakoi rasseiannyi" (Scatterbrain), by Samuil Marshak, there are mentions of Leningrad, Basseinaia Street, Bologoe, Popovka, Dibuny, and Yamskaia. The last four are train stops on the route Scatterbrain thinks he is taking; more importantly, these toponyms provide end rhymes, the same way the word *Kalamazoo* is drafted to serve as an end rhyme in several poems by Dr. Seuss. In my translation, rhyming names gives way to plain rhyming, since it is inessential that these particular train stops be presented in the story. "Eto chto za ostanovka— / Bologoe il' Popovka?" becomes "What's this little whistle-stop? / Is this my stop? Did I miss my stop?" The name of Scatterbrain's home street, Basseinaia, is Anglicized and made Splatter Lane. Basseinaia is not a fictional street: currently, there is a Basseinaia (Basin) Street in Saint Petersburg and another Basseinaia in one of its suburbs. The Leningrad Street where Mr. Scatterbrain lives forever in Soviet culture had been called Basseinaia before it was renamed.[1] Basin Street is an evocative, watery name, befitting the city of Leningrad and its many rivers, canals, and channels; however, the main purpose of using that name in the poem, again, is in the rhyme it provides to the word *rasseiannyi* (scattered). It is common for Russophone children who read the poem aloud in Russian to mispronounce the street name as *Basseiannaia*, thus making it a full rhyme. My solution to the place-name quandary was to settle the forgetful Mr. Scatterbrain on Splatter Lane, suitably wet sounding and well rhyming. The only toponym transferred unchanged to the target text is Leningrad. Leningrad was a major world city (and remains one under its original name, Saint Petersburg); for those children who do not know this fact, the name is made more decipherable by the handy inclusion of the word *gorod* in the original—made a *town* called Leningrad in the translation. All the above place-name solutions leave Mr. Scatterbrain accurately situated—geographically and historically—without getting him mired in a place too obscure for young US readers.

Elsewhere, other tactics to deal with the obscure were used. Let's look at the following excerpt from "On zhivoi i svetitsia" (He's alive and he glows):

> "So, can I have your dump truck?"
>
> "Get lost, Mishka."
>
> Mishka said:
>
> "I'll trade it for stamps! One Guatemala and two Barbadoses!"
>
> I said:
>
> "Your Barbadoses are no match for my truck."
>
> Mishka went:
>
> "Wanna take my swim ring?"
>
> I said:
>
> "It's bursted."
>
> Mishka went:
>
> "You'll fix it up!"
>
> That made me a little angry.
>
> "Where would I swim? In the communal bathtub? On Tuesdays when it's our turn to use it?"
>
> Mishka got huffy again. After a while, he said:
>
> "Oh, whatever. Remember my kindhood! Here, take this!"
>
> He offered me a matchbox. I took it.

In the original, "one Guatemala and two Barbadoses" appears unaccompanied by any explanation that they are postage stamps from

Guatemala and Barbados. For Soviet children of the time, no explication was needed, since philately was a common hobby, if not a craze. In the original, there is also no mention of the characters taking turns to use the bathtub, nor is the bathtub described as communal. The protagonist simply says the only place and time he can swim is in the bathtub on Tuesdays; communal apartments used to be common in Soviet housing, which contemporary readers knew intimately and which today's adult readers might know, but which modern children in the United States very likely do not. I introduced clarifications directly into the target text to avoid adding footnotes, which would interrupt a child's reading experience. (The words *lopnutyi* and *dobrost'* are ungrammatical in the original, so they become *bursted* and *kindhood* in translation.)

In my view, cultural and historical content and form demand progressively less domestication or explication in translation the older the age of the prospective readers: four-year-olds and seven-year-olds inhabit different worlds, while four-year-olds and twelve-year-olds inhabit different galaxies. It is often texts for the youngest children that are the most demanding, especially when they are rhymed and metric, since such texts must meet the criteria for successful children's verse in the target language. Let's look at an example of a short rhyme to see what transformations were done in translation to make it a working children's rhyme in English and what in fact makes a rhyme for young children work.

Agniia Barto's 1935 poem "Rezinovaia Zina" (literally: The rubber Zina) is metric, rhymed, alliterative, and accessible. It would typically be read or recited to preschool-age children, and countless Soviet kids memorized it. My first task was to select a doll name that is short, easy to articulate, and well suited for rhyme and alliteration. *Molly* sounds like a good name for a dolly—but could it be admissible in a Soviet children's poem? Writing about a real Soviet girl named Molly would require a considerable stretch of the imagination; with doll names, we could allow more latitude, especially if we consider the plethora of English literature in translation available to Soviet readers. Perhaps, the name for our Molly could have come from Charles Dickens. If many Soviet dogs in the 1970s were named Lassie after the rough collie in the eponymous US television series broadcast on Soviet TV in 1974, would it be so wrong to name one Soviet doll Molly?

Next, we must account for any connotations the name may have in the target language. Do any connotations exist for the name Molly, and would they pose a problem? The derived common noun *moll* came to mean a "gangster's girlfriend" or "prostitute" in the first half of the twentieth century in the United States; those negative Prohibition era connotations are now obsolete. The name Molly saw a surge in popularity in the United States in the 1980s and 1990s; currently, it appears to be read as neutral. (It is worth noting that our original toy, Zina, is not without sin, either. In the late Soviet years, the expression "rezinovaia Zina" was jokingly used to denote an inflatable sex doll. Perhaps, Molly's seedy gangster moll past could add a trace of innuendo to the translation to match the late overlay of the lewd in the original.)

Molly is a believable doll; her name rolls off a child's tongue. Molly is more transnational than Zina, but there is no reason Molly can't appear in this poem intended for young children. By contrast, in Barto's poem "My s Tamaroi" (Me and Tamara), the Russian names Tamara, Tanya, and Vanya are simply transliterated. "Me and Tamara" was written for school-age children; an older child possessing a better awareness of the world and its many countries should have an easier time pronouncing those names and imagining their owners.

Rezinovaia Zina the doll keeps falling and getting dirty. The narrator implies that this trait is both a nuisance and a moral failing. Therefore, the doll is threatened with a washing that is both hygienic and punitive: the narrator promises to wash the doll in gasoline. In the eyes of the average modern Western child, gasoline is not associated with cleaning. However, rubbing alcohol is a familiar household substance that can be applied to skin as a disinfectant and that does burn a little. The translator's decision, then, is to have our rubber doll cleaned with rubbing alcohol.

Finally, for alliteration, *razinia* is turned into a *flubber*. *Razinia* is an unfocused person who has her mouth open often: a gawky gaper. A flubber (unrelated to the eponymous substance from the 1997 Robin Williams comedy) can be easily imagined as a person who often flubs. Persons who gape and persons who flub tend to have many commonalities. The word *flubber*, while an occasionalism, is transparent in meaning, and in the context of the poem it serves well and instantly. And so, off goes our newly minted Molly the Flubber:

. . . She was a little flubber,
That Molly Made of Rubber,
Kept falling if we dropped her,
Kept plopping in the slop.
We'll rub with alcohol
That muddy rubber doll,
We'll scrub the doll with alcohol
And tell her she must stop
And not be such a flubber,
That Molly Made of Rubber . . .

In my view, it was essential to keep children's poems in new translations suitable for the age groups for which they were originally written. I found that many—though not all—earlier translations of Soviet kid rhymes into English, while inventive in their own right, sacrifice the simplicity required for the given reading levels. Kornei Chukovsky's "Mukha-Tsokotukha" (Tsokotukha the fly, 1924) was issued in English in Dorian Rottenberg's translation by Raduga Publishers (Moscow) in several editions as "Buzzy-Wuzzy Busy Fly." In Rottenberg's rendering, this poem, recommended for children aged two through seven, gains complex vocabulary and inverted syntax that are not found in the very simple original. Here are Rottenberg's lines describing a brave mosquito slaying an evil spider and thus saving a fair young fly from death:

In a jiffy, up he flies,
Pulls his sabre out and cries:
"Now, you brute!" and at full gallop
Deals the pest a deadly wallop!

Once the mosquito has dealt his deadly wallop, he eloquently asks the fly for her hand in marriage:

By the hand he takes the fly,
To the window leads her, spry:
"Now the villain's dead and perished.
Now I've freed the one I cherished!"

A literal translation of the original would have no "perished," "cherished," "deadly wallop," "in a jiffy," "pest," "spry," or "you brute"; the syntax of the original is direct and clear and would pose no difficulty for a three-year-old, while the syntax of "to the window leads her, spry" just may.

In my new translation ("Zizzy Lizzy the Fly" in this volume) I opted for direct word order and simple vocabulary:

He takes out his sword and makes
One quick dash!
He takes off the Spider's head
With one quick slash!

Now, he saved the Fly from harm.
Now, they come out arm-in-arm:
"I have killed the Deadly Beast!
You are saved! You are released!
Now, my darling, on my knee
I'm asking you to marry me!"

The following passage describing an insect dance party in Rottenberg's translation introduces adult innuendo into a stanza that is quite PG in the original. In it, a partygoer Ant

> . . . Blows the Girl-Gnats stealthy kisses:
> "Oh you naughty gnats,
> Oh you saucy brats,
> Cocky Cockroaches in your Stetson hats!"

While the "saucy brats" in Rottenberg's translation sport Stetson hats fit for a hoedown at a saloon, the insects in the respective stanza in Tom Botting's translation of the same poem ("Little Fly So Sprightly"; Malysh Publishers, Moscow, 1977) favor both Irish reels and Latin dances—which they dance in inverted word order, as well:

> . . . Ant at little insects winks an eye,
> "Mites, how nice you are!
> I spy there on far
> Cucaracha, cha-cha-cha,
> Cucaracha-cha!"

As an adult reader, I am amused by the decorative touches in these two translations; however, the age of the target readership was a deciding factor in selecting the language for my own, simpler, translation:

> Leafhoppers dance in twos.
> They might wear out their shoes!
> Leafhopper gives his missus hugs,
> Winking at the Ladybugs:
> "Hey there, ladies,
> Lovely ladies,
> Lovely pretty spotty ladies!"

In his "Trinadsat' zapovedei dlia detskikh poetov" (Thirteen commandments for children's poets), the prominent Soviet children's author and translator Kornei Chukovsky sets forth requirements and advice for creating poetry for kids.[2] He urges poets writing for the very young to adhere to certain rules of composition. His technical advice can be economically paraphrased as follows: think child, think folk, think picture, think action, think tune, think speech, think simple, think rhyme, think syntax, think game, and, also important, think of adults.

Chukovsky postulates that thinking about folk traditions will help a children's poet compose, since those oral traditions had proved successful in child education and entertainment long before the proliferation of the written word. Thinking about the child's psyche and interests will help the poet choose the optimal literary path to the child's mind. Thinking about the verse in terms of what illustrations it would require will help the author keep the rhyme graphic, dynamic, stimulating, and arresting to the young imagination: the more changing pictures, the better. Thinking about action and refusing static descriptions will help the story move quickly, capturing the child's attention. Thinking about whether the verse can be sung or danced to will help the poet focus on musicality. Thinking about the ease of pronunciation—that is, eliminating large consonant clusters—will help the writer craft poems that small kids can easily repeat, recite, and remember. Thinking about the simplicity of the text involves, for instance, doing away with excessive epithets and reserving ample adjective use for poems for older children, who have better capabilities for contemplating the qualities of objects at length. When thinking about what rhyme scheme to employ, the poet should favor rhyming couplets, which are easy and appealing to younger children; moreover, the end rhyme words in the stanzas should carry the semantic focus of the line. With that in mind, the poet should think about syntax and devise the poem so that each line is syntagmatically complete. (Chukovsky describes his own technique of covering the left side of the poem with his palm to see if just the rhyming part on the right would give him a good idea of the story; if it did, the poem was structurally successful.)

A children's poem works best, according to Chukovsky, when a child's propensity to play meets a game in the poem, whether it is physical play accompanying rhymes for the littlest kids or word play in poems for the more verbal child. Thinking of adults means remembering that children's poetry is created by adults for the purposes of child-rearing and education, and so, however juvenile in form, rhymes must not simply pander to kids but serve teaching goals and developmental tasks. Finally, children's poems must work for grown-ups if they are to work for kids; adults must recognize the verse as good poetry and, while Chukovsky's other recommendations are specific to certain age groups and levels of reading competence, this last commandment holds forever and for all audiences.

Now, perhaps, we could return to our Molly Made of Rubber but armed with the lens of the fourth addressee of the translation: the expert evaluator. Can this poem work for preschoolers in English? We could consider Kornei Chukovsky's commandments in our review and search for child-friendly line breaks, for musicality, for play. We could cover the left side of the poem with a sheet of paper and see if the syntax is clear enough for the story line to be deduced, or we could test the rhyme on the first addressee of the translation, that is, a preschool-age child. If the child laughs, claps, stamps her feet, or at least listens through without getting distracted, this translator will consider the task she had set for herself—the task of keeping children's literature *children's*, despite the challenges arising from differences in history, culture, and context—well accomplished.

Notes

1. Curiously, there was no Basseinaia Street in Leningrad in 1928 when Marshak wrote his "Mr. Scatterbrain." The name of the street referred to in the poem was changed to Nekrasov Street in 1918 to commemorate the Russian writer Nikolai Nekrasov. In 1954, a new Basseinaia Street appeared in a different area of Leningrad. The new Basseinaia Street is now home to Samuil Marshak Central Children's Library.

2. Chukovskii, "Trinadtsat' zapovedei dlia detskikh poetov," 3–19.

"I Am Running, Running, Running, and I Cannot, Cannot Stop!"

Meter in Translation

Dmitri Manin

Almost all translation strives for equivalence to the original. Behind this seemingly trivial statement, however, hides the perennially thorny question of what exactly the notion of equivalence is supposed to mean. Since translation, by definition, differs from the original by being written in a different language and functioning in a different culture, what are the core aspects of the original that define its individuality and that can be reproduced in the translation?

Two complementary approaches to this problem that are widely recognized today are usually referred to as *formal* versus *functional equivalence*, or *foreignization* versus *domestication*.[1] Roughly speaking, formal equivalence places the emphasis on reproducing surface linguistic structures, while functional equivalence shifts the attention toward semantics and pragmatics. This distinction is easy to illustrate with the example of translating idiomatic expressions. The formal method would require translating "ves' do nitochki promok" as "got wet to the (last) thread" (a literal translation), whereas the functional method would replace it with the idiomatic English "got wet to the bone."

It is important to note that formal and functional equivalence are not always opposites. For instance, something like "I love you," when translated literally from Russian, is also as functionally equivalent as it can be. But, of course, the cases when the two equivalences come into conflict are more important, because that's where the translator is forced to make a choice.

In this chapter, I consider only one aspect of a poem: its metrical structure. The issues of equivalence can be defined and treated much more precisely here than on the holistic level, but they still retain much of the complexity and controversy of the larger topic.

Prosody and Rhythm

The prosody in both English and Russian versification is based on counting stresses and syllables as salient features of speech cadence. When only stresses are counted, we get accentual verse, like G. M. Hopkins's sprung rhythm or the meter of the Russian folk genre *bylina*.[2] When both are counted, standard accentual-syllabic meters result, such as iambic pentameter. An intermediate class of meters, such as the English ballad meter and the Russian *dolnik*, allows some variation in the syllable count with strict stress count.[3] Purely syllabic verse, in which only syllables are counted, is possible in both languages, but it does not sound regular enough to the untrained ear, so its use has been very limited.

Thus, the definitive features of verse prosody are quite common for Russian and English. It should, then, be straightforward to define formal equivalence in the domain of rhythm: let the translation simply follow the pattern of stressed and unstressed syllables of the original. Should that be the beginning and end of it? Do we even need the notion of functional equivalence in this area—does it make sense here?

Of course, as any practicing translator knows, the reality is much more interesting. It would be next to impossible to achieve this strict stress-for-stress equivalence between English and Russian for a number of reasons that I will discuss below. It is also not needed. Formal equivalence with regard to rhythm is actually defined at the level of the poetic *meter*.

Meter and Rhythm

Many different ways of analyzing and classifying the rhythm of poetic speech have been proposed. The Anglophone tradition mostly inherited the classical treatment of a poetic line as consisting of feet, usually two- or three-syllable clusters with a specific pattern of stressed and unstressed syllables in each foot.[4] For example, the following famous line from *Hamlet* could be analyzed as three iambs, a trochee, another iamb, and an extra syllable forming a feminine ending:

To be or not to be, that is the question
– / | – / | – / | / – | – / | –

The entire line is then considered to be in iambic pentameter, with trochee substituted for iamb in the fourth foot. On the whole, this method admits too much arbitrariness in determining foot boundaries. To the native ear in either English or Russian, the acoustic reality of a metric foot is too tenuous.

A different approach developed by the Russian formalists provides a better theoretical framework.[5] It is based on the distinction between meter and rhythm. Meter is the ideal pattern of stressed and unstressed syllables (or strong and weak places, respectively), whereas rhythm is the actual stress pattern of a line. The meter of Hamlet's line above, then, is pure iambic pentameter with feminine ending, –/–/–/–/–/–, while its rhythm differs from the pattern in shifting the fourth stress from the strong place to the preceding weak place.

The main benefit of this approach is that it explains how accentual-syllabic verse works, with its inevitable tension between meter and rhythm. Meter defines the metrical expectation in the reader/listener's mind, and the actual stress positions are then perceived as either matching or violating this expectation. These meter violations, when they are limited, can work as expressive devices. In other words, the meter's acoustic reality is, to employ a musical analogy, an underlying beat, like a drumbeat, on top of which interesting syncopation becomes possible.

Rhythm in Russian and English

Although the basic linguistic features pertinent to poetic rhythm are similar in Russian and English, there are also enough differences to make the feel of the same accentual-syllabic meters quite distinct in the two languages. Word length is, perhaps, the most important one.

It is well known that Russian words are longer on average than English words. This happens primarily because of Russian morphology: though word roots are rarely long, both grammatical endings and word-forming prefixes and suffixes can add significant syllable count. Another reason is that the Russian language does not use auxiliary verbs to form verb tenses, it has no articles, and it uses fewer prepositions, because the case system takes care of some of their function.[6] So, the density of frequently occurring short words in Russian is also much lower. For a short example illustrating this, compare two equivalent sentences:

Give a bone to the dog: 5 words, 6 syllables, 22 characters

Дай кость собаке: 3 words, 5 syllables, 16 characters

Though Russian words are longer on average, they still only bear one stress each. Even such monsters as the proverbial *vykarabkivaiushchimisia* (vy-kah-RAHB-ki-vah-iu-shchi-mi-sia, "scrambling out of" in the plural instrumental case) do not have any appreciable secondary stresses. Meanwhile, English words of three or more syllables typically acquire secondary stresses on every other syllable.

The significance of these secondary stresses is such that they can even carry a rhyme, as in Robert Frost's "The Road Not Taken" (the rhymed syllables are marked in bold):

> Somewhere ages and ages **hence**:
> Two roads diverged in a wood, and I—
> I took the one less traveled by,
> And that has made all the diff**erence.**[7]

As a result, the speech stream in Russian has a lower stress density. In the most common, disyllabic meters, every other syllable is a strong place. Typically, there are not enough stresses in a Russian line to fill all the strong places with stressed syllables. This creates a pleasant variability in the way iambic lines can sound in Russian. Here is an example of the canonical Pushkin iambs (the beginning of *Eugene Onegin*):

> Мой **дя**дя **са**мых **че**стных **пра**вил,
> Ког**да** не в **шут**ку *за*не**мог**,
> Он *у*ва**жать** се*бя* за**ста**вил
> И **луч**ше **вы**ду*мать* не **мог**.[8]

Here, the stressed syllables are in bold, and unstressed strong places are italicized. No two lines in this quatrain have the same stress pattern, but the only way the metric expectation is violated is by stress omission.

With short English words (especially in children's poetry) and secondary stresses, most strong places are naturally filled with stresses. Compare the canonical example of English iambic tetrameter from a William Wordsworth's poem (here, the stressed syllables are in bold, and unstressed strong places are italicized):

> I **wan**dered **lone**ly *as* a **cloud**
> That **floats** on **high** o'er **dales** and **hills,**
> When, **all** at **once**, I **saw** a **crowd,**
> A **host,** of **gold**en **daffodils**.[9]

To be fair, not all the stresses are equal here. For example, it can be argued that "once" and "crowd" in the third line bear stronger stresses than "all" and "saw."[10] Still, English accentual-syllabic rhythm would tend to sound too monotonous if other types of violations were not employed. That is why two other types of meter violation are common in English, though they are virtually prohibited in Russian verse: stresses shifted to a weak place and extrametrical syllables (or half syllables) inserted. As an illustration, consider an example from John Keats's "Ode on a Grecian Urn":

> **Thou** *still* un**ra**vish'd **bride** of **quiet***ness*,
> **Thou fos**ter-**child** of **sil**ence *and* **slow time**,
> **Syl***van* his**to**rian, *who* **canst thus** ex**press**
> A **flower**y **tale** more **sweet**ly *than* **our rhyme**.[11]

Here, the stressed syllables are in bold, unstressed strong places are italicized, and instances of stress shift are underlined; extrametrical syllables (or half syllables) occur in the words "historian" and "flowery."

Functional and Systemic Equivalence

It should be clear from the previous section that strictly equirhythmic translation between Russian and English in either direction, even if it were possible, would sound strained and clumsy. This is what the foreignizing approach would probably strive for, with its emphasis on foregrounding the text's alien pedigree. Though an interesting possibility, this approach is hardly appropriate if the goal is to translate children's verse *as* children's verse. For that reason, we chose to translate Russian meters into corresponding English meters. Even if their sound is somewhat different, it is equally natural, and that's what counts. Both of these approaches, the rhythm-based and the meter-based, fit under the formal equivalence rubric.

What, then, is functional equivalence? Some meters have well-defined roles that they play in the poetry of certain periods. For example, in both Russian and English traditions, iambic pentameter is the meter of blank dramatic verse, such as Shakespeare's *Hamlet* or Pushkin's *Boris Godunov*. It is also the most common meter of sonnets in both literatures. On the other hand, trochaic tetrameter is perceived as a light, bouncy meter often used in children's and folk poetry in both Russian and English (even though it can be used for other purposes as well). Thus, one could say that iambic pentameter and trochaic tetrameter in Russian are functionally, as well as formally, equivalent to their English counterparts.

However, there are other valid considerations that further muddle the picture. Not all standard accentual-syllabic meters are equally in use. For example, in Russian poetry, iambic hexameter is fairly common, mainly owing to translations and imitations of the French alexandrine.[12] In English, this meter is exceedingly rare, and when the French alexandrine is translated metrically, iambic pentameter is typically used.[13] So, formal equivalence dictates translating Russian hexameters into English hexameters, but functional equivalence arguably suggests English pentameters.

Yet, suppose we are translating two Russian poems, one pentametric and the other hexametric. Should we translate both into English pentameters? If we do, we will lose an important distinction that exists between them in the original. What about a long poem where some parts are pentametric and others hexametric?

This suggests a third equivalence type—what I term *systemic equivalence*.[14] The basic idea is that, when translating, one should try to preserve the superstructure of similarities and differences that exist in the original. When one translates a poem consisting of parts written in different meters, it may not be as important to reproduce those exact meters as to keep the parts *somehow* metrically different in order to convey the compositional structure of the whole.

In the practice of Russian to English poetry translation, a violent clash between functional and systemic equivalence occurs when the translator makes a basic, but key decision: whether to translate metrically. Indeed, free verse dominates contemporary English poetry, whereas Russian poetry covers a spectrum of varying degrees (and kinds) of metrical regularity. English free verse can be considered functionally equivalent to any Russian meter in contemporary poetry, and, indeed, standard practice is to translate metrical poetry into free verse. However, from the point of view of systemic equivalence, this practice obliterates an important distinction between poems originally written in different meters, thus erasing some of their individual character.

Translating Rhythm

Children's poetry is one of two genres (the other is humorous poetry) in which meter is still commonly used in English; thus, it was not a question for us *whether* to translate metrically. However, because of the differences in the prosody of the two languages, the question of *how* to translate metrically did arise.

By far the most common meter of Russian children's poetry is trochaic tetrameter. For example, half of the poems in Marshak's *Detki v kletke* (Babies in cages, translated in this volume as *Who Is Who at the Zoo*) are written in this meter, as well as eight out of eleven poems in Barto's *Igrushki* (Toys). This meter is not as prevalent in English children's poetry but is still common enough. Let's take a look at some examples of this meter in Russian and English. "Gruzovik" (Truck) is a poem from *Toys* (I have given its metrical scheme below):

Нет, напрасно мы решили
Прокатить кота в машине:
Кот кататься не привык—
Опрокинул грузовик.

/–/–x–/–
x–/–/–/–
/–/–x–/
x–/–x–/

Its metrical scheme shows the rhythmic variety achieved by omitting stresses on strong metrical positions (denoted by *x*'s), as is common in Russian versification.

The following English example comes from *Mother Goose*:

Every lady in this land
Has twenty nails, upon each hand
Five, and twenty on hands and feet:
All this is true, without deceit.

/– /– x–/
–/– /– /–/
/– /– –/–/
/– –/– /–/

Here, we see quite a different pattern of variability. Only one stress is omitted (on the preposition "in" in the first line), but each of the remaining lines has an extra unstressed syllable in different places.

Compare these to the English translation of "Truck" in this volume:

It was silly that we tried
To give the cat a merry ride:
All he knew was fight and buck,
Run away and crash the truck.[15]

x–/–x–/
–/–/–/–/
/–/–/–/
x–/–/–/

Its rhythm hovers halfway between the native English and Russian patterns: it omits more stresses and inserts fewer extrametrical syllables than the former.[16] In other words, it attempts to strike a balance between domesticating and foreignizing the character of trochaic tetrameter.

Kornei Chukovsky's poems present harder problems with respect to meter. His rhythms, inherited from Russian folk tradition, are idiosyncratic and immediately recognizable. His longer poems are usually polymetric, and it is important to convey the rhythmic transitions in translation. Here is an excerpt from "Fedorino gore" (Fedora's woes, translated in this volume as "Old Theodora's Trouble and Horror"):

И кастрюля на бегу
Закричала утюгу:
«Я бегу, бегу, бегу,
Удержаться не могу!»

Вот и чайник за кофейником бежит,
Тараторит, тараторит, дребезжит . . .

Утюги бегут, покрякивают,
Через лужи, через лужи перескакивают.

– –/– – –/
– –/– – –/
– –/–/–/
– –/– – –/

– –/– – –/– – –/
– –/– – –/– – –/

– –/–/–/– – –
– –/– – –/– – –/– – –

The first quatrain here is nominally in trochaic tetrameter, but, in typical Chukovskian fashion, it systematically omits the first and third stresses (the only exception is in line 3), which turns the meter into what is known as *third paeon*.[17] The same paeonic rhythm is sustained over the longer lines 4–8, with the last two lines sporting endings with three unstressed syllables (hyperdactylic), unusual even in Russian poetry and virtually unheard of in English.

What makes these paeonic rhythms possible in Russian is its abundance of long words and its lack of secondary stresses. It would be very hard to replicate them exactly in English, especially in children's poetry. However, systemic equivalence only requires indication of some change in rhythm, preferably in the same direction as in the original.

And a pot shouts to the iron,
With a skip and with a hop:
"I am running, running, running
And I cannot, cannot stop!"

And a teapot races swiftly, all a-clatter,
With a coffeepot behind it, pitter-patter,
And the heavy irons tumble
Over mud, and groan, and grumble.[18]

– – // – – /–
– – /– – – /
– – / – / – / –
– – / – / – /

– – / – / – /– – – /–
– – /– – – /– – – /–
– – / – / – / –
– – / – / – / –

Systematically omitting the first stress and occasionally other odd-numbered stresses does the job here quite successfully. This is done without using long English words, which would be out of place in children's poetry. Instead, the translator of this poem (Anna Krushelnitskaya) utilized short auxiliary words, plentiful in English and usually unstressed.[19]

Of course, we don't actually sit around counting syllables and stresses while translating. Most of the practical work is done by ear, but the ear in question has been trained and tuned in advance by analytical work.

Different types of equivalence in translation are not mandates; they can agree or disagree with each other, and in the latter case, some have to be violated. But even then, they are useful tools that give the translator conscious control over the choices that need to be made, as well as awareness of the losses incurred and tradeoffs made.

Notes

1. Venuti, *Translator's Invisibility*, 19–22.

2. On sprung rhythm, see Greene et al., *Princeton Encyclopedia of Poetry and Poetics*, 1354. On the *bylina*, see Jones, *Language and Prosody*, 9–15.

3. On *dolnik*, see Attridge, "Enduring Form," 147–87.

4. Of course, the classical quantitative versification was not based on the distinction of stressed versus unstressed but of long versus short syllables.

5. See Žirmunskij, *Introduction to Metrics*, 18–23.

6. Curiously, three of the important prepositions, "in(to)," "to(ward)," and "with" are zero-syllable words in Russian: "в," "к," and "с," so they don't affect syllable count.

7. From "The Road Not Taken" in Frost, *Poetry of Robert Frost*, 105.

8. From *Evgenii Onegin* in Pushkin, *Izbrannye sochineniia*, 127.

9. From "I Wandered Lonely as a Cloud" in Wordsworth, *Wordsworth*, 14.

10. Generally, though weak stresses can be identified in both languages, English appears to present more distinct gradations of stress strength.

11. From "Ode on a Grecian Urn" in Keats, *Complete Poems*, 221.

12. The French alexandrine is twelve-syllable verse with a caesura.

13. It is mostly used in isolated lines amid pentameters, whether occasional or regular, as in the Spenserian stanza.

14. Note that this term exists in linguistics, but we use it here in a different sense.

15. Translated by D. Manin.

16. Because of the fluidity of English stresses, the claim that "all" in line 3 is stressed while "run" in line 4 is unstressed is somewhat tenuous. Both could be considered carrying weak stress, but that would not invalidate the overall conclusion.

17. A four-syllable foot with the stress on the third syllable.

18. Translated by A. Krushelnitskaya.

19. Note also the stress shift in the first line, from the fifth to the fourth syllable, similar to the examples above from Shakespeare's and Keats's verse.

Part IV

Scholarly Essays

To Keep and to Expand

The Canon of Soviet Children's Literature in Contemporary Publishing in Russia

Svetlana Maslinskaya

The discussion of the classics and the canon in children's literatures has a long history of being centered on so-called best texts from adult literatures that were repurposed, at some point in time, for reading by the young. In that discussion, first teachers and then researchers focused their attention on texts not originally written for young audiences but eventually read by them. For Russian literature, the supposed best texts in question were the works of such classic authors as Alexander Pushkin, Vasily Zhukovsky, and Nikolai Gogol. In other national literatures, the works of William Shakespeare, Johann Wolfgang von Goethe, and Victor Hugo, among others, were similarly employed. However, a distinct new direction in canon studies has gained prominence in the past thirty years; it features scholarship on the formation of canons of twentieth-century children's literature proper for all world literatures, including Russia's.[1]

In some cases, a radical revision of the existing canon of children's texts came as a result of social cataclysms giving rise to new nation building. Germany's children's literature canon was significantly reshaped after the National Socialists came to power; Israel's, after the new nation-state was formed; and Russia's, after the Bolshevik Revolution.[2] Less prominent yet still observable alterations in the canon can arrive when a nation attempts to free itself from the influence of a "strong neighbor"; Canada's children's literature of the 1920s is one example of such change.

In times of drastic social change in nation-states, reformers tend to address children as "future citizens" of either the nation under a new government or even a completely new nation. As a rule, the new literature created specifically for young audiences becomes an overt propaganda tool in service to the nation's new value systems and proposed development paths. A substantial reshaping of children's literary corpora may lead to marked revisions of the canons formed earlier. In the USSR, in particular, this transformation took place in the 1920s, when both the poetics of children's texts and the rosters of participants in the literary process changed significantly.

How It All Began

Samuil Marshak, one of the founding fathers of the new Soviet children's literature in the 1920s, once declared, "We can't live by our heritage alone, however great it may be. We ourselves must make our today and tomorrow—that new literature that will fully reflect our time and even peer into the distant future."[3] Such declarations of the need to create a new children's literature led to a marked departure from the prior practice in children's publishing. Bans imposed on certain books, coupled with prescriptions to publish certain other books, significantly altered the natural course of development of Russian children's literature. Works of many domestic children's authors from the modernist 1890s to 1910s were forcibly discarded. Those deprived of the opportunity for their work to reach the reading circles of the Soviet young included authors who contributed to the children's periodicals *Galchonok* (Baby jackdaw), *Tropinka* (The little path), and *Zadushevnoe slovo* (The heartfelt word); writers of adventure books about WWI; authors of junior novels for girls, including Lidiia Charskaia and Klavdiia Lukashevich; authors of didactic fiction, such as Vladimir Nemirovich-Danchenko and Vasily Avenarius; and authors of picture books, such as Valery Carrick. As Samuil Marshak wrote, "The Revolution could not conserve this entire heritage of the past."[4] During the 1920s, not a single title by Fyodor Dostoevsky, Vasily Zhukovsky, Charles Perrault, or Selma Lagerlöf was published for children.

Of all the writers whose books were in print in 1918 and 1919, only twenty-five had their work published after 1930 in the USSR.[5] This list includes works by the classic Russian authors Ivan Krylov, Alexander Pushkin, Mikhail Lermontov, and Nikolai Gogol, as well as works by such European and New World writers as Henry Wadsworth Longfellow, Charles Dickens, Jonathan Swift, Hans Christian Andersen, Ernest Thompson Seton, Charles G. D. Roberts, and Daniel Defoe. Only a handful of writers, including then-living authors, who had been active and published before the Revolution were still published as children's authors after the Revolution; this list features Yakov Perelman, Dmitrii Mamin-Sibiriak, Vladimir Korolenko, Maxim Gorky, and Alexandra Bostrom.

The renovation of children's literature was not a linear process. Between 1924 and 1929, the list of published children's titles grew significantly to include books by authors who joined the literary process as new recruits to children's literature only briefly, writing just a few texts and then abandoning this particular creative arena. These were primarily adventure stories and novellas with plots centered on the 1917 Revolution, the subsequent civil war, and the first steps in building the new Soviet government and life. The output produced by this subset of authors remained in steady and regular print during the latter half of the 1920s, with new publications appearing annually. Among these authors were Sergei Auslender, Rodion Akulshin, Pavel Bliakhin, Nikolai Karintsev, Fedor Kamanin, Andrei Irkutov, Larisa Larina, Aleksei Kozhevnikov, Nikolai Bogdanov, Iakov Meksin, Sergei Shervinskii, and Sergei Zaiaitskii. Eventually, however, numerous critical articles condemning "red adventurism" and cheap stereotypical depictions of teen factory workers prompted many authors who worked in the dime novel sector of children's literature in the mid-1920s either to leave the domain by 1930 or to attempt to change their writing in response to the new demand for more realistic representations of young builders of communism.

The only writer whose books were consistently published year after year, from the moment of his entry into children's literature in 1922 up until 1940, was Samuil Marshak. Marshak's publishing history progressed from a scant few early career editions to a peak twenty-three titles in print in 1930. In the early 1930s, his publishing growth slowed down to a degree, but its pace soon picked up again. By 1938, there were over three million copies of Marshak's books in print. The only other children's author whose books were printed and disseminated on the same scale was Agniia Barto. By contrast, Kornei Chukovsky's publishing history took a different turn. Chukovsky became a children's writer before the Revolution; the publication of his poem "Krokodil" (Crocodile) in 1917 marked a distinct new development in Russian children's rhyme. In 1923, Chukovsky overtook Marshak in the number of print copies of children's texts produced; however, in the aftermath of the 1928–29 critical campaign for "eradicating fairy tales," not a single children's title by Chukovsky was published in 1932.[6] In 1933, nevertheless, Chukovsky's name once again returned to the top of the list of most published authors.

Until 1930, the roster of children's authors kept changing: more and more new names joined the literary process, and both the variety and the print runs of books for young audiences increased. In 1931 and 1932, the publishing output in the children's literature segment was markedly reduced. The decrease in print volume was caused in part by the personnel changes that took place within the Communist Party once Andrei Bubnov succeeded Anatoly Lunacharsky as head of the People's Commissariat for Education, in part by the reorganization of the State Publishers in 1930 and in part by a crisis within the guild, which was precipitated by the critical campaigns of the late 1920s. In 1932, the numbers of writers new to the field of children's literature dropped sharply, while the print runs of books by those authors who did manage to continue practicing increased considerably. The list of writers who successfully weathered the changes include Agniia Barto (whose first children's text was published in 1925); Valentin Kataev (in 1925); Sergei Rozanov (in 1925); Mikhail Il'in (in 1926); Arkadii Gaidar (in 1927); L. Panteleev (in 1927); Zinaida Aleksandrova (in 1927); Konstantin Paustovskii (in 1930); and Lev Kassil' (in 1930). This was the slate of fiction writers and poets representing the new Soviet children's literature, the stability of which was underpinned by large print runs. As the number and the variety of authors shrank, the expansion of print runs between 1935 and 1940 led to predictable outcomes: books by the aforementioned slate of writers kept being released by national and regional publishing houses and disseminated throughout the country, making the names of these writers familiar to large numbers of young Soviet readers. Only a few new authors who joined the Soviet children's writers' guild in the 1930s were published as widely as the authors above; among them are Ruvim Fraerman, Sergei Mikhalkov, and Lev Kvitko.

Thus, the nucleus of the canon of Soviet children's literature was formed in the 1930s.

The ideological and publishing collapse of the early 1930s triggered a process of ideological and aesthetic filtering, during which many authors active in the 1920s were forced out, while writers in possession of useful personal connections and acceptable aesthetic platforms cemented their professional positions and came to be seen as "real" Soviet children's writers.

A Hundred Years Later

Of all the authors named above, only a few are featured on the A-list in contemporary publishing in Russia. Who are those few?

In recent years, the Russian Book Chamber has released statistical data on the most widely published and sold children's books.[7] Since 2005, reports on the top ten authors whose books are released in the largest print runs have been made available annually; since 2012, reports on the top twenty such authors have also been made public. The analysis of the pool of the ten most published writers shows that overall print runs have been steadily decreasing in the past fifteen years for all children's titles. In 2006, nearly sixteen million copies of children's titles were printed; in 2019, that number hovered around seven million. The overall share of Soviet books in the top ten children's titles remains at or near 50 percent (the three-year average stays within 45 percent and 55 percent), with occasional sharp increases and dips, which can probably be ascribed to various external or random factors. For instance, the sharp 2006–7 plunge to 35 percent in the share of Soviet titles is attributable to the concurrent wide release of J. K. Rowling's books. Among the top ten authors who enjoyed successful careers in children's literature during the Soviet era and passed away before 1985 are Kornei Chukovsky, Agniia Barto, Samuil Marshak, Nikolai Nosov, and Aleksandr Volkov. Sergei Mikhalkov, who rose to fame in the 1930s and died in 2009, also makes this list.[8] This roster of the most published authors indicates that, in the past fourteen years, books by poets who wrote for the very young (Chukovsky, Barto, Marshak, and Mikhalkov) and by writers who wrote fiction for preschoolers and for elementary and middle school children (Nosov and Volkov) have remained in high demand with consumers.

The overall market share of rhyme for preschoolers has stayed around 40 percent, and the share of fiction for young schoolchildren around 10 percent. In other words, four-fifths (80 percent) of the volume of the most published Soviet kids' books comprise rhyming books for preschoolers, primarily written by Barto and Chukovsky, although there is an observable trend toward a gradual decrease in that share. One obvious explanation for the publishers' response to the readers' interest rests on the fact that books for kids ages two through five are normally picked out by the adults in charge, and these adults are usually the parents—or, somewhat less often, preschool teachers and elementary school teachers—whose fondness for Soviet children's classics must be taken into consideration. Viewing rhyme as the preferred literature for children ages two through five is a broader tendency in pedagogies of children's literacy than it may appear at a first glance. The long-standing practice of parents reading rhyme to kids is not culturally specific to Russia; however, the significance of rhyme in books for very young children in contemporary Russia must be noted.

What specific publishing trends can be identified with regard to the aforementioned bestselling authors?

Since 2005, Kornei Chukovsky has kept his first place as the most republished Soviet author, with the print runs of his titles peaking at over 3.5 million copies in 2010 and dipping just below 2 million in 2019. Agniia Barto follows in second place, with the number of copies highest in 2008, at just over 2 million, and lowest in 2019, at about half a million. Other Soviet authors from the top list remain practically in a tie in terms of print runs, with occasional rises and dips, like the one observed for Marshak in 2014. A sharp decline in print volume is seen for titles by Sergei Mikhalkov; after 2008, his name dropped from the list of the most published completely, only to return to it briefly in 2016 and 2017, albeit with the print runs cut nearly by half. The Soviet authors Vitaly Bianki and Vladimir Suteev made the top twenty in 2016, with print runs on par with those for Viktor Dragunskii's and Aleksandr Volkov's books. Previously, Bianki and Suteev qualified for the list, and the new ascent could be attributed both to an independent rise in their own popularity and to the departure of certain names, such as Mikhalkov's, from the leaderboard against the background of a general decrease in publishing volumes and a rise in market diversification.

Nevertheless, the trend of repeatedly reissuing works by children's poets who began their writing careers in the 1920s and by children's fiction writers who published their first books in the 1930s and continued working through the first two postwar decades calls for commentary.

After two decades of harsh criticism and forced conformism, poets practicing in various genres—be it Chukovsky with his long poems and tales; Barto with her short nursery rhymes, such as her cycle of poetic miniatures titled *Igrushki* (Toys); or Marshak with his narrative poems, such as "Pozhar" (The house fire), "Bagazh" (The luggage), and "Pochta" (The post office)—saw their popularity and their print runs peak in the 1950s and 1960s, and they kept their dominance in the domain of publishing until the demise of Soviet rule. They enjoyed phenomenal renown, if not cult status, during their lifetimes. It must be noted that both the foundations of worship and the communities of worshippers of the writers' talents varied greatly, depending on the tastes and worldviews of people across different Soviet social groups and strata. In this way, the reputations of these three authors as the main Soviet children's writers were solidified.

Sergei Mikhalkov—who occupied high administrative positions and who jealously watched his literary competition and wrote ideologically servile verse—was as popular as the Big Three (Marshak, Chukovsky, and Barto) in Soviet times. In recent years, however, he has lost a considerable number of fans: Mikhalkov's publishing ratings keep falling, and this trend is expected to continue.[9] At the same time, the status of authors who were in the avant-garde of Soviet children's poetry in the 1920s proved to be more stable than the status of those writers who worked in circumvention of the contemporary proscriptions in the later decades (such as the OBERIU writers in the late 1920s and 1930s and the members of the Lianozovo group in the 1950s and early 1960s), as well as the status of other authors who faithfully followed in the titans' footsteps, such as Boris Zakhoder, Valentin Berestov, and Elena Blaginina, to name a few. The founding fathers Chukovsky and Marshak, together with the founding mother Barto, created precedent texts, which received such wide distribution that most Soviet and post-Soviet readers can still recite the respective titles and quote their rhymes from memory. Repeated rereading of their texts, revisited year after year—most often involving adults reading the texts aloud to children and eventually to grandchildren—helps keep the names of the authors at the top of Russian publishing.

The popularity of the authors of fairy-tale novel series—Aleksandr Volkov and Nikolai Nosov—is of a slightly different origin. (It must be noted that Nosov's humorous short stories also add to his fame.) It appears that the main reason their texts remain in the canon has to do with the inclusion of their titles in summer reading lists for Soviet and modern-day schoolchildren, although this consideration cannot be cited as exclusive. Both writers were truly popular during and after WWII; ample readers' testimonies from the 1940s through the 1980s confirm this. Moreover, the print runs of Aleksandr Volkov's "Volshebnik izumrudnogo goroda" (Wizard of the Emerald City) were consistently large both during Soviet times and in the 1990s; between 1997 and 2012, in Moscow alone, this book was issued in eighty-five editions, for a total of around 1.5 million copies.[10] Several possible explanations for this immense popularity may be advanced, but none can transcend speculation: Nosov was not the only author writing humorous stories for elementary school kids at the time, nor were Nosov and Volkov the only writers offering fairy-tale novel series. The main reason fairy tales are always popular may be that, as Samuil Marshak explained, fairy tales are "a little bit beyond time."[11]

As things stand, Chukovsky, Marshak, Barto, Volkov, and Nosov are the authors whose works make up the nucleus of the Soviet children's literary canon at this juncture and are among the key texts of Russian literature in general. The literary scholar Mariia Litovskaia proposes that Soviet children's texts be counted as key texts along with the classics included in secondary school curricula:

> In Russia, through the established practice of early introduction of reading to children, through fostering the attitude of

treating books as sacred objects, through outlining the compendia of required reading for preschoolers (including the rhymes of Agniia Barto, Elena Blaginina, Samuil Marshak, Sergei Kozlov, Sergei Mikhalkov, and Kornei Chukovsky), it is specifically children's literature that proves to be the most popular reading. Repeated revisiting of the same texts, characteristic of the way children become exposed to literature, creates conditions for these most loved children's favorites to be best absorbed. It is at this stage that many stereotypical ideas and images, speech clichés and formulas enter and remain in the worldview of a participant of a particular culture.[12]

Is It Soviet and/or Is It Children's?

Approaches to the planning and design of reissues of canonical Soviet children's books differ across publishers. One approach that invites particular interest is the combining of texts into series. Examples of such series that exploit the idea of the Soviet children's literary canon include *Liubimaia mamina knizhka* (Mommy's favorite book) and *Liubimaia papina knizhka* (Daddy's favorite book), both from Rech Publishers; *Vsia detskaia klassika* (All children's classics), from AST and Astrel; and *Novye starye knizhki* (New old books), from Enas-Kniga. Publishing houses believe, not without merit, that when adults buy books for children, they rely on their personal recollections of the books they themselves read as children. As Nataliia Erofeeva, the chief editor of children's publishing at Enas-Kniga, puts it, "The New Old Books series re-creates the classics of our domestic literature for kids, so that we remember it, so that we appreciate it, so that we feel proud."[13] Whether the remembered childhood in question is Soviet or post-Soviet proves not entirely essential. People of different generations—including those who grew up in the 1990s and now buy books for their own children—pick from the selection of titles they themselves read in childhood, be that childhood Soviet or not.

Adult readers buy Soviet children's classics in bookstores for the same reasons they seek out lists of the same titles online: to remember their own childhoods. The following is a representative sample of recent online comments about and reviews of Soviet children's books :

> Ah, the books of my childhood! Rech Publishers' series [Mommy's favorite book] was the biggest most wonderful surprise!! The books look exactly like how they were published originally! Excellent quality both of paper and of execution! Super! (from an online review of a Nosov title).[14]

> A book from my childhood. I read it so often I wore holes in it. Bought it for my daughter, but I also leaf through it from time to time, sinking into nostalgia (from an online review of a Marshak title).[15]

> This was my favorite book when I was a child. I remember listening to this tale with bated breath and asking for it again and again (from an online review of a Chukovsky title).[16]

> A marvelous book! The art by Konashevich is familiar to me from childhood☺ Soon as I saw it, it all came back to me. The print quality is excellent. Thanks to Melik-Pashaev Publishers for the reprint (from an online review of a Marshak title).[17]

> Read this book with pleasure together with my first-grader son in two days, taking turns! It's impossible to pull myself away from this text, from these most wonderful illustrations by V. Chizhikov, illustrations straight from my childhood!!! My sons share my love for Chizhikov's art, we are putting together a collection of books with his pictures!" (from a web review of a Chukovsky title).[18]

Most comments and reviews by adult readers feature typical statements: "I bought the book out of a feeling of nostalgia—I had one just like it when I was a child."

Rosman Publishers released a series with the title *Ta samaia knizhka* (That very book), which comprises reprints of books by Arkadii Gaidar, Nikolai Nosov, and Gennadii Tsyferov, among others. Here is the publisher's address to prospective customers:

> Dear Mommies and Daddies, Grandmas and Grandpas! Think of the warmth and love we feel when we occasionally recall the books of our childhood, which have left indelible marks on our souls! When we chance upon a book like that in a secondhand bookstore or in a market bookstall—a well-worn book, with a ratty cover—think about the pleasure with which we pick it up, leaf through it, remember the moments of joy the book gifted us once upon a time. . . . That very book! That's what we feel like exclaiming when we want to share the joy of encountering this book from our childhood with our own kids and grandkids, so that they, too, might discover the book for themselves and feel the same feeling. But those books from our childhood are becoming more and more rare. The *That Very Book* series is double the joy! It brings joy to our children when they first meet the wonderful book characters they won't ever forget, and it brings joy to us when we meet our good old friends again. The *That Very Book* series creates an opportunity for several generations in the family to discover the best children's books together. Once you read them, both you and the kids in your family will have precious memories and new experiences to share.[19]

This publishing manifesto reveals the foundations of the nostalgic discourse on childhood books: it refers to tactile memory, invokes the emotional experience of recognition, channels intergenerational and interpersonal connection through similarity, and promises shared experiences.

Recognition is a key category in describing the social practices involved in republishing Soviet books. One aspect that draws immediate attention is the regular practice of consumers' comparing just bought new reissues or reprint editions to corresponding old books kept in libraries since Soviet times or to reissues bought in the interim. As one reader puts it, "I came by this book by chance, and what a storm of emotions I felt!!!! It looks exactly like the book I had as a child and I loved it so much!!!! All the pictures are totally the same. I'll absolutely order a copy, mine is lost without a trace."[20]

Because of these histories of processing children's literature, readers meet any deviations from the original texts in reeditions of titles by the top ten authors with vigilance. For instance, in 2018, a reader discovered a word substitution in Kornei Chukovsky's "Moidodyr" ("Gottascrub" in this volume), released as part of the *Mommy's Favorite Book* series by Rech:

> I found a small difference in the text; right here it says:
>
> А за ним и бутерброд:
> Подбежал—и прямо в рот!
>
> [This translates literally as:
> After it, a slice of buttered bread
> Ran up—and straight into my mouth![21]]
>
> We are more used to "бутерброд подскочил" ("the slice of buttered bread jumped up"), but that's no big deal.[22]

Here, the benevolent evaluation of the substitution is less salient than the emblematic concern for precise reproduction of the original text. So modest are these texts in size and so well preserved in the memories of readers—Marshak and Chukovsky are revisited in contemporary Russian-speaking culture more often than Pushkin and Lermontov by an order of magnitude—that the general public's requirements for exact replication in print approximate academic requirements for classic texts included in textbooks.[23] (As an aside, it should be pointed out that no academic publications of the works of the aforementioned authors exist.) The texts are reviewed not by research institutions but by the general adult reading audience, who have memorized the texts to the point of instant recognition. A flawlessly faithful replication of *that very book* the reader remembers from childhood is a sufficient criterion for high praise for a given edition. The availability of several historical versions of the same texts, or versions of the same texts accompanied by different art, typical of Soviet production practice, makes room for minute examinations of pages, performed to identify the best reprint. In customer reviews on booksellers' websites, the reviewers compare color rendering, the positioning of illustrations, and the care in detailing. The earnest attention the readers pay to the design of reissued books is exemplified, for instance, in customer reviews of Volkov's *Volshebnik izumrudnogo goroda* (Wizard of the Emerald City) published by Malysh, an imprint of AST, in 2020:

> The main surprise was waiting for me when I opened the book—Vladimirskii's illustrations, familiar to the last line, shone with new colors of the rainbow, here they are lighter and more airy than the ones I had in my childhood copy. Compared to modern children's publications, which often have more bright pictures than text, this one does not have too many illustrations; however, they are positioned nicely, although not on every page, of course. The illustrations are all of different colibers [*sic*]—some large, some medium, some small. The flaps are colorful, traditionally representing maps of Goodwin's land. The paper in this reissue is wood-free uncoated, white, medium thick. The type is very clear, large, most suitable for children's independent reading. For comparison, I'm posting several illustrations from my old copy (Sovetskaia Rossiia, Moscow, 1971).[24]

Or another review reads:

> While checking this copy against the 1980 edition, I discovered several, in my view, drawbacks in the new edition.
>
> 1. Several illustrations turned out to be "torn apart" and their parts were placed on two separate pages (see photos 7 and 8). In principle, this new placement of the pics does not affect the perception of illustrations, but I think they looked more unified in the old version.
>
> 2. The new book is missing about 3 illustrations, for instance, I was not able to find this wonderful Strashila (photo 9).[25]

Readers scrupulously compare the Soviet editions from 1958, 1971, and 1985 with the newest reeditions. The publishing house released the title featuring the same art by Leonid Vladimirskii that illustrated the Soviet era editions. One can observe that the most active reader response is generated by books reissued with the established, popular Soviet design: reprints featuring art by once-famous illustrators, such as Vladimir Lebedev, Vladimir Konashevich, Valeri Alfeevskii, Viktor Chizhikov, and Leonid Vladimirskii, prompt more vigorous discussion than the respective reissues illustrated by less prominent artists or those not illustrated at all. Minuscule deviations from "the original source" are met with customer disapproval and even outrage. Internet commenters compete in levels of scrutiny to which they subject the new reprint, compare versions of the same book within the series when different sizes or formats are available, and review the book against editions of the same title released by other publishing houses. On occasion, they enter dialogue, but generally, such comment threads tend to consist of isolated posts: readers share their analysis of the new reissue without trying to engage with the previous commenters. Readers tend to wish to air their own individual observations and evaluations of the book they just bought for their home library, rather than juxtapose their own position with the positions of other readers. Group identity here becomes less important than the opportunity to look at the past through the lens of the present and to see a book from one's childhood in its new material manifestation. (However, this type of reader engagement must be partly conditioned on the format of reader reviews on booksellers' websites, who, as a rule, do not encourage debate.)

This preservationist discourse dominates evaluations of present-day editions in comparison with the old Soviet ones. As mentioned before, all deviations are seen as damaging or even violating childhood memories:

> Is it really impossible with the existing technology of publishing we have not to distort, I can't find any other word, this book because it became our heritage, more than one generation grew up with this fairy tale and love it to this day. . . . Folks let's respect our past whatever it may have been, our literature and art, and children's literature especially, for what was read in childhood will never leave the memory. We must preserve and carefully treat fairy tales, other big literature, and poetry. In that way we pay the dues of memory to our ancestors.[26]

Framing recollections of books read in childhood as absolute ("will never leave the memory") and general ("the dues of memory to our ancestors") sets the axiological bar devised to enhance the symbolic capital of books once read and to establish their place among other unimpeachable symbols of the past. In this line of reasoning, the subtle mechanisms of individual memory (reproducing an emotion experienced earlier through tactile and visual associations) are obscured by preservationist rhetoric designed to monopolize the right to recycle material and symbolic objects of times past. This rhetoric is distinguished by an instrumentalization of technological advancements ("the existing technology of publishing"): the achievements of the present must be employed for exact reproduction of the products of the past.[27]

Thus, in constructing their retro-identity, consumers of Soviet reissues are determined to receive literal replicas of texts that are seen as exact character sequences (in which the texts are fully compliant with the authoritative originals, typically the ones remembered from childhood), complete collections or cycles of texts, and true reprints of illustrations.[28] A precise reactivation of tactile and visual sensations associated with remembered childhood experiences assists with the reproduction of the text, image, and meaning.[29] The childhood experience is not problematized in this discourse; it is presented as devoid of trauma, as fragmented, and as collapsed into a single childhood artifact—namely, a book once read.

Readers of Soviet era reprints are people whose identities are rooted in "happy childhoods filled with books." The so-called book guard not only monitors how carefully the traditions of Russian book publishing for kids are being preserved but aims to ensure that the replication and multiplication of artifacts and meanings of the past are done with the utmost reverence for the originals. Defending the past means, in part, defending one's childhood and, therefore, securely defending the current self in a world that constantly challenges the self to identify with a group. Reflecting upon *those very books* may present a return not to the tribe, not to the family, but to self-as-a-child. Having read good books becomes less relevant because the reader's identity, according to booksellers' websites, is constructed specifically around having read *those very books*, the *right books*. The word *those* in this case is a demonstrative pronoun, that deictic element marking the correlation between *these* and *those very* books. To know *those* books from *not those*, one must see them, touch them, read *those* texts, and thus find oneself.

Clarifying the (Un)clear

Another way that reissues of Soviet children's books foreground childhood memory is by supplying commentary. Thanks to this commentary, it is the content of the text, as opposed to the exactly reproduced form of the text (and the accompanying illustrations), that becomes the focus for adult readers. The commentary creates another layer of data: for adults, it provides information about daily life in *those* times in order to help adult readers *recall* and *recognize* them; for children, the commentary is intended to help them *understand* the text correctly.[30]

The inclusion of commentary in children's books is a long-standing tradition in Soviet publishing. In a 1940 article titled "O klassikakh i ikh kommentatorakh" (On classics and commentators), Aleksandra Liubarskaia and Lidiia Chukovskaia announced, "It is high time the craft of commentary was elevated to art."[31] Their lengthy article was dedicated to a critical overview of then-contemporary practices in the writing of commentary for classic works, including those for children. The authors, with characteristic pedantry and sarcasm, expounded the tasks of commentary, which were, according to them, to explicate and decipher the text: "Today's reader must not end up more helpless than the reader for whom the author intended his text back in his day; together with the inheritance, [the reader] must receive the key to the inheritance."[32] This argument contains an important premise: an individual reading a text at a significant temporal remove will almost invariably have difficulty understanding the text. In this respect, there is little difference between classic texts written in antiquity, nineteenth-century classic texts, and Soviet classics.

Liubarskaia and Chukovskaia were not consistent in this view, however. They considered the publication of works by Jules Verne without historical commentary entirely appropriate because, in their assessment, "the reader will understand everything even with no restoration of historical and biographical connections," whereas the publication of Jonathan Swift's *Gulliver's Travels* without such commentary was unacceptable to them.[33] The distinction is obvious: commentary is necessary when there is a possibility that the reader will misinterpret or simply ignore the ideological content of the text: "[*Gulliver's*] *Travels* requires not footnotes but an article with detailed commentary telling the reader about Swift's biography, re-creating the historical background, and explaining political allusions."[34] Many modern-day Russian publishers and readers disagree with this distinction. Labirint Press, which created the series *Kniga+Epokha* (Book+epoch), published several editions of children's world classics, such as Jules Verne's *Around the World in Eighty Days*, Robert Louis Stevenson's *Treasure Island*, Lewis Carrol's *Alice in Wonderland*, and Arthur Conan Doyle's *Adventures of Sherlock Holmes*, all of which include a sizable commentary on the historical content and the realia in the texts. The commentary appears as inserts, maps, 3D pop-ups, and other supplements enclosed in special pockets and flaps in the books. Such editions are devised to create a literally multilayered narrative structure in which the idea of "enclosed" knowledge is hypertrophied.

When publishing houses turn to reissuing Soviet children's literature, significant space in the editions is allocated to ideological commentary in which editors employ specific approaches to re-create historical backgrounds, as well as point out and explain to children the hidden political hints and smirks written into the books by Soviet writers. One example of said approach is a book series produced by Ilya Bernstein's publishing project A i B (A and B).[35] The commentary provided in the series seems to suggest that the editors did not just aim to give young readers an idea of the multifaceted everyday background against which the book's plot develops, including, perhaps, a depiction of a Soviet midcentury small-town movie theater or a list of cigarette brands available for sale at the time. The editors were also concerned with ensuring a "correct" reception of ideological meanings and, more generally, with regulating the mechanisms of text perception.

The widespread idea that commentary for children is a special kind of commentary—mainly tasked with explaining the unclear, interpreting the obscure, and essentially casting light on the dark spots in the text—has recently undergone a radical revision. More and more often, commentary becomes a venue for delivering adult views on the Soviet past (or other pasts) to young readers, thus eventually moving away from being limited to remarks on the particulars of the text or the respective realia and instead becoming broadly pedagogical, defining a normative reading of a given text. Editors compiling the commentary may employ different optics and supply different evaluations, but what is noteworthy is the fact that editors take it upon themselves to supply evaluations as a matter of course.

The proliferation of contemporary commentary (on occasion as lengthy as the commented-upon text itself, thus necessitating publishing the commentary as a separate volume[36]) brings to mind the original practice of commentary on sacred texts—that is, texts that must be interpreted correctly rather than completely. Some of those who study the practice of commentary attest that "overall, commentary must be concise and contain only that without which the text will be hard or impossible to understand. Otherwise, commentary turns into a source of independent content."[37] Modern-day commentary on editions of children's literature, then, can be confidently termed "a source of independent content." This, again, confirms the status of children's literature in the modern world: as ever, it remains a tool of ideological indoctrination. The "key to the inheritance," which contemporary commentators pick for Soviet children's literature, and the motives and the pragmatics of employing that key are inextricably connected to the ideological profiles of the commentators.

It is important to point out that publishing houses are aware of the fact that the target audience for such commentary, especially when issued as a separate volume, will not always be the child reader: "The addressee of the commentary is not necessarily the contemporary child or teen (although young appreciators of encyclopedias, footnotes, and detailed annotations do exist, they are in the clear minority), but rather it's the parent, the teacher, the librarian who employ these books to meet the goals of education and edification."[38] It is evident, however, that publications of this kind also satisfy other goals—namely, the desire of adult readers to revisit their childhoods and reimmerse themselves in the realia of Soviet daily life. Here is a reader's review of a recent edition of Iurii Koval''s *Vasiia Kurolesov* trilogy: "An excellent book! Our kid is engrossed in Vasiia's adventures, and I and my husband had SUCH fun reading the commentary! It is not all boring and detailed, but so vivid, giving us the opportunity to remember the signs and the daily life of those times. Highly recommended☺."[39]

"Those times" to which the reader seems to refer must be either the 1970s or the 1980s, since the first book in the trilogy was originally published in 1971. However, scholars of the trilogy point out multiple anachronistic elements in Koval''s text: "The material world of the 1960s in *Prikliucheniia Basi Kurolesova* (Adventures of Vasiia Kurolesov) incorporates realia from an earlier time."[40] Koval' himself affirms this: "It is very hard to say what time my detective stories are from. They are kind of from today, but also kind of from yesterday, hard to figure it out. . . . I'm trying not to include any signs of time. Let's say it's of today. A little bit of yesterday, too, though."[41] For the reader, "those times," all those different times, appear to be compressed into one solid past, which can be "recalled" through perusing the commentary that is illustrated with photos of everyday objects and the cultural landscape. In this phenomenon, there is paramnesia, or false memory. This kind of memory, however, is sufficient for the reader to identify with the aficionados of children's books of the so-called Soviet century. The *Soviet* here is nonspecific: it is from the day before yesterday but not from too long ago; it is not from the times immemorial but from the times memorial, the times of one's childhood, when books were beautiful and good.[42]

Not all readers react positively to commentary, however, as can be seen in the comments on Labirint's website:

> Maybe I'll be the only person who did not like the part of the book with the commentary, but to my mind it was not very professionally done. The only interesting part is the one about Iurii Koval''s parents and also certain signs of the past, when

> the novellas were being written. The rest of it is an attempt to attach sometimes debatable allusions and too detailed explanations to nearly every phrase in the book, and I thought it was excessive. Why, for example, did they quote an entire page from Kataev's *Beleet parus odinokii* [A lone white sail], etc. Maybe older schoolchildren will appreciate that, but I am a grown man, and the world described by Koval' is not familiar to me, and I have no interest whatsoever in what different kinds of cigarettes they had in the '60s–'70s; that explanation will add nothing to Koval''s magic.[43]

The reader who does not aim to "dive into the past" is disappointed by didactic commentary interfering with their aesthetic pleasure. Such statements expose meaningful differences in the positions of readers of such editions. Editions with commentary are addressed to adults for whom remembering is part of the reading process. It is noteworthy that Soviet books for adults are not currently seen as meriting commentary in reissues. Previously, Tamara Gabbe and Aleksandra Liubarskaia stated that books intended for adults require commentary whenever their target audience changes. Nowadays, the situation is reversed: books originally written for children by Iurii Koval', Viktor Dragunskii, and Aleksandr Neverov, for instance, are supplied with commentary with the switch in target readership (from children to adults). In one discussion of the current commentary practices employed in reeditions of Soviet children's literature, literary scholar Olga Vinogradova muses:

> Commentary on, specifically, Soviet kids' books, in my view, is part of a larger process, a process of rediscovery, reconceptualization of Soviet mass culture, as well as the growing scholarly interest in it (in addition to multiple inquiries into the Soviet avant-garde practices of the 1920s and '30s and the late Soviet underground). Here, children's literature appears as a pure, platonic example of a mass culture text, not only

> because of its wide dissemination but because of the a priori naïveté and the abstract perception of the text by the (naïve, unpoliticized, fantasizing, young) reader. An unexpected, estranged look at this very familiar "innocent" text uncovers in it multiple, previously unseen markers of the social and the political, encrypted spaces of freedom and unfreedom, spaces of criticism and manipulation—that is, it really discovers the text anew.[44]

Such rediscovery of Soviet children's literature by now grown Soviet children is a very curious example of children's literature not only functioning in adult reading circles but being strategically used in reading to achieve mnemonic effects.

Conclusion

The works of many Soviet children's authors who, in their time, enjoyed large print runs and literary awards bestowed upon them did not manage to cross the cultural gap of the 1990s. Books by Agniia Barto and Aleksandr Volkov stayed in print, while books by Iosif Likstanov and Antonina Golubeva did not.[45] The titles that made it across the threshold of the new century remain in print not only because of the inertia of publishing houses but also because of the characteristic features of "key texts" that they possess. First, they are easily retained in memory through being read aloud by older generations to younger ones (the dominant content of reissued Soviet classics are the plots of 1920s nursery rhymes and 1950s fairy-tale novels). Second, their success is bolstered by the attending cult of Soviet children's book design, primarily that of the illustrated children's book—a cult that was formed during Soviet times and has been kept alive since. As a result of this cult, contemporary readers express the need to have the visual and tactile experiences they had when reading Soviet editions in childhood re-created for them. On the other hand, the cultivated memory of a happy childhood, and happy childhood reading as part of it, plays an important role. It appears that the fabled literature-centricity of Russian culture has recently manifested itself in the trend of consuming *those very books*, the list of which includes more than—and actually fewer of—works by Alexander Pushkin and Piotr Ershov.

Several factors affect the longevity of books in retail: relevant or timeless content, which must be devoid of any topical political messaging (thus, further obsolescence of Sergei Mikhalkov's books may be forecasted); illustrations added to preserve the emblematic look that at one point was viewed by experts as the pinnacle in book design (thus, books once illustrated by successful artists have a better shot at longevity); and the collective desire of adults, nostalgic for their Soviet childhoods, to be reminded of its material and cultural world. It is the combination of the above factors that explains why not all Soviet children's books ended up in long-term storage in public libraries or in recycling centers to serve as a mere source of paper and cardboard pulp.

Notes

1. In recent research, see Kümmerling-Meibauer and Müller, *Canon Constitution*. I would like to express my gratitude to the Internationale Jugendbibliothek (International Youth Library) in Munich, Germany for affording me the opportunity to gather material for this section of the article. The article was prepared with the support of the Russian Science Foundation, project no. 19-18-00414 (Soviet Culture Today [Forms of Cultural Recycling in Russian Art and Aesthetics of the Everyday Life], 1990s–2010s).

2. On Israel's children's literature, see Darr, *Nation and the Child*.

3. Marshak, "Literatura—detiam," 196. Unless otherwise indicated, all translations from Russian are by A. Krushelnitskaya.

4. Marshak, "Literatura—detiam," 196.

5. Statistical data on the publishing of children's literature in the 1920s and 1930s are based on Ivan I. Startsev's indexes. See I. Startsev, *Detskaia literatura: Bibliografiia 1918–1931*, 19 vols. (Moscow: Molodaia gvardiia, 1933–89); and I. Startsev, *Detskaia literatura 1932–1939* (Moscow: Detizdat, 1941).

6. All numbers are quoted based on the bibliographic data featured in the indexes compiled by Ivan I. Startsev and his cohort; see his eighteen-part volume *Detskaia literatura*.

7. For these statistics, see the website of the Russian Book Chamber, accessed November 29, 2022, http://www.bookchamber.ru/statistics.html.

8. The Russian Book Chamber lists of top writers also include Eduard Uspenskii, Grigorii Oster, and Andrei Usachev; however, a discussion of the popularity of their works is beyond the scope of this chapter. Since 2012, Viktor Dragunskii's name also makes the list.

9. We may hypothesize that Mikhalkov's lower publishing ratings have to do not only with the overt ideological messaging in his poems but also with the poems' firm rootedness in Soviet everyday life. More inquiry into the poetics of all the authors under discussion is needed to establish whether the presence of obsolete Soviet realia in a given children's text affects the text's current popularity. For instance, Marshak's "Rasskaz o neizvestnom geroe" (Tale of an Unknown Hero) and Mikhalkov's "Diadia Stepa" (Uncle Stepa) have fallen out of favor with contemporary readers, while Marshak's translations into Russian of English children's rhymes have not.

10. Goncharova, "Istoriia izdaniia skazochnoi," 47.

11. Marshak, *Sobranie sochinenii*, 8:155.

12. Litovskaia, "Kliuchevye teksti," 68–69.

13. Nataliia Erofeeva, "O chuvstve nostal'gii i liubimykh starykh knizhkakh: Interv'iu s N. Erofeevoi," accessed October 13, 2022, https://www.labirint.ru/child-now/novaya-staraya-knizhka.

14. Lidiia Sergeeva, "Retsenziia na knigu 'Zamazka' Nikolai Nosov," accessed October 13, 2022, https://www.labirint.ru/reviews/show/1854989/. This and the subsequent excerpts from reader reviews were collected from the website of the online bookseller Labirint, Labirint.ru. The English translation has tried to preserve the quirks of the original Russian. Translation by A. Krushelnitskaya.

15. Marina Kuznetsova, "Retsenziia na knigu 'Ot odnogo do desiati. Veselyi schet' Samuil Marshak," accessed October 13, 2022, https://www.labirint.ru/reviews/show/1401905/.

16. Elena Petrova, "Retsenziia na knigu 'Doktor Aibolit' Kornei Chukovskii," accessed October 13, 2022, https://www.labirint.ru/reviews/show/1308086/.

17. Mariia Timashchuk, "Retsenziia na knigu 'Ot odnogo do desiati. Veselyi schet' Samuil Marshak," accessed October 13, 2022, https://www.labirint.ru/reviews/show/740776/.

18. Ekaterina Arapova, "Retsenziia na knigu 'Doktor Aibolit' Kornei Chukovskii," accessed October 13, 2022, https://www.labirint.ru/reviews/show/2078837/.

19. Rosman Publishers, address to potential customers of T. Aleksandrova and V. Berestov, *Katia v igrushechnom gorode*, accessed October 13, 2022, https://www.livelib.ru/book/1000927594-katya-v-igrushechnom-gorode-tatyana-aleksandrova.

20. Iuliia Divanidova, "Retsenziia na knigu 'Kubik na kubik' Iakov Taits," accessed October 13, 2022, https://www.labirint.ru/reviews/show/1869842/.

21. Translations by A. Krushelnitskaya.

22. Olala, "Retsenziia na knigu 'Moidodyr' Kornei Chukovsky," accessed October 13, 2022, https://www.labirint.ru/reviews/show/1375877/.

23. For instance, in 2007, 163 editions of Chukovsky's titles were published, with a total of 3,289,500 copies, compared to only 57 editions of Pushkin, with a total of 520,400 copies. Even with the general decrease in print runs, this proportion remained constant in 2019, with 131 Chukovsky editions, 1,380,470 copies to 70 Pushkin editions at 379,180 copies; see data provided by the Russian Book Chamber: https://www.bookchamber.ru/statistics.html.

24. ELOIZA, "Retsenziia na knigu 'Volshebnik Izumrudnogo goroda' Aleksandr Volkov," accessed October 13, 2022, https://www.labirint.ru/reviews/show/693774/.

25. Niu4a, "Retsenziia na knigu 'Volshebnik Izumrudnogo goroda' Aleksandr Volkov," accessed October 13, 2022, https://www.labirint.ru/reviews/show/699317/.

26. Aleksandr Saf'ianov, "Retsenziia na knigu 'Volshebnik Izumrudnogo goroda' Aleksandr Volkov," accessed October 13, 2022, https://www.labirint.ru/reviews/show/2131618/.

27. This strategy of redesign is employed in other contexts and discourses as well, including the reuse of brand logos, e.g., "Sdelano v SSSR" (Made in the USSR), GOST (State standard), etc.

28. Readers pay particular attention to whether "all" or "not all Deniska's stories" are included in reeditions of Viktor Dragunskii's books, specifically in his *Rytsari i eshche 60 istorii. Sobranie Deniskinykh rasskazov.*

29. As one reader's review puts it, "The book came out nice and pleasant to touch, I get the full impression I'm holding a Soviet edition in my hands, it'll be hard to find fault with it even for picky customers." Anna, "Retsenziia na knigu 'Vitia Maleev v shkole i doma' Nikolai Nosov," accessed October 13, 2022, https://www.labirint.ru/books/591774/.

30. See the following works on contemporary issues in young readers' perception of Soviet literature: Iu. Belysheva, P. Kliushin, and E. Markasova, "'Neponiatnye slova' v rasskazakh V. Dragunskogo," in *Problemy ontolingvistiki—2013: Materialy mezhdunarodnoi nauchnoi konferentsii*, 26–29 iiunia, Sankt-Peterburg, pp. 332–37. Sankt-Peterburg: Izd-vo RGPU im. A.I. Gercena, 2013; Markasova, "'Deniskiny rasskazy,'" 138–47; Dudko, "Problemy vospriiatiia tekstov," 125–30.

31. Liubarskaia and Chukovskaia, "O klassikakh i ikh kommentatorakh," 172.

32. Liubarskaia and Chukovskaia, "O klassikakh i ikh kommentatorakh," 165.

33. Liubarskaia and Chukovskaia, "O klassikakh i ikh kommentatorakh," 169.

34. Liubarskaia and Chukovskaia, "O klassikakh i ikh kommentatorakh," 169.

35. See Koval', *Prikliucheniia Vasi Kurolesova*. See also, Dragunskii, *Rytsari i eshche 60 istorii*; and Nekrasov, *Prikliucheniia kapitana Vrungelia*. Previously the editor-publisher collaborated with other publishing houses on similar projects. For the full list of his projects of this type, see Bernshtein, "Detskaia literatura sovetskoi epokhi," 122–23.

36. See Gelfond, *Trilogiia A. Ia. Brushtein*, as an example of commentary on a children's text issued as a separate volume, without the attending original children's text.

37. Zharkov, *Tekhnologiia redaktsionno-izdatel'skogo dela*.

38. Bernshtein, "Detskaia literatura sovetskoi epokhi," 108–9.

39. Elena Zolina, "Retsenziia na knigu 'Tri povesti o Vase Kurolesove' Iurii Koval'," accessed October 13, 2022, https://www.labirint.ru/reviews/show/1480214/.

40. See the commentary to Koval', *Prikliucheniia Vasi Kurolesova*, 198.

41. See the commentary to Koval', *Prikliucheniia Vasi Kurolesova*, 198–99.

42. See the misdating of book illustrations by Vladimir Konashevich in a reader's review of a 2017 reedition of Samuil Marshak's *Veselyi schet* (Fun counting): "Since I'm a mommy of a 3-year-old boy, I bought this book to combine business with pleasure☺ Thanks Melik-Pashayev Publishers for your series Small Masterpieces for the Littlest Ones, you bring our kids good books from the distant 1980s." Illustrations for this title were created by Konashevich much earlier, but here the reader sees the moment of her own introduction to the book as the point of origin. Vikusha-mama, "Retsenziia na knigu 'Ot odnogo do desiati. Veselyi schet' Samuil Marshak," accessed October 13, 2022, https://www.labirint.ru/reviews/show/739823/.

43. Bathsheba, "Retsenziia na knigu 'Tri povesti o Vase Kurolesove' Iurii Koval'," accessed October 13, 2022, https://www.labirint.ru/reviews/show/1640002/.

44. "Anketa DCh," 19–20.

45. Likstanov's *Malyshok* (Teeny kid) and Golubeva's *Mal'chik iz Urzhuma* (A boy from Urzhum) were regularly republished in sizeable print runs until the mid-1980s.

In the Interlude

The Search for Form and Method in Early Soviet Children's Poetry

Serguei Alex. Oushakine

> *The term poetry, circulating widely in our language and scholarship, has by now lost all concrete reach or content and become a value judgment.*
>
> —Yuri Tynianov, "Promezhutok"

Reading critical reviews of early Soviet poetry almost a hundred years after they were published is a rare delight, a pleasure in its own right. These reviews reflect the logic of the period that could be tentatively bookended by the publication of Lev Trotsky's *Literatura i revoliutsiia* (Literature and revolution) in 1923 and the official birthdate of socialist realism in 1934. Yuri Tynianov (1894–1943), a key Russian formalist, commented on the very beginning of this "interlude" (*promezhutok*), as he called it, in 1924, observing that it was a time when postrevolutionary poetry had not yet been "pulled off."[1] Its genre specifics were still in flux, and slowly but consistently, poetry was acquiring a recognizable outline, building a stable inner structure, and exploring the paths of its future development.

In such a context, the scholar of literary development—or "literary evolution," to use another term coined by Tynianov—was forced to play the role of a chronicler rather than a researcher. While critics meticulously documented every period and every stage in the life of poetry, determining their precise meaning and mission was still almost impossible to do. Each new change of direction could turn into the beginning of a qualitative breakthrough—or of a drawn-out dead end. The literary ends had not yet started to justify the means, and the appeal of the literary process was not in its direction but in its dynamism. Today, these century-old literary debates are interesting precisely because they are emphatically disengaged from any concerns about teleology, directionality, or tradition. The literary history of the interlude is the history of literature's possibilities. The participants of the literary process—as opposed to us now—could only speculate about the consequences of their actions. For them, "nothing had ended yet," as Viktor Shklovsky, another leader of the formalist school, wrote in his book *Revoliutsiia i front* (Revolution and the front; 1921), though in a different context.[2]

Tynianov, however, offered a slight correction to his colleague's words in 1924: "For poetry, the period of inertia has ended. Belonging to a school or holding a poetic passport won't save the poet any longer. The schools have disappeared, the movements have . . . ceased to be. . . . The ones surviving are the solitaries."[3] Curiously, it is in the practices of such solitary survival that Tynianov saw the possibility of (poetic) discovery. The abrupt stop of the steamroller of poetic inertia might look like a historical dead end, but this dead end—as the formalist insisted—is an illusion itself. The language's "new dimension," or the new poetic vision, could arise only "in the interludes when inertia loses its grip."[4]

As a result, Tynianov viewed the poetry of the interlude as undergoing a difficult, slow, but utterly necessary transformation of poetic optics and vision, poetic materials and techniques, and poetic timbre and intonation, followed by the transformation of the poets as well as their audiences. As the poetry of the interlude was shifting its boundaries and modifying its approaches, its historical significance, according to Tynianov, stemmed not so much from successes and "accomplished works" as from an active quest for a possible escape from the apparent dead end. The "*interludic*" pieces themselves might be "unsuccessful," but what was important was their ability to further the "possibility of 'successes'" (italics in original).[5]

A little later, in a brief article in the July 1927 issue of *Leningradskaia pravda*, Boris Eikhenbaum (1886–1959), a formalist colleague of Shklovsky's and Tynianov's, transferred the logic of Tynianov's interlude onto the tracks of literary criticism proper. Like Tynianov, Eikhenbaum diagnosed the institutional implosion of literary scholarship. And like him, he noted the general striving toward solitary survival: "There are no vibrant literary debates anymore, there are no literary 'groupings'—each poet is for himself, but collectively, they are just a rabble. . . . The old literary and paraliterary fights, which used to motivate some critics quite recently, have completely exhausted themselves by now."[6]

In contrast to Tynianov, Eikhenbaum was much less optimistic about the creative possibilities offered by the interlude. For him, the lack of a common arena of literary struggle gave rise to more than just strategies of individual survival. The absence of shared platforms quickly led to progressive fragmentation, to a splintering of the literary field and literary labor into autonomous enclaves. Or, to be more precise, it led to "specialization, as in medicine. Having acquired a special field of expertise (say, sexual issues and topics), a specialist naturally expects to be treated with respect."[7] The competition of ideas was giving way to the competition of statuses.

In other words, the indeterminacy of genres and the individualism of solitary survival in the literature of the 1920s and early 1930s were exacerbated by the lack of a literary environment that could generate a set of common criteria for evaluating the "successes" and "failures" that were mentioned by Tynianov. Without clear common goals, strategies of solitary survival paved the path for the increasing thematic and professional feudalization of the literary community.

The children's literature of the interlude added an important dimension to the picture painted by the formalists. There was no inertia of literary tradition or of literary criticism to speak of: a steamroller of poetic inertia was nowhere to be seen—there wasn't even a road where such a steamroller could have stalled. This effectively doubled the complexity of the situation. A way out of the drawn-out dead end had to be sought in the edifice of children's poetry, which was yet to be built.

Boris Bukhshtab (1904–85), a second-wave formalist, explained the essence of the problem clearly in his article "Stikhi dlia detei" (Poems for children; 1931). The broad challenge was not that the edifice of children's poetry had to be created from nothing. The preliminary work at the children's poetry "site" had been started long before; it was the overall plan of the construction that generated questions. Bukhshtab saw "prerevolutionary children's poetry" (overpopulated by "knights, mermaids, and fairies"[8]) and the literature of "high school humor"[9] as catering to extremely narrow social circles. Targeting mostly "the children of wealthy classes, the natives of the separate kids' quarters" with their "'greenhouse' upbringing" and "carefully filtered experiences," this poetry demonstrated an "astonishingly limited thematic range."[10]

Of course, Bukhshtab's observations about the class and thematic constraints of prerevolutionary children's poetry are easy to write off as bowing to the political demands of the 1930s. However, one should not rush to do so. Complaints about the thematic scarcity of poetry for children were linked with specific structural properties of this poetry and not with particular historical circumstances of its existence. The basic problem of pre-Soviet children's poetry was its constitutive principle: the specificity of this genre was defined exclusively in terms of its subject matter. The "children" dimension of "prerevolutionary children's poetry" was entirely determined by a certain repertoire of poetic topics. Since "this poetry had no specific formal characteristics of its own," its thematic boundaries defined the limits of children's poetry as a whole.[11]

With all its apparent radicalism, Bukhshtab's perception of children's poetry of the pre-Soviet period as being thematically limited and methodologically underdeveloped was fairly true to the actual state of affairs. Without going into details, I cite only one representative example from a review written by Elizaveta Tikheeva (1867–1943), an educator and later vice-president of the Saint Petersburg Society for the Promotion of Preschool Education and a professor at the Petrograd Pedagogical Institute of Preschool Education. The article was published in 1898 in the journal *Vospitanie i obuchenie* (Nurture and education; published in Saint Petersburg since 1877) as a survey of poetry books for children that came out in the mid-1890s.

After a thorough review of seven single-author volumes, Tikheeva came to a discouraging conclusion: "All the analyzed poetry examples have to be recognized as mediocre. . . . The general impression . . . is that of a lackluster humdrum routine."[12] Tikheeva's generally negative outlook on the state of the "poetic guild" is instructive. Even more telling are the aesthetic and pedagogical demands that the critic placed on poetry in general and children's poetry in particular:

> According to its fundamental purpose and meaning, poetry must affect readers' emotion, the spiritual need that forces them to seek beauty in the world around them . . . and cling to it; poetry must engage readers with its beauty and power; it must capture them, make them temporarily break loose from the mundane and prosaic existence and rise above it. . . . At the same time, it is imperative that we strive to sow into the young soul the seeds of love for poetry as the most beautiful branch of literature, to nurture the right attitude in [the soul] from the very beginning, and to see poetry not as idle entertainment, not as something indifferent, insubstantial and unnecessary, but as an ever-accessible source of communing with the best manifestations of the human spirit.[13]

And a bit later:

> The child needs to be introduced into the realm of the best poetry as soon as he is capable of perceiving and memorizing. From the outset, he needs to be given exemplars springing from lively and free-flowing inspiration. His internal gaze needs to get used to exemplars of immaculate beauty. Only those lines should fall on his ear that give poetry the right to be called "the language of gods."
>
> . . . The music of every new verse should not be a fleeting visitor to his ear but be well understood and thoroughly felt; it should help him rise to the next rung of his aesthetic development. And to that end, we need to do away with everything extraneous by cleaning the mind, memory, and imagination from all the deadweight and garbage. Admit nothing that is too pale, nebulous, vague, and hazy.[14]

Certainly, for Bukhshtab (and other like-minded critics), overcoming this (thematic) orientation of poetry toward "the language of gods" and "exemplars of immaculate beauty" was part of the program for creating genuine children's poetry whose purpose would not be "breaking loose" from life's prose. Yet, merely renouncing the traditional "nothing extraneous" approach (as voiced by Tikheeva), even when coupled with Bukhshtab's conscious desire to make artistically available "all the topics accessible to the child's mind,"[15] could hardly alter the nature of (pseudo-)children's literature.

As Bukhshtab explained, the topics, even the most important ones, could not be revolutionary or nonrevolutionary in and of themselves, "*without considering their organization and focus* [*obrabotka i osveshchenie*]" (italics in original): "a May Day celebration [can be pictured] so that it would seem dull, gray, and bureaucratic."[16] Creating genuine children's poetry required "finding *methods* of artistic refraction [of the subject matter] that would be specific for children's literature" (italics in original).[17] Moreover, it was the method (as opposed to themes) that would chiefly distinguish children's poetry from "Soviet literature 'at large.'"[18] To support his position, Bukhshtab provided an illuminating example of "interrelations between 'children's' and 'adult' literature":

> Preeminent masters of contemporary poetry write for children: on the covers of children's books, we encounter the names of Mayakovsky, Aseev, Pasternak, Mandelstam. . . . So, there is a certain possibility for literary skills and mastery to be carried over from adult to children's literature. Yet we should also note that "children's poets" beat the preeminent poets hands down on this front. The "guest acts" yield to professional children's poets both in popularity and in artistic mastery. Apparently, having considerable literary skills doesn't really suffice. To succeed as a children's author, the poet also needs a distinctive set of psychotechnical qualities.[19]

In 1930, Anna Pokrovskaia (1878–1972), then director of the Institute of Children's Reading, pointed out a similar problem in a (favorable) review of Vladimir Mayakovsky's children's poetry. Relying on her pedagogical experience, Pokrovskaia observed that "children appeared not to notice" Mayakovsky's poetry, while parents and teachers "did not accept" it—most likely because Mayakovsky's books for children were "more of a literary than a pedagogical phenomenon."[20] A year later, the literary scholar Leonid Timofeev (1904–84) directly outlined the essence of the general problem using Eduard Bagritskii's poems as his examples: "Strictly speaking, Bagritskii still doesn't write poems for children; he tries to simplify poems written for adults so that they would speak to children. . . . But the little ones require a different treatment of image and poetic word; straightforward simplification of the standard poetic language is not enough."[21] In 1934, in a speech at the First Congress of Soviet Writers, Samuil Marshak unequivocally advocated an active search for a "genuine children's language" that could be used for writing books "about the [Russian] civil war or about the stars."[22] The methods of "artistic refraction"[23] promoted so insistently by Bukhshtab were to become a tool for operationalizing "a different *kind* of image *treatment*"[24] (italics in original), a different methodology of verbal work, and a different understanding of the verbal resonance that poetic words might generate in the child.

It is easy to trace, behind the facade of Bukhshtab's dichotomy of topics versus methods, the classical formalist opposition of form and content or, in a slightly modified form, of the material and its organizing principles. Yet, for the formalists, this opposition was tactical rather than essential. In 1924, Tynianov, for instance, stated with a sense of relief, "We have recently . . . done away with the notorious analogy 'form—content = glass—wine.'"[25] In the field of poetry, the formalists resolved the conflict between form and content by a "dual" approach to its verbal material.[26] In verbal arts, the word took on two different roles: it was a common, colloquial, everyday word, and it was a treated, processed word that was built into the framework of an artistic text. As Tynianov noted, the "verbal material" of poetry was dynamized with the help of the so-called *constructive* principle. "A sharp line" was drawn "between the verse word and the prose word": the constructive action of the rhythm transformed "the speech word" into "the metrical word."[27]

Of course, this process could not be reduced to a simple rhythmic reorganization of the raw verbal mass. Poetic transformation also signified a conscious shift of priorities. During the process of poetic ordering (with the help of metrical structure, strophic composition, etc.), speech gradually extricated itself from the dictates of the informational (communicative or semantic) function of language. According to Tynianov, "the *semantic importance* of a word in the poem" was reconfigured by subjecting it to "the importance of *rhythm*" (italics in original).[28] Or, to put it a little differently, for the formalists, poetry's orientation toward the rhythmic arrangement of words was expressed not only in "the obscuring of the semantic aspect" but also in its "sharp deformation."[29] And so, "as a result, the word became *hindered*" (italics in original).[30] Its expressive—pronunciational (*proiznositel'naia*)—aspect was foregrounded.[31] The speech material started showing some resistance as it was being transformed into "a material with a perceptible shape."[32] Sound, rhythm, rhyme, and intonation were ultimately emerging from the shadow of semantics.

Roman Jakobson, also a formalist, noted in his very first paper on the new Russian poetry that poetic language was characterized by the tendency toward *zaum'* (transense) speech, which drives the word to its "phonetic limits": "In the history of all times and peoples, we observe again and again that the poet cares about 'chime only,' to use Trediakovskii's words."[33] Kornei Chukovsky's "Trinadtsat' zapovedei dlia detskikh poetov" (Thirteen commandments for children's poets), published in 1929, can serve as a perfect illustration of the "acoustic approach to verse" proposed by the formalists.[34] Chukovsky's commandments are essentially a protocol for transforming "a poem for children" into a phonetic object—or into what Chukovsky called a "verse picture," a "verbal painting," or a "cinematic" creation.[35]

Notably, Chukovsky carefully avoided a situation where the perception of a poem could be reduced to reading only: "The poet who depicts must also be a poet who sings. The child is not content with seeing a certain scene depicted in verse; he also demands that this verse contain a song within a dance."[36] Of course, saturating poetry for children with painterly, cinematic, musical, and choreographic qualities was just the beginning of a long journey. Moreover, for Chukovsky, verse also had to have the quality of activity or, more precisely, play.

It is hardly by accident that the final requirement on Chukovsky's list of commandments responds to the formalist agenda. The content of the poetic play, or game, is utterly and irreversibly specified: the game becomes a game of speech and words, where "pronounced sounds" become toys.[37] Importantly, what mattered for the poet in this gamification of children's poetry was not "chime only" but also its effects—that is, the ability of these sounds and chimes to actualize the forms of activity that allow children to not so much "rise above" the mundane as participate in mastering the surrounding world by all the means at their disposal.

Chukovsky's consistent orientation toward working with the nonsemantic affordances of words and his emphatic insistence on giving poetry the *children's* character by flooding its structure with word game elements could not remain unchallenged. His publications clearly exposed that same professional watershed in literary studies that was the subject of Eikhenbaum's writings. As if reviving the "elevated" aesthetic demands of poetry as formulated in the late nineteenth century by Tikheeva ("poetry is not an idle entertainment, not something indifferent, insubstantial and unnecessary"[38]), a number of critics viewed "Chukovism" as primarily a cult of "gibberish" (*bessmyslinki*)[39] that suffered from a "paucity of contentivity" (*malosoderzhatel'nost'*) in the narrative structure.[40]

At the same time, these distinctive features of Chukovsky's poetry gave another group of critics reason to talk about the emergence of genuine children's poetry. For instance, Mikhail Malishevskii (1896–1955), secretary of the library subsection of the State Academic Council at Narkompros (Ministry of Education) and author of a book on versification theory,[41] noted in his review of children's poetry that the "gamification" of a poem is enabled largely by its "rhythmically organized" structure, rather than by its content.[42]

The dominant role of "rhyme and sonority in the content" of verses intended for children was linked with two important functions. The "verse aspect" rhythmically organized a ludic interaction (the play); it thereby also compensated for the "paucity" (if not "meaninglessness") of its narrative. Or, as Malishevskii himself put it:

> How does one translate into prose this rhyme:
>
> One-two-three, one-two-three,
> Little bunny under the tree.
> But the hunter, he comes running,

Takes his gun and shoots the bunny.
Boom! boom! oh me, oh my!
Little bunny, will you die?

It would be naïve to conclude that this poem relies on a verse structure just to "tell the story" of the poor bunny. In fact, the poem is inextricably interwoven with the process of the game; the poem's content is synonymous to the content of the game. It is impossible to subtract from the poem its rhythmic sound without ruining the game, while subtracting the bunny's story would do only a little damage.[43]

Such specialization between the supporters of "contentivity" (*soderzhatel'nost'*) for children's poetry on one end of the continuum and the supporters of "poetics" on the other largely continued to define the direction and tenor of scholarship—and squabbles—in the field of twentieth-century children's poetry.

To view the opposition of poetics and thematics or of form and content as only a Soviet phenomenon would not be accurate. Osip Brik, another formalist scholar of literature, emphasized in a 1927 article that the struggle between "the two approaches to verse"—the rhythmic and the semantic—had a long history, becoming especially intensified "at pivotal moments of poetic culture."[44] It is not the extremes, however, that are particularly interesting but the space between them: the interlude. Quite a few authors of the early Soviet period were able to stay "above the fray," maintaining—with varying degrees of success—the analytical "duality" in their perception of poetry, in which the *contentitvity* (*soderzhatel'nost'*) principle (semantics, content) was consciously put in a dialogue with the *constructivity* (*konstruktsionnost'*) principle (poetics, sonority). Coming from different perspectives, these texts made an effort to explore the substantive role of the form and the formative role of the substance.

Boris Bukhshtab's 1931 article "Stikhi dlia detei" (quoted earlier) was by all indications the very first Soviet attempt at a systematic analysis of late 1920s children's poetry.[45] To a great degree, the importance of this article has to do with its charting of a yet unexplored literary terrain. That is why Bukhshtab's analytical optics privilege sharp contrasts, capturing the most notable and readily apparent features, as is typical of trailblazers. Bukhshtab's essay shows another common trait of trailblazing enterprises: the striving to work out the good, the bad, and the ugly in the field of children's poetry. As a result, an examination of the cornerstones and pinnacles of the early Soviet literary field—exemplified by the poetry of Kornei Chukovsky, Samuil Marshak, and, to a lesser degree, Daniil Kharms—is complemented here by the critical analysis of "signs of slapdash work" in the output of the "opposing lineup of poets," such as Agniya Barto and Sofia Fedorchenko.

Another review article of the same period, Mikhail Malishevskii's "O poezii dlia detei" (On poetry for children; 1935), largely converges with Bukhshtab's review in its tone and analytical methods. But it differs in some respects: in the four years that had passed since the publication of Bukhshtab's work, the analytical optics were fine-tuned to discern more nuances. Children's poetry was increasingly perceived in relation to the stable outlines of the social and artistic institution of children's literature at large that was taking shape at the time. Malishevskii could not just see the peaks and valleys of the literary landscape, but he could also separate settlements, as it were, in the form of organized, or rather self-organizing, communities of children's literary magazines (such as *Pioner*, *Murzilka*, and *Chizh i Ezh*). However, in the course of his review, Malishevskii comes to a disheartening conclusion: the institutionalization of children's literature by itself does not yet guarantee the emergence of original works of art—"not a single new children's genre was discovered in these magazines."[46] The formation of new literary traditions, as Tynianov predicted, was taking place through solitary work.

Such general reviews present useful temporal snapshots, documenting the deployment of forces at the time not contaminated by later revisions and recoveries. For instance, it is not hard to determine the four front-runners among the children's poets whose books received the most reviews at their time of publication. Chukovsky and Marshak come out far ahead; Barto and Mayakovsky, far behind; and the OBERIU poets appear as but a speck on the horizon.

These surveys of books of poetry highlight another important dimension of the literary evolution: the comparative analysis of children's magazines undertaken by Malishevskii in 1935 suggests a significant correction to today's ideas about those magazines' aesthetic and political orientation. Ranking the magazines by the "ideological and political charge carried by their poetry," Malishevskii did not give first place to *Pioner* (the magazine "totally failed in mastering its reader, being pedagogically very passive") or to the "ideologically vague" *Murzilka*. Going against the contemporary perception of the literary process of that time, Malishevskii gave first prize to the ideology-forward *Ezh* for its politically charged children's poetry and its opening "doors into political issues."[47]

These hierarchies and evaluations made by contemporaries are important. It is, of course, equally important to understand that the disposition (and evaluation) of the players in the literary field was completely determined by the viewpoint that took shape within the period. Chukovsky correctly noted in a 1925 diary entry that "every writer whose works stay alive through multiple eras is subject to being viewed in every new era through a different grid or framework; therefore, each time, different features of the writer's profile become revealed or remain hidden."[48] Four additional important critical essays devoted to individual poets are instrumental for understanding the work of the grid of the interlude period and the process of canonization of the poetic practices of children's literature of the time. I will single out only one aspect in this process of shaping poetic norms and methods—namely, the reviewers' consistent attunement to the techniques of the craft of writing and to the devices used to organize children's poetry.

For instance, as Bukhshtab correctly notes in his essay, the universal belief that "children's poems must be written in singsong rhythms, with syntax subjugated to rhythm, as is typical of songs"—that is, the "new rhythmics" that formed the foundation of Soviet children's poetry—was not simply "given" or "discovered." It was created by concrete authors. It was Chukovsky who "linked" children's poetry with song, in the same way that Nikolai Nekrasov in his time "linked" poetry for adults with vaudeville, parody, feuilleton, and comedy of all sorts.[49] The songlike rhythmic structure of children's poetry pioneered by Chukovsky was ultimately canonized in the work of Marshak, who was also instrumental in shaping the compositional structure of children's poetry. As Bukhshtab reminds us, Marshak's important contribution to children's poetry was the introduction of "persistent repetitions modeled after song choruses and strict semantic parallelism corresponding to rhythmic parallelism."[50]

The origin and the gradual strengthening of the general rhythmic and syntactic contours of Soviet children's poetry are important. But they should not overshadow some other—less dramatic—discoveries that eventually became commonplace notions. For example, in his article "Tvorchestvo S. Marshaka" (S. Marshak's oeuvre), Samuil Bolotin juxtaposes Marshak's and Chukovsky's poems to observe a substantial commonality in the poets' practices.[51] Both Chukovsky and Marshak build their poetry on "defamiliarization, puns, [and] humorous substitution of meanings" in order to estrange the familiar in their poems and to present "unexpected facets of common things" to the young reader.[52] There are major differences, though. According to Bolotin, the improbability of the "topsy-turvy world" in Chukovsky's poems and all his "twists and turns" are held together "only by the logic of trochaic tetrameter and rhyming couplets"; in Marshak's poems, the gradual uncovering and demystification of riddles is built on finding a realistic resolution "within any fantastic situation."[53] Paradoxical displacements and deformations were goals in themselves for Chukovsky; Marshak took them further: to the eventual reconstitution of order and the normalization of rational purposiveness.

I want to single out yet another tendency in children's poetry that is clearly identified in reviews of the time. Soviet children's poetry is, to a large degree (though not exclusively), the domain of laughter and the comical. Displacements and deformations lie at the base of its playful—inter*ludic*—effect. What is somewhat unusual is the deployment of these devices: the jokingly absurdist streak is in dialogue with topical satire. For example, the critic and literary scholar Boris Begak (1903–89), in his article "Kornei Chukovsky," describes the "comedic construction" of Chukovsky's children's poems as an intrinsic feature of his "every book."[54] In Marshak's practice, this pancomical setup undergoes functional specialization, turning first into laughter induced by displacement and culminating later in "laughable" images of eccentrics, fools, and other Mister Twister–like characters.[55] In Mayakovsky's comical fables, the social function of humor is, again, different: acting as a "pedagogical tool," laughter is transformed into mockery and ridicule. For Anna Grinberg, Mayakovsky's use of grotesque deformation is to intensify "the opposition between proletarian virtues and bourgeois vices."[56] He melds comedy and mockery.[57] With time, this type of mockery would be "mellowed down" and "normalized" in Barto's works, creating a new subgenre of the "feuilleton in verse."[58] Riddles and playful confusions would be replaced by teases and taunts. The comic relief that played the central role in Marshak's or Chukovsky's poems would be overshadowed by a different concern: the sharp precision of laughter hitting its target.[59]

The debates on children's poetry of the 1920s and 1930s enable us to trace not just the poetic evolution of the key authors but also the peculiar evolution of their social role in the field of children's poetry. Chukovsky's work, with his interest in the poem-as-play and his distance from topical problems, could be viewed, in Bukhshtab's words, as the Soviet analog of Western European "classics." Accordingly, Marshak, for whom it was so important to pin down in verse form all the details of the transition from "yesterday's" tradition to "today's" reality, was identified (by Bukhshtab again) as "an active fellow traveler of the socialist culture."[60]

In turn, for the literary scholar Vera Smirnova (1898–1977), Agniya Barto's poetry presented a perfect case of a journey of ideological education and maturation. As a "representative of the intelligentsia," Barto initially lacked the "native ear for class issues"; her development was a process of "working out" an adequate "sonic approach to poetry." Step by step and poem by poem, she asserted her "right to the title of a Soviet children's author."[61] Finally, in Anna Pokrovskaia's article "Maiakovskii kak detskii pisatel'" (Mayakovsky as a children's author), Mayakovsky is described as completing the circle of the brightest stars in the field of children's poetry. As Pokrovskaia points out, in his children's fables, the poet remained true to his reputation as a revolutionary futurist poet: if "Chukovsky broke the mold of traditional children's writing," then Mayakovsky had nothing else left but to ruthlessly parody Chukovsky's own molds.[62] In this way, futurism ceased to be a substantial aesthetic and political program and turned into a formal device.

Yuri Tynianov began his article "Interlude" (Promezhutok) with a complaint: "These days, writing about poems is almost as hard as writing them. And writing poems is almost as hard as reading them."[63] Thanks to the formalists, we know now that when literary work becomes difficult, this usually means two things: the ossification of old traditions and the beginning of the search for the way out of the dead end. Early Soviet discussions show how the difficulties of the interlude period were overcome in practice, transforming a potential dead end into an aesthetic and methodological breakthrough and turning stylistically and thematically incoherent children's texts into superior children's literature.

Notes

1. "Interlude" in Tynianov, *Permanent Evolution*, 173. English-language quotations in this article from Tynianov's "Interlude" are from this English translation.

2. Shklovskii, "Revoliutsiia i front [1921]," 1:149. Unless otherwise noted, all translations from Russian are by D. Manin.

3. Tynianov, *Permanent Evolution*, 175.
4. Tynianov, *Permanent Evolution*, 175.
5. Tynianov, *Permanent Evolution*, 216.
6. Eikhenbaum, "Vmesto 'rezkoi kritiki' [1927]," 167–68.
7. Eikhenbaum, "Vmesto 'rezkoi kritiki' [1927]," 168.
8. Abramovich, "Detskii mir," 35.
9. For more details on high school humor in children's poetry of the time, see Loshchilov, "Detskaia poema Petra Potemkina"; and Golovin, "Zhurnal 'Galchonok.'"
10. Bukhshtab, "Stikhi dlia detei," 103.
11. Bukhshtab, "Stikhi dlia detei," 104–5.
12. Tikheeva, "O spetsial'nykh sbornikakh," 312.
13. Tikheeva, "O spetsial'nykh sbornikakh," 290.
14. Tikheeva, "O spetsial'nykh sbornikakh," 313.
15. Bukhshtab, "Stikhi dlia detei," 105.
16. Bukhshtab, "Stikhi dlia detei," 105.
17. Bukhshtab, "Stikhi dlia detei," 105.
18. Bukhshtab, "Stikhi dlia detei," 105.
19. Bukhshtab, "Poeziia Marshaka," 16.
20. Pokrovskaia, "Maiakovskii kak detskii pisatel'," 16.
21. Timofeev, "O stikhakh dlia detei," 12.
22. Marshak, "Sodoklad o detskoi literature," 25.
23. Bukhshtab, "Stikhi dlia detei," 105.
24. Timofeev, "O stikhakh dlia detei," 12.
25. Tynianov, *Problema stikhotvornogo iazyka*, 9.
26. Tynianov, *Problema stikhotvornogo iazyka*, 7.
27. Tynianov, *Problema stikhotvornogo iazyka*, 40, 117, 40.
28. Tynianov, *Problema stikhotvornogo iazyka*, 76.
29. Tynianov, *Problema stikhotvornogo iazyka*, 117.
30. Tynianov, *Problema stikhotvornogo iazyka*, 40.
31. Shklovskii, "O poezii i zaumnom iazyke [1925]," 137.
32. Tynianov, *Problema stikhotvornogo iazyka*, 16.
33. Iakobson, "Noveishaia russkaia poeziia. Nabrosok pervyi [1921]," 303.
34. Tynianov, *Problema stikhotvornogo iazyka*, 4.
35. Chukovskii, "Trinadtsat' zapovedei dlia detskikh poetov," 13.
36. Chukovskii, "Trinadtsat' zapovedei dlia detskikh poetov," 13.
37. Chukovskii, "Trinadtsat' zapovedei dlia detskikh poetov," 17.
38. Tikheeva, "O spetsial'nykh sbornikakh," 291.
39. Kal'm, "'Kuda nos ego vedet,'" 2.
40. Timofeev, "O stikhakh dlia detei," 11.
41. See Malishevskii, *Metronika*.

42. Malishevskii, "O poezii dlia detei," 8.
43. Malishevskii, "O poezii dlia detei," 7–8.
44. Brik, "Ritm i sintaksis," 833.
45. Bukhshtab, "Stikhi dlia detei."
46. Malishevskii, "O poezii dlia detei," 10.
47. Malishevskii, "O poezii dlia detei," 10.
48. Chukovskii, *Dnevnik*, 367.
49. Eikhenbaum, "Poet-zhurnalist [1928]," 581.
50. Bukhshtab, "Stikhi dlia detei," 112.
51. Bolotin, "Tvorchestvo S. Marshka."
52. Bolotin, "Tvorchestvo S. Marshka," 2.
53. Bolotin, "Tvorchestvo S. Marshka," 3.
54. Begak, "Kornei Chukovskii," 2.
55. Mister Twister (Mister-Tvister) is the main character of the eponymous satirical poem by S. Marshak; he is a cartoonish American industrialist. See also Bolotin, "Tvorchestvo S. Marshka," 4.
56. Grinberg, Review of *Skazka o Pete tolstom rebenke*, 257.
57. Pokrovskaia, "Maiakovskii kak detskii pisatel,'" 17.
58. Kon, Review of *Devochka chumazaia*, 12.
59. Chumachenko, "Veselaia knizhka."
60. Bukhshtab, "Stikhi dlia detei," 112.
61. Smirnova, "A. Barto," 20.
62. Pokrovskaia, "Maiakovskii kak detskii pisatel,'" 17; and Grinberg, Review of *Skazka o Pete tolstom rebenke.*
63. Tynianov, *Permanent Evolution*, 173.

Agniia Barto's Fun Rhymes
Lost Toys, Torn Paws, and Emotional Maturation

Marina Balina

> *I love you and I wrap you in paper, and when you tore up one time, I glued you back together.*
>
> —Excerpt from a child's letter to Agniia Barto[1]

Agniia Barto (1906–81) is one of a handful of children's poets of the Soviet era still enjoying popularity among contemporary readers. Some twenty-first-century young readers first encounter Barto's rhymes through their grandparents, who were raised on Barto's substantial oeuvre; others are introduced to her poetry by parents, whose generation was exposed to a much narrower selection of Barto's work. Barto's famous school satire, her poems inspired by international politics, and, in fact, most of her prolific socialist realist output—which was recognized with such prestigious government literary awards as the 1950 Stalin Prize and the 1972 Lenin Prize—as it turned out, did not stand the test of time. It is the poet's early work, written in the 1920s and 1930s (in particular, her 1936 cycle of poems published under the eminently child-friendly title *Igrushki* [Toys]), that remains in steady demand with readers born after the year 2000. Today, numerous musical and animated renditions of Barto's *Toys* populate the Internet media space. Parenting websites host scores of video recordings of young children reciting rhymes from *Toys*, with the quality of footage ranging from samples of professional videography to unabashedly homemade displays of parental pride. To keep up with reader demand, commercial publishing houses offer a variety of editions of *Toys*, including a reprint of the 1950 issue of the collection featuring rare historical illustrations by Vladimir Konashevich (Melik-Pashaev Publishers, 2017), an edition illustrated with new art by Irina Sharikova and Nataliia Burkot (Rosman Press, 2015), an interactive edition (AST Publishers, 2018), and even a puzzle book published in China in 2017.[2]

This steady interest in *Toys*—the revisiting of the work in various media available to the contemporary reader—calls for a reevaluation of certain critical approaches to the collection, as well as for new commentary based on the present-day criticism of children's literature. Depictions of the toy world as a space in which emotional, interpersonal, and social attitudes are formed has been a long-standing theme in children's literature. According to Marina Kostiukhina, a contemporary researcher of children's literature, the negative view of toys typical of the Enlightenment era was succeeded by Romanticism's heightened interest in toys and games.[3] "To fulfill its tasks," Kostiukhina postulates, "literature endows games with ethical and spiritual content. The facets of the child's soul—be it virtues or vices, sensitivity or indifference—manifest in the child's treatment of toys. Toys help the child form a system of values underlying human relationships."[4]

Barto's *Toys* stands apart from Soviet children's poetry of the 1920s and 1930s. The collection lacks the revolutionary rhetoric permeating the poet's earliest children's verse. As the literary scholar and critic Evgeniia Putilova points out, "The elegant, laconic, nimble and fun verse of *Toys* joined two worlds—the real world and the toy world—together in harmony; playing games served as that ever-important 'life arena' where kids' characters were expressed and where kids were on occasion seriously tested in their personal qualities."[5] But what were the personal qualities in question? In what way were they the subject of young Barto's self-described "fun verse"? Why did the poet recruit toy characters to open a conversation about human values? My commentary on the poems that are included in the 1936 collection is an attempt to analyze the resilience and the timelessness of the verse of *Toys* as well as to assess its relevance in the modern literary space, which is radically different from that of the 1930s.

Barto's perhaps best-known rhyme is "Mishka" (Teddy bear):

Уронили мишку на пол,
Оторвали мишке лапу.
Все равно его не брошу—
Потому что он хороший.[6]

[Teddy Bear left on the floor,
One paw missing, sad and sore.
I won't leave him lying there!
He's the best, my Teddy Bear.][7]

In analyzing this collection by Barto, the literary scholar Iuri Domanskii identifies two "vectors" along which the poems in *Toys* can be sorted: the "destructive tendency" vector and the "creative tendency" vector.[8] In "Teddy Bear," Domanskii perceives a third vector—that of "reduction of harm." The poor tattered toy suffers a series of negative acts—someone throws it on the floor, someone tears off its paw—yet the reader never finds out who the perpetrator of the harm is. If there is no one available to punish for this behavior, then whom does the toy owner address with her stubbornly optimistic remark? If "I won't leave him lying there" is polemic, then with whom is the narrator's argument? I posit that this four-line stanza is in fact interior dialogue, a conversation with self, and that it presents an early lesson in empathy, which the unnamed lyrical hero of the poem takes well.

In her work on narrative empathy, the Australian scholar Kerry Mallan identifies children's literature as a tool for creating and cultivating empathy, which is foundational for a society in which care and compassion are an important, perhaps even crucial, part of daily life.[9] "Reading children's literature is often considered important for developing (among other things) children's ethical and empathic understanding of society and its people," Mallan writes.[10] Citing the work of the contemporary philosophers Martha Nussbaum and Margrethe Bruun Vaage, Mallan suggests that children's literature be dedicated to the task of nurturing empathic readers.[11]

Agniia Barto's "Teddy Bear" is truly about that specific task, the task of nurturing a compassionate, empathic reader, not only able to feel the pain and hurt of someone else—in this case, an old toy—but, through the act of empathic reading, capable of taking the relevant moral step of saving the toy from being destroyed. It is interesting to follow the stepping-stones Barto lays to lead young readers to narrative empathy. The first lines of the original Russian poem have verbal predicates in the third-person plural (an impersonal verb form, rendered in the passive voice in Manin's English translation): *uronili, otorvali*—"[they] dropped," "[they] tore off the paw." The act of destruction performed on the toy is thus presented as the work of a faceless collective; no individual actors are pointed out. It looks like such acts of destruction are commonplace and frequent; by contrast, the act brought forth by a desire to combat destruction is a personal act rooted in empathy. "I won't leave him no matter what" (Все равно его не брошу), says the narrator as if to mean, "no matter what my playmates may think."

The Soviet scholar Vanda Razova, in her analysis of Barto's work, writes that this short verse about the teddy bear contains "not simply a scene from a child's daily life but a lesson in ethics: the feelings of pity and compassion prevail."[12] Kindness toward an old broken toy becomes an early step toward maturity, toward experiencing the pain of others as if it were one's own. Domanskii, in his article about the damaged toy, points out that the tradition of speaking to the reader's sense of empathy already existed in prerevolutionary poetry. Citing children's rhymes written by Sasha Cherny, Sergei Gorodetskii, and

Alexander Blok, Domanskii argues that this literary device had long been part of the poetic toolbox pre-Barto.[13] Barto herself began to include calls for empathy in her earliest rhymes, such as "Kitaichonok Van Li" (Little Chinese boy Wan Li; 1924) and "Bratishki" (Little brothers; 1925).[14] However, it was specifically social class–based care and compassion that the reader was called to feel toward the poor, cruelly exploited little Wan Li and toward the international family of "brothers" from different countries struggling under colonial rule. The didactics of compassion were rooted in class theory; however, even appearances of class-based empathy were rare in the children's literature of the 1920s. Consider, for instance, Vladimir Mayakovsky's *Skazka o Pete, tolstom rebionke, i o Sime, kotoryi tonkii* (A tale of Petya the fatty and Sima who was skinny), which was originally published in 1925 as a single-poem book illustrated by Nikolai Kupreianov.[15] In the poem, a fat and gluttonous capitalist boy named Petya simply bursts as a result of his gluttony, after which the October kids (*oktiabriata*), the good children of the Revolution, receive delicious treats falling out of Petya like from a piñata and eat them:

Нет,
        не чудо это, дети,
а—из лопнувшего Пети.
Все, что лопал Петя толстый,
рассыпается на версты.
Ливнем льет
                        и валит валом—
так беднягу разорвало.
Масса хлеба,
                        сласти масса—
и сосиски,
                    и колбасы!
Сели дети,
                    и отряд
съел с восторгом всё подряд.[16]

[That was no magic,
like you thought first:
It all fell out when Petya burst.
All that Petya the Fatty ate in piles
Kept piling on for miles and miles.
It rained, it poured,
It lasted and lasted—
That's how hard the poor fatty got blasted.
Tons of bread,
Sweets by tons—
Rolls, sausages,
Meats and buns!
The kids sat down,
And the troop
Ate it all up in one fell swoop.]

The scholar Miron Petrovskii writes that, in this final scene of the tale, "Petya explodes and vanishes from the story once and for all. Mayakovsky has no intention of putting Petya back together, or of resurrecting him, or, especially, of pitying him. Mayakovsky has no feelings for the class enemy, and the fact that the little capitalist is of a tender age makes no difference to him."[17] Such poems, without a doubt, met the new revolutionary didactic aims, but they could hardly be employed as vehicles for fostering empathy in young readers. Against the background of children's poetry of no mercy, Barto's rhymes about toys are appealing for their focus on small-caliber emotions, devoid of revolutionary slogans and mottos and free of any and all ideologies.

Loss and grief are bound up with the phenomenon of empathy. The contemporary anthropologist Serguei Oushakine argues, "The theme of loss was not a leading one in the culture of Soviet childhood; [however,] its presence and significance should not be underestimated."[18] In Barto's *Toys*, the motif of loss accompanies the emergence of empathy, but no dominant model for the depiction of loss can be discerned. Barto employs every form of narration available, be it imaginary dialogue in "Miachik" (The ball); the voice of an omniscient, rather emotionally uninvolved narrator in "Zaika" (The bunny) and "Bychok" (The calf); or the first-person voice of the collective "we" in "Samolet" (The airplane). "The Ball" shows both a fear of losing a favorite toy and a fear for its fate if it escapes the narrator's control.

Наша Таня громко плачет.
Уронила в речку мячик.
—Тише, Танечка, не плачь:
Не утонет в речке мяч.

[Tanya cries and sobs and squeaks:
She dropped her ball into the creek.
Tanya, smile and wipe your cheek:
Bouncy balls don't sink in creeks.][19]

The exposition of the poem states a fact: the ball has been dropped into the creek. Tanya, the protagonist, however, is crying specifically about the uncertain fate of the ball and not her own bad luck. The adult character, observing but not included in the scene, then enters to offer comfort to the protagonist: her ball will not drown, and it will not "die"; instead, it will continue to "live" and, possibly, keep bringing joy to its owner.

The verse opens with a depiction of an act of empathy, of little Tanya's compassion toward and fear for the "life" of another, however inanimate that other is. What prompts Tanya's emotions becomes evident to the reader only in the last lines of the stanza, from the dialogue, in which this cause is implicit. In almost all the poems in *Toys*, creating the empathic reader occurs step by step, from a statement of fact in the beginning to a personal emotional experience. The loss of or the damage suffered by a favorite toy does not immediately induce compassion or a desire to help, to rescue, or to stave off destruction. Forming empathy takes time, which Barto offers to her readers in the space between the two opening and the two closing lines of "The Ball," thus creating an impetus for the relevant feelings to grow.

At moments, the four-line poem holds that emotional impetus holistically, leaving the empathic response to form and express itself postreading, beyond the text. In the poem "Zaika" (The bunny), the narrative empathy requires that the child analyze the story of what happened independently in order to arrive at feeling compassion without being explicitly prompted to do so by the text:

Зайку бросила хозяйка,
Под дождём остался зайка.
Со скамейки слезть не мог,
Весь до ниточки промок.

[In the garden little Bunny
Was left behind when it was sunny.
Then it rained and he got drenched:
He couldn't climb off the garden bench.][20]

There is perhaps not a single rhyme in *Toys* in which Barto would point out any character flaws in members of her young audience, although in general she never shied away from criticizing her little readers in her work. Certain early poems by Barto carry an explicit critical attitude in their very titles: "Devochka chumazaia" (The grimy girl; 1929) and "Devochka-revushka" (The crybaby; 1930), both poems written in collaboration with the writer's first husband Pavel Barto), and "Pro Lentiaia Ivanovicha" (Lazybones, son of Ivan; 1930).[21] The poem "The Bunny" does open with an accusation: the toy's owner left her bunny; she forgot it. A description of the toy's misfortunes resulting from the owner's neglect and lack of care follows. The bunny got drenched; the bunny was not able to get off the bench—and the young reader understands that to be true since, by the conditions set in the poems of *Toys*, the child understands very well that the bunny is a toy and yet at the same time perceives the bunny as a living being. The drenched bunny is a victim whose plight evokes an array of emotions: anger on behalf of the toy, outrage at its owner's negligence, and a desire to come to the rescue. The Barto scholar Igor Motiashov writes about the tears that the poem prompts: "Little kids cry. . . . And those are blessed tears. The rhyme helps them experience the neglectful treatment of a toy as a betrayal of a friend."[22] Thus, an act of creating empathic readers is performed, and the "blessed" cathartic tears need not be supplemented with any clarifications or lectures on what is right and what is wrong.

I do not aim to provide commentary on all the rhymes in *Toys* in this chapter; however, one more poem, a "happy" one in which narrative empathy is complete in form and fortified with the action it causes, merits mention. It is "Kozlenok" (The baby goat):

> У меня живёт козлёнок,
> Я сама его пасу.
> Я козлёнка в сад зелёный
> Рано утром отнесу.
> Он заблудится в саду—
> Я в траве его найду.
>
> [Look: I have a baby goat
> And I let him out to graze.
> He is light enough to tote
> To the green, and if he strays
> In the tall grass in the garden,
> I will always find and guard him.][23]

The poem, written as a first-person narrative, clearly outlines the stance of its lyrical heroine. There are two characters in the poem: a young girl and her toy, which she evidently sees as a living baby animal in her imagination. The toy, a baby goat, is given her constant care and attention; the narrative empathy here takes the form of a sense of responsibility for the toy and creates the atmosphere of a harmonious coexistence between the animate and the animated in the play space. The empathic lyrical heroine leads the empathic reader into this space, thus making the reader, too, responsible for the toy's well-being. The baby goat must be pastured, and to that end it must be brought into the garden; if it ever gets lost, the heroine must find it *herself*. In this way the poem presents the final stage of emotional maturation, whereby the child, without the assistance of an adult, is ready to take on responsibility for another being, even if that other being is only a toy for now.

In his analysis of *Toys*, Iurii Domanskii concludes, "At the level of ethical problem-setting, Barto's cycle of poems reveals itself to be very multifaceted, representing various aspects of being."[24] Can this "multifaceted" ethical representation be unintentional? Many Barto scholars explicate the connections between her children's rhymes and the poetic tradition established by Samuil Marshak and Kornei Chukovsky. In her diaries, titled *Zapiski detskogo poeta* (Notes of a children's poet), Barto counts Kornei Chukovsky, Vladimir Mayakovsky, and, with a caveat, Samuil Marshak among her influences in the chapter "U kogo ia uchilas' pisat' stikhi" (Who taught me to write rhyme).[25] It is challenging, however, to find poems in the body of children's poetry of the first Soviet decade that would match Barto's in fostering empathy. A review of statements Barto made in print and onstage late in her writing career reveals the significance the writer saw in fostering empathy and compassion in children as a foundational principle of her creative work. In her speech at the Fourth Congress of Soviet Writers in 1967, Barto, already a distinguished writer roundly respected by the Soviet literary establishment, announced at the lectern, "We lack poetry capable of unsettling the mind and the heart of children, capable of bringing tears to their eyes. . . . Should we really be so vigilant in keeping kids away from strong feelings? Protecting childhood does not at all mean deadening the child's sensitivity to deep emotional experiences that enrich the soul."[26] It is remarkable how this statement made in 1967 echoes the early works Barto created in 1936, at the very beginning of her career as a children's writer. *Toys* is a clear testament and outcome of Barto's mission to teach children compassion and empathy, those perennial values inherent in the ethics of human coexistence.

The famous children's poet Mikhail Iasnov (1946–2020), in evaluating the effect of the works of Soviet children's poets on contemporary readership, arrived at a rather accurate summation: "I see constantly that children no longer understand many writings by Marshak, Barto, and Mikhalkov. The world has changed; the school [life] about which Agniia Barto wrote so spiritedly does not exist anymore, and that is why her school poems stopped working, while her fabulous *Toys* survives era after era: her poetic language, intonation, and sense of utmost sincerity are what's most important in them."[27]

Barto's school poems belong to the genre of "spiky words," per Motiashov's definition; they criticize those human behavioral traits of which, according to Barto, her young readers had best rid themselves as expediently as possible. The poems are satire, a genre to which Barto turned rather early in her career. One of her first satirical poems, "Boltunia" (Chatterbox) was published in 1934. Throughout her writing life, Barto turned to school satire, and on occasion Soviet literary critics took Barto to task for her "spiky rhymes." To wit, in a 1949 article titled "Bol'shie zaprosy malen'kikh chitatelei" (Big demands of little readers), Barto was accused of "slandering children," and her satirical poetry was labeled "unwholesome."[28] At the same time, it was children's satire that earned Barto high praise from Kornei Chukovsky. In her *Notes of a Children's Poet*, Barto quotes excerpts from Chukovsky's letter to her in which he calls her "a true Shchedrin for kids."[29] A more elaborate assessment of Barto as a children's satirist is from a 1956 letter by Chukovsky, in which he explains to her why her "spiky rhymes" are so popular with children: "Your satire is written from the point of view of children, and you speak to your Yegors, Katyas, Lyubochkas not as a pedagogue and a moralist but as a friend distressed by their bad behavior. You metamorphose into a child artistically, and so lively is your reproduction of children's voices, intonations, gestures, and their very mindset, that all children begin to see you as their classmate."[30] Both Chukovsky and Iasnov notice the presence of "utmost sincerity" and the absence of moralizing in Barto's poetry for children. For nearly one hundred years now, her little readers have been feeling them as well.

Barto's satirical verse stays in print, although it is less popular than *Toys*. Barto's capacity for showing a child's world specifically from the child's perspective, through eyes looking up at the big world outside (which is how her lyrical heroes see things), without a doubt requires great mastery; it is this mastery that made it possible for Barto to join the highest rank of Soviet children's poets—her contemporaries. Notably, in addition to having won many Soviet literary prizes, Barto was a recipient of the 1976 international Hans Christian Andersen Award—and Andersen himself would never miss an opportunity to criticize and mock his fairy-tale characters.[31] Still, Barto's children's satire never eclipsed or diminished her focus on creating empathic readers keenly aware both of the world and of their own role in it. Three poems that Barto wrote later in her career illustrate this well. The poems were included in different collections, separate in time and in theme, yet all of them respond to the important task of creating empathic readers. [32]

In her 1957 article "O poezii dlia detei" (On children's poetry), which sets forth Barto's authorial principles if not her entire creed, the poet writes:

> I must confess I never feel that I'm writing for children only. It seems to me that a children's poem is always addressed to the adult as well, and, just like folktales, which have underlying meanings not always clear to kids, children's poetry has subtext. Also, a child grows with every new day, while the poems stay in his memory, so, every time he revisits the poem, he understands it in a new way. That means [the poem] must offer . . . something that can be reinterpreted.[33]

The poem "Lebedinoe gore" (Swan grief), from the 1968 collection *Ia rastu* (I'm growing up), fits in this category of double address, and the subtext to be decoded here provides the child with a path to understanding basic facts of life—namely, that the world is imperfect and there are things in it that cannot be "fixed."[34] The lyrical hero of "Swan Grief" takes a walk in a winter park and sees a solitary swan that, for some reason, did not migrate in the fall with the rest of the flock:

> В холодном парке
> Среди льдин
> Зимует лебедь.
> Он один.
>
> [The park is cold.
> A swan, alone,
> Sits on the ice.
> His flock has flown.]

Here, sympathy for the swan begins at the level of cognition but quickly moves to the level of emotion, prompting a succession of concerned and compassionate acts characteristic of empathic readers raised on *Toys*. The poem continues,

> Решил я
> Притвориться:
> Я тоже
> Лебедь-птица,
>
> Я тоже белый,
> Весь в снегу.
> Я выгнул шею,
> Как могу.

[And so, I started
Playing
Like I'm a swan
Who's staying.

I'm also white
Without a speck.
I'm stuck in snow.
I bend my neck.]

The lyrical hero of the poem moves through all the stages of imaginative empathy as formulated by Margrethe Bruun Vaage. The first is "feeling as the other": the child sees a solitary swan and immediately recognizes that the bird is lonely.[35] Here, cognition comes to the reader's aid in interpreting the situation as anomalous—swans usually live and migrate in flocks. The next stage is "feeling with the other," arriving as a premonition of possible disasters that may befall the solitary bird intertwined with the almost instantaneous urge to help the swan; this comes in tight connection with "feeling for others while making them part of our concern."[36] This feeling, however, comes packaged in a child's fantasy: "I, too, am a swan bird!" The situation calls for further decisive steps to help the swan out of his distressing loneliness: "I bend my neck," "I shout . . . 'We'll swim together.'" But Barto will not leave her lyrical hero mired in fantasy: here, fostering empathy and fostering realism go hand in hand. The attempt at a fairy-tale transformation of the character into a swan, intended to help the bird, ends in failure and with a rather severe moral:

Я поднял руку
Как крыло,
Но ничего
Не помогло.

[I flapped my arm,
Just like a wing.
But nothing helped him.
Not a thing.]

This poem might teach a classic lesson in "the cold hard truth of life" in a somewhat harsh form, yet it offers the child a path to understanding that sometimes nothing helps no matter how much effort is expended. Nonetheless, the "swan grief" of loneliness is experienced on par with the reader's own human grief, thus showing the living world as one cohesive whole. While continuing to cultivate empathy in her reader, Barto introduces a philosophical category of the surrounding world as a living entity capable of suffering and requiring both recognition and insight. It is a new lesson in ethics offered by the poet to her characters as well as to her readers and their parents.[37]

Barto's poem "My ne zametili zhuka" ("We never even saw the bug," from her 1970 collection *Za tsvetami v zimnii les* [Off to the winter forest for flowers]) offers a similar invitation:

Мы не заметили жука
И рамы зимние закрыли,
А он живой,
Он жив пока,
Жужжит в окне,
Расправив крылья . . .
И я зову на помощь маму:
—Там жук живой!
Раскроем раму.[38]

[We never even saw the bug.
We sealed our windows: winter's coming.
The bug's alive.
The seal is snug.

The bug is flapping,
Buzzing, thrumming . . .
I call my mom: "It's time you came!
This bug's alive!
Unseal the frame!"]

Just like in "Swan Grief," here the reader witnesses the lyrical hero move from compassion to action. If *Toys* only hints at this progression, in Barto's late-career poetry the progression becomes a behavioral pattern for her characters. The lives of everything living are worth preserving and helping—it is a rule by which not only Barto's empathic readers live but also their parents. The child knows that to keep the bug alive they must go to their mother for help: the latter will offer physical assistance and understand the horror of the potential loss of life. In this short poem, the didactics of the empathic progression from observation to action is presented on two narrative levels, one addressed to a child and the other to an adult. In it, Barto actualizes her idea of "poetry to grow into": her adult reader also goes to empathy school and learns to share their child's feelings no matter how insignificant the cause of the feelings may seem; it can be as small as a bug stuck inside a window frame sealed for the winter. Igor Motiashov identifies this quality of Barto's poetry: "Barto's rhymes are poetry one grows into; children who seem to have grown out of them reread the poems with appreciation, and it is only after years pass that they grasp [the poems'] true meaning, their foundational idea, occasionally shining in its completeness and its many facets."[39]

Besides empathy, the question of behavioral ethics is a major theme in Barto's writing. The beginnings of that theme are evident in *Toys* (e.g., in "Teddy Bear"), and its exploration is furthered in her school satire (e.g., in "Lovely Lyuba"). In her lyrical poetry of the 1970s, the poet continues to engage with ethical issues, and she introduces her readers to the code of coexistence within the living world, which for the writer extends beyond the world of human relationships. The world of plants, for instance, is also part of the ethical sphere for Barto. It is shown as autonomous, and its autonomy is shown as worthy of respect, in the poem "Vpolgolosa" (Softly and quietly):

> Два цветка, два гладиолуса,
> Разговор ведут вполголоса.
>
> По утрам они беседуют
> Про цветочные дела . . .
>
> Но подслушивать не следует,
> Я подальше отошла.
>
> [Two big gladiolus flowers
> Have been murmuring for hours.
>
> Each and every morning, quietly
> They are talking flower-shop . . .
>
> I have stepped away politely:
> It's not proper to eavesdrop.]

Limiting the description of the poetic means used by Barto to straightforward anthropomorphizing would not do the poem justice. Endowing inanimate objects with human qualities is not part of Barto's writerly toolbox: to her, as to her little readers, there simply are no inanimate objects.

The soft and quiet conversation between two flowers represents, to a child, the privacy and agency of others, which must be respected. It is much easier to formulate a social rule and simply affirm that eavesdropping is not okay—but will that affirmation work? Will it prove memorable? Two gladioli privately conducting a quiet conversation, on the other hand, create a vivid image that appeals to a child's imagination—real live talking gladioli!—and that, at the same time, teaches a valuable lesson in ethics.

American philosopher Martha Nussbaum asserts that the "narrative imagination is an essential preparation for moral interaction."[40] Children's poet Agniia Barto manages to create a special world of narrative imagination in her poems; appealing to children's fantasy, the writer endows the real and the imaginary with equal rights in order to establish in her readers the sense of the importance of the experience they acquire through reading her work. Barto tirelessly cultivates empathy and compassion toward her characters in her readers, preparing them for future moral interactions in the larger world. To Barto, empathy is a perennial human value; her writings teach children to see, hear, and empathize from the youngest age. In this lies the significance of her writings, which remain in demand to this day. Her deceptively light verse is indeed intentional in teaching children human values. To quote Motiashov, her "poems betray how complex the inner world of a small child is. . . . In it, there are worlds for cheery imitation of adults, for fantasy and games, for the proverbial seven million 'whys' that, day after day, become deeper and more serious, and for delicate and complicated feelings."[41]

Notes

1. *Dnevniki 1974*, in Barto, *Zapiski detskogo poeta*, 5. Unless otherwise indicated, all translations from Russian are by A. Krushelnitskaya.

2. In the late 1990s, the then-popular Russian band Masha i Medvedi (Masha and the bears) recorded an original song with Agniia Barto's 1945 poem "Liubochka" used as lyrics. The song was in heavy rotation on FM radio; the accompanying music video, which shows the band's soloist Masha Medvedeva performing in front of the Khajuraho Temples in India, helped revive and refresh Barto's name and the poem in the listener's memory.

3. Kostiukhina, *Igrushka v detskoi literature*, 8.

4. Kostiukhina, *Igrushka v detskoi literature*, 6.

5. Putilova, *Chetyre veka russkoi poezii detiam*, 49.

6. "Mishka" in Barto, *Sobranie sochinenii v 3-kh tomakh*, 15.

7. Translation by D. Manin.

8. Domanskii, "Povrezhdennaia igrushka," 179–96.

9. Mallan, "Empathy," 106–14.

10. Mallan, "Empathy," 105.

11. For more on empathy and young readers, see Nikolajeva, "Guilt, Empathy and the Ethical Potential."

12. Razova, *Fol'klornye istoki*, 60.

13. Domanskii, "Povrezhdennaia igrushka," 194–95.

14. "Kitaichonok Van Li" was first published in *Pioner* no. 10 (1924). "Bratishki" was published by GIZ, with illustrations by G. Yechistov, in 1928 and again in 1929 and 1936.

15. For the original publication, see Vladimir Maiakovskii, *Skazka o Pete, tolstom rebionke, i o Sime, kotoryi tonkii* (Moscow: Moskovskii Rabochii, 1925).

16. Maiakovskii, *Skazka o Pete*, 191–206.

17. Petrovskii, *Kniga nashego detstva*, 140.

18. Oushakine, "My v gorod izumrudnyi idem dorogoi trudnoi," 44.

19. Translation by D. Manin.

20. Translation by D. Manin.

21. See A. Barto and P. Barto, *Devochka-revushka* (Moscow: Detizdat, 1930); and A. Barto and P. Barto, *Devochka chumazaia* (Moscow: GIZ, 1929).

22. Motiashov, *Zhizn' i tvorchestvo Agnii Barto*, 31.

23. Translation by D. Manin.

24. Domanskii, "Povrezhdennaia igrushka," 186.

25. It is worth noting that the scholars Vera Smirnova and Igor Motiashov somewhat overestimate the role Samuil Marshak played in forming Agniia Barto's poetic voice. Since the earliest days of her practice as a children's author, Barto rejected Marshak's editorial input and his attempts to influence her style; in turn, Marshak often criticized Barto for sloppy verse and imperfect rhyming. "I can't be Marshak, and I won't be Marshak's underling," Barto famously declared. The relationship between the two children's writers remained complicated for years. Barto, *Zapiski detskogo poeta*, 31.

26. "Rech' na 4-om s"ezde pisatelei" in Barto, *Sobranie sochinenii*, 4:298–300.

27. Mikhail Iasnov, "Deti meniaiutsia, i uzhe ne ponimaiut mnogoe iz Marshaka i Barto," interview by Vitalii Kotov, accessed March 2, 2022, sobaka.ru /entertainment/books/37171.

28. Quoted in Motiashov, *Zhizn' i tvorchestvo Agnii Barto*, 99. For the original article, see *Oktiabr*, no. 7 (1949).

29. Barto, *Zapiski detskogo poeta*, 24–25.

30. Barto, "Zapiski detskogo poeta," 24–25.

31. Barto's poetry is currently published in Russia by such publishing houses as ROSMEN, Melik-Pashaev, Makhaon, Astrel, and Samovar. Present-day collections

of Barto's poetry include both poems for early readers and satirical verse for school-aged children.

32. It is beyond the scope of this chapter to comment on Barto's attitudes and politics toward her fellow writers, such as Boris Pasternak and Lidiia Chukovskaia. Barto's actions are just one of the many examples of the tactics of complex compromise typically employed by her creative (and not only creative) contemporaries.

33. Barto, *Sobranie sochinenii v 4-kh tomakh*, 4:220.

34. "Lebedinoe gore" in Barto, *Prosto stikhi*, 6.

35. On imaginative empathy, see Vaage, "Fiction Film," 158–79.

36. Vaage, "Fiction Film," 161.

37. Since 1965, Barto hosted a radio show, *Naiti cheloveka* (To find the person) on Mayak Radio. The impetus for the show was originally Barto's 1947 long poem "Zvenigorod," in which Barto describes the life of children in an orphanage after they lost their families and loved ones in the war. Barto helped restore the memories of the children bit by bit; in the weekly twenty-five-minute radio broadcast, Barto spoke about the lives of the orphans, based on the stories and vague recollections of lost families the children were able to summon. The radio show was broadcast till 1973; it brought more than nine hundred families together. In a way, encouraging empathy was more than a didactic task for Barto; it was her personal ethos.

38. "My ne zametili zhuka" in Barto, *Za tsvetami v zimnii les*, 10.

39. Motiashov, *Zhizn' i tvorchestvo Agnii Barto*, 49.

40. Nussbaum, *Cultivating Humanity*, 90.

41. Motiashov, *Zhizn' i tvorchestvo Agnii Barto*, 278–79.

People's Stories for the Kids

Folklore in Soviet Children's Literature

Sibelan Forrester

In prerevolutionary Russia, folklore was already something for children, since nurses and nannies (usually peasant women) in well-off families would naturally tell their charges the same children's stories and rhymes and sing the same lullabies that they were accustomed to using with their own children. Wealthy families who employed governesses to raise the children as speakers of English, French, or German would acquire a second body of children's lore,[1] though educated governesses were more likely to bring printed stories. Grown-ups later recalled the stories, and some literate men—Aleksandr Pushkin, Pyotr Ershov, Konstantin Aksakov, Leo Tolstoy—turned folktale plots into works of literature that are still offered to Russophone children.[2] Given all this, by the turn of the twentieth century educated citizens of Russia had come to associate folklore with childhood: it was dear, domestic, even Edenic, but at the same time primitive and meant to be outgrown. This feeling may underlie the comment in the Brockhaus-Efron *Encyclopedic Dictionary* that by the late nineteenth century folktales had become the province of the very young and the very old, no longer of interest to mature educated people unless they had undergone "artistic reworking."[3]

When Bolsheviks took over literary policy after 1917, they tended to look at folklore with a more suspicious eye: it was, as noted, associated with backward peasant women (who could potentially spread the ideas of Russian Orthodoxy or other religions) and with the conservatism of traditional society. As Evgeniia Putilova notes, "In 1920, the Political-Education Department of the People's Commissariat for Education issued an 'Instruction' removing from circulation all books that extolled monarchy and the church, failed to meet ideological and pedagogical standards, or were sentimentally and emotionally oriented. The list was so long it made up an entire book."[4] Nadezhda Krupskaya, wife and then powerful widow of Vladimir Ilyich Lenin, strove to drive folklore (especially peasant folklore) out of the repertoire of readings available to children. In the early 1930s, however, folklore made a comeback in Soviet literature across the board, thanks especially to Maxim Gorky's famous declaration at the First Congress of the Soviet Writers' Union in 1934 that folklore had to be the basis of Soviet literature.[5] The result was a body of children's tales that incorporated significant folklore elements; this chapter will look at some well-known examples of Soviet works for children that incorporate folkloric elements, after a brief discussion of the transition from folklore to literature and its particular nature in the Soviet Union.

Folklore from Russia to the USSR

Every culture in the past had children's folklore, with songs or stories that adults sang or told (such as lullabies, quickly picked up by the slightly older sisters deputized to watch babies while their mothers stepped out to work in yard and field or factory) as well as the little rhymes or charms created by and shared among children themselves.[6] Oral lore serves both to calm and entertain children and to teach them, integrating them into the ways of the group. In his book *The Russian Folktale*, Vladimir Propp stresses that children are often exquisite tellers of tales from the community repertoire.[7]

One exceptional element in the shift from oral bedtime stories to Soviet literature for children is that it accompanied a huge push for universal literacy, which meant a general shift from oral culture (the source of folklore of all kinds) to literate culture, from oral tales to children's literature proper. The text in a book or magazine would be approved by Soviet censors, printed, and distributed to bookstores, libraries, and schools, ensuring that one single correct version of any story reached all children wherever they encountered print or heard reading aloud. If an older tale or story was edited for children, changes were generally not announced or described. Even the most traditional oral tales varied from one telling or teller to the next,[8] but printed children's literature would now dependably tell the proper stories to the younger Soviet generation.

The folktales in Aleksandr Afanas'ev's collection, equivalent in cachet to the German tales of the Brothers Grimm, were printed in new and approved selections for children to read, and kindergartens were often decorated with panels depicting scenes from well-known tales, especially the animal tales that did not involve tsars and princesses. This too separated the printed tales from their oral variants; Afanas'ev provided variants of several tales, but the full three-volume edition of his collection that supplied variants was aimed at scholars and serious adult readers, not at children.[9] The almost inevitable variation of oral performance would threaten a story's ideological acceptability: the story had to be correct, since its task was to form the New Soviet Person. In print, on the other hand, a tale would be the same each time it was read, although comfort with the idea that folklore belonged to everyone and could be adjusted as needed did mean that different retellings of individual tales, all passed by the censors, might read differently. A silently edited folktale would take the place of whatever versions had come before; even books for Soviet adults (such as Aleksandr Bogdanov's *Red Star* and Fedor Gladkov's *Cement*) were edited over time without notice. Meanwhile, propaganda posters hailed libraries and literacy, and it was highly socially acceptable to read to children, who would not yet find sources like the official newspaper *Pravda* engaging. At the same time, the shift into near-universal literacy did not mean the end of nannies, even though many sources from the Soviet era and after state that nannies were no longer part of the new society. The possibility of working as a nanny saved the lives of many girls from farming families who were repressed or exiled during collectivization in the early 1930s, and the author Tatyana Tolstaya (born in 1951), describes a perhaps fictional family governess in her story "Любишь—не любишь" ("Loves Me, Loves Me Not"), though this woman is neither a peasant nor a good storyteller.[10]

Propp proposes in another book, *The Historical Roots of the Magic Tale*, that wonder tales (the kind that in English are usually called fairy tales and in Russian *volshebnye skazki*, or "magic tales") descended from elements of adolescent rites of passage.[11] Whether or not we agree here with Propp, folktales and other folk genres can definitely serve a pedagogical function and help to lead a child toward adulthood. They often highlight peasant virtues: intelligence, persistence, patience, and expertise in handling animals, agricultural work, and crafts. Even a princess may need to spin and weave or to gather the fruits of an orchard to attain her happy end; Vasilisa the Beautiful relies on the doll her dying mother gave her to complete chores at Baba Yaga's house and then wins a tsar as her husband with her outstanding spinning, weaving, and tailoring skills. It is no innovation to use narratives to teach children things, and in that way the Soviet project welcomed elements of folklore into literature for children. Elements of the tales that made them entertaining or amusing could be the spoonful of sugar for the lessons conveyed, while including a more or less explicit "moral" at the end would feel familiar from Ivan Krylov's (or Aesop's) folklike fables.

Gaidar's "Tale of the Military Secret"

Arkadii Gaidar and Valentin Kataev both wrote, among other works, tales for Soviet children that included significant folkloric elements and became popular with children. The tales employ some folk language and incorporate narrative features familiar from folktales: plot repetitions and repeated catchphrases or rhymes that create a musical texture children can enjoy. Unlike Pushkin's almost exclusively rhyming versions of Russian folktales, traditional tales include only short rhymes, such as this one in which a frog princess in one of Afanas'ev's versions greets Prince Ivan as he arrives to report a new, seemingly impossible request for her to complete: "Что ж ты, князь, не весел, / Буйну голову повесил?" (Why, prince, are you cheerless, / Hanging your wild head?). Soviet children's tales also offer implicit or explicit lessons in correct behavior—some of them resembling the messages of traditional folktales. Reusing or transforming narrative material fits in the tradition of folklore, though ascribing authorship (as opposed to recognizing an outstanding performance of a story that belongs to the community) is a sign of literate culture, in which the written and then printed story guarantees ongoing recognition of its author. The pedagogical impulse of some of the folk-inflected Soviet stories recalls a nanny or teacher whose job it is to contribute to children's upbringing rather than merely to entertain them.

The title of Gaidar's "Tale of the Military Secret" ("Сказка о военной тайне," 1933[12]) identifies it as a *skazka*, an oral and folk form as opposed to a story in more general generic terms, *rasskaz*. Gaidar's tale employs an interesting framing narrative that situates the tale in terms of realism: the tale itself belongs to Al'ka, a boy in a summer camp, but it is actually told by a young woman, Natka, who is older than the children listening. The story begins with the folktale locution "жил да был" ("Once there lived," a genre marker comparable to "Once upon a time"), and it introduces the hero, Mal'chish-Kibal'chish. The first part of the hero's name, Mal'chish, is almost the same as the Russian word for "boy," *mal'chik*, and the tale goes on to refer to other boys as *mal'chishi*, generalizing the term. The second part of his name, Kibal'chish, will remind an adult (though not a child) of Nikolai Kibal'chich, who built the bomb that killed Tsar Alexander II in 1881 and was hanged for his part in the assassination.

The name is at once associated with protorevolutionary heroism and self-sacrifice. As Olga Bukhina notes (citing Larissa Rudova), "Soviet literature valued heroism above all else and accepted it in almost any form, whether James Fenimore Cooper's Indians, Alexandre Dumas's musketeers, or the homegrown Pavlik Morozov. They all fed into the 'model of "heroic" masculinity' needed by the new Soviet state (Rudova, 2014: p. 88)."[13] The setting of "'heroic' masculinity" is underlined in Gaidar's story: Mal'chish-Kibal'chish lives with his father and brother. They have no mother, and their home village, which is flourishing farmland as the tale begins, appears to have no women, only old men, men of the father's age, older brothers, and then *mal'chishi* of our hero's age. The tale even belongs to a boy, Al'ka; the girl who tells it defers to Al'ka several times during the narration to make sure she is doing it right. In a weird echo of the assignment of folktales to nannies and other women, the role of the girls in this tale is to repeat the story of male heroism and make sure they get it right.

At the same time, Natka is a wonderful storyteller, able to speak in rich wording that evokes fairy-tale rhyming and rhythm: "Тихо стало на тех широких полях, на зеленых лугах, где рожь росла, где гречиха цвела" (It grew quiet in those broad fields, on the green meadows, where the rye grew, where the buckwheat flowered). The Red Army and the evil *burzhuins* (bourgeois) are clearly identified, but the setting's local features are generalized: the Black Mountains, the Blue River (preparing the reader for the red star on the headgear of the rider who summons successive generations of menfolk?). Lest the reader forget that this tale is being told (evoking the oral nature of a traditional tale), the narrative is interrupted three times so that Al'ka can confirm that it is being told well and individual children can be mentioned—including a few who generally misbehave and a Bashkir girl, Emine, who doesn't understand Russian well ("только кое-как понимала по-русски") but is still magically transfixed by the story. In later years, the tale was often shortened in children's textbooks and readers by removing the frame narrative and associated interruptions of the main story.

Gaidar's 1933 tale predates socialist realism proper by a year or so, and yet its villains are entirely socialist realistic, especially the internal traitor and wrecker, Mal'chish-Plokhish, whose name means simply "Bad Boy." For no reason other than the requirements of his role, he is filled with the desire to "betray," and in a foreshadowing of certain moments in Narnia (or *The Matrix*) his reward is a whole cask of jam and a whole basket of cookies, which he devours on the spot. Meanwhile, Mal'chish-Kibal'chish is captured, put in chains, and tortured, offstage, as he grows more Romantic and adult with each report to the head Burzhuin ("бледный он стоял, Мальчиш, но гордый" [pale he stood, Mal'chish, but proud]). The head Burzhuin asks questions in beautiful and elevated language, while he refuses to dirty his hands with the actual torture; Mal'chish refuses to reveal the Military Secret, laughing in the faces of the Burzhuins and finally putting his ear to the stone slabs of his fairy-tale tower cell, where he can hear the distant hoofbeats of the Red Army approaching.

Then they kill Mal'chish-Kibal'chish! The children are stunned into silence and disturbed whispers. Natka continues with the victory of the Red Army and then ends the tale with a brief poetic description of how ships, airplanes, trains, and Young Pioneers passing the grave of Mal'chish-Kibal'chish greet and salute him. The tale appears not to call on its hearers to emulate Mal'chish's heroic resistance but rather to recall and retell his story, which becomes something like a saint's life in the pantheon of Soviet resistance to bourgeois evil. The very brief final line, "Вот вам, ребята, и вся сказка" (And there's the whole tale for you, kids), recalls the formulaic endings of traditional tales that announce the end rather than assert the heroes' happily-ever-after. The cover of the first edition of the book says that it is for children of younger, preliterate age: it was originally intended to be read aloud, though its lively plot, sometimes beautiful language, and (in some editions at least) wonderful illustrations surely made it popular with older, literate children as well.

Kataev's Folkloric Tales

Valentin Kataev is best known for his writing for adults, but two of his stories for children offer a different incorporation of folk elements from that in Gaidar's "Tale of the Military Secret." "Дудочка и кувшинчик" ("The little pipe and the little pitcher," 1940; made into a cartoon in 1950) begins as an ordinary story: a family of four goes to pick strawberries in the woods. Zhenya, the daughter, is given a little pitcher to fill with berries. Her father says that he has a sort of incantation to use while picking: "Одну ягодку беру, на другую смотрю, третью замечаю, а четвёртая мерещится" ("I take one berry, I look at a second, I notice a third, and a fourth shows itself to me"). Zhenya says the words once and gathers four berries; twice, and gathers a second four—but then she grows weary, walks to find a clearing with better fruit, and runs into a woodland creature. She addresses him as "дяденька" (uncle), but he replies, "Я не дяденька, а дедушка. Аль не узнала? Я старик боровик, коренной лесовик, главный начальник над всеми грибами и ягодами" (I'm not an uncle but a granddad. Didn't you recognize me? I'm old man boletus [mushroom], native wood goblin, the main boss of all the mushrooms and berries), with nice rhymes in "eek." He represents the edible forest wealth that grows by itself independent of agriculture and that is deeply important to a traditional Russian household's foodways. Zhenya trades her pitcher for his magic pipe that plays by itself (a very folkloric magical acquisition!) to make the berries peek out from beneath the leaves. There is a beautiful description of how various plants and animals respond to the pipe's music—entirely not typical of a traditional folktale. But now Zhenya has no way to hold the berries she sees, so she returns to get her pitcher in exchange for the pipe. Now the berries are hiding under the leaves again, and she hates bending to find them under the leaves. The girl's own refrain is, "Так собирать мне совсем не нравится. Нагибайся да нагибайся. Пока наберёшь полный кувшинчик, чего доброго, и устать можно" (I don't like picking this way at all. Bend over and bend over. While you pick a jugful, chances are you can get tired).

She goes back once more to the magical forest creature, demanding the pipe, and Old Man Mushroom (whose resonant full title repeats each time, no doubt pleasing children as they listen to the story) declares that she is simply lazy. He stamps his foot and disappears. Yet this final encounter has somehow taught Zhenya her lesson: she returns to the clearing her mother had found for her, busily fills her pitcher with berries, and returns to her parents. When her father says she must be tired after all that work, she says no, not at all. But she tells no one about the pipe. How has the peasant or communist virtue of hard work been inculcated in the child? Did the magical creature's declaration that she was lazy prick her developing conscience? The story may suggest that an encounter with magic, or simply with folklore, can make such a salutary difference.

Kataev's tale "Цветик-Семицветик" (The rainbow [literally: seven-colored] flower, also 1940, with an animated cartoon treatment in 1948) features the same girl Zhenya as its heroine. Here we see that she lives in a town or city, not the countryside. She is sent to buy seven *baranki* (bread rings smaller, thinner, and drier than bagels) for her family but gets distracted walking home, and a dog follows her and eats the *baranki*. She chases the dog, gets lost, and starts crying; an old woman takes pity on her (commenting that she can tell Zhenya is a good girl even though she gets distracted and makes mistakes) and gives her a seven-colored flower from her garden. The kind old woman explains how to make wishes with the flower: tear off one petal and recite this rhyme:

Лети, лети, лепесток,
Через запад на восток,
Через север, через юг,
Возвращайся, сделав круг.
Лишь коснешься ты земли—
Быть по-моему вели.

[Fly, fly, little petal,
Through the west toward the east,
Through the north, through the south,
Come back, having made a circle.
The moment you touch the ground—
Let it be as I desire.]

Such an extended rhyme is not characteristic of folktales or even of folk *zagovory* (magic spells), but the way it repeats through the rest of the story is indeed folkloric: traditional tales rarely stint on repetition, and Pushkin's tales in verse reproduce this element with great fidelity.

Zhenya uses her first wish to get home with her bagels restored, then breaks her mother's favorite vase and fixes it; wishes herself at the North Pole; discovers that the North Pole is cold and dangerous (seven bears, each one described individually, are about to get her!) and wishes herself back home; wishes for all the toys in the world—an obvious recipe for disaster (has Zhenya never listened to folktales!?); unwishes the toys; and finds herself with a single unused petal—the light blue one, the color devoted to daydreams and the heart's desires. The motif of wishes that are poorly employed and then must be used up to fix the situation is very common in folktales. Usually, the wisher ends up with all the wishes wasted, but Zhenya suddenly turns sensible, pondering what to do with the final wish. She sees a nice boy and wants to play with him, but he is lame and cannot run and play. Of course, Zhenya then uses her final wish to heal him, and the story ends with the boy running so fast that Zhenya can never catch him. The moral is implied but clear: she has used her wish to improve someone else's life, and her reward is a wonderful new friend who, moreover, owes his new mobility and happiness to her. At the same time, the new friend (a boy) is now faster and thus better than the girl who helped him: yes, she has been selfless in the end, has transcended the earthboundness or silliness of her other wishes, but what is the pleasure in the game if they are still not equals? Nevertheless, the story encourages the listener to applaud Zhenya's generosity and offers a very clear lesson.

Both of Kataev's "folkloric" tales turn on an initial difficulty or loss, followed by an encounter with a donor who offers a magical object as assistance; both these elements are classic functions of wonder tales (as described in Propp's *Morphology of the Folktale*). Zhenya's continuing childish errors and indeed her continuing childhood instead of adolescent maturation, on the other hand, are realistic rather than folkloric elements in the tales.

Other Folkloric Works for Children

These three tales are far from the only Soviet literary works for children that incorporate folk elements: there are folk elements (Russian or otherwise) in a great deal of Soviet children's poetry (Agniia Barto, Kornei Chukovsky, Vera Inber, Samuil Marshak), and some outstanding Soviet cartoons and live action films were based on folk topics or on these very stories by Gaidar and Kataev. (The Soviet repertoire also includes some disappointing films that twist together folk elements in campy pastiches involving folktale characters, entirely mixing up the traditional plots.) One folk-inflected story that really feels authentic is "Малахитовая шкатулка" [The malachite box], one of a series of stories by Pavel Bazhov based on Ural miners' folklore and the Ural dialect of Russian, which was influenced by Bashkir. Despite its many realistic elements and strong protosocialist tendencies, emphasizing workers' experience and the folklore of Ural miners (an early proletarian body in Russia), the story really does read like a folktale; this is partly because the very believable folk language recalls the genre of the *skaz*, which continued to be popular in the Soviet period (for instance, the narrator always refers to the city "Sankt-Peterburg" as "Sam-Peterbukh"). The story's adult themes (mistresses, marriages through trickery), however, would discourage a teacher or parent from offering it to children, and the specific language and (again) adult themes make it more suitable for older children, if at all. The story has also been made into a cartoon, and it has an unusual happy end: the beautiful heroine escapes marriage to the wealthy and decadent mining heir, who looks like a hare. She joins the Lady of the Mountain whom she so resembles, becoming a sort of deity and embodiment of malachite rather than an ordinary wife. With regard to Soviet treatments of folklore, the charming 1947 film version of *Cinderella* (Zolushka) directed by Nadezhda Kosheverova and Mikhail Shapiro should be noted too. Its departures from the standard Western versions of Cinderella (in this case, the Perrault version of the fairy tale rather than that of the Grimms) are part of the pleasure, perhaps especially for Western viewers. The film's happy ending is a good socialist ending.

What is the impact of stories like these? Children who heard or read them remember them later and associate them with traditional folklore—the connection through plot similarity or verbal texture is vital enough that they sense it. Gaidar's and Kataev's stories remain an important element of Soviet children's literature and interesting reading for children, parents, and scholars of the topic.

Notes

1. Marina Tsvetaeva describes the competing Russian versus French techniques for finding lost objects in her autobiographical essay "The Devil."

2. Pushkin's folktales in verse, Ershov's "Little Humpbacked Horse" (1834), and (to a lesser extent) Aksakov's "Little Scarlet Flower" (1858) were more or less credited to the peasant women who had told them to the writers. Tolstoy's primers for peasant children made free with plots from both folklore and elite literature. Although these works were not part of Soviet children's literature, they continued to be read to, read by, and even memorized by Soviet children. By setting folktale plots to verse, Pushkin deeply impacted formal perceptions of folktales, which in the wild include only short stretches of verse. Soviet literary politics eventually agreed that Pushkin's tales, like Afanas'ev's collection published in the nineteenth century, did not need to be purged of their royalty: they belonged to an earlier

historical period, when feudal elements were not yet incompatible with correct socialist politics.

3. From the article "Skazki" by N. Sumtsov: «Интеллигенцию онѣ [сказки—SF] занимают лишь в художественной обработке (повести Л. Толстого, Квитки, Стороженка), а в простом виде обращаются в низших слоях населения, преимущественно среди старых и малых» [They (folktales—SF) interest the intelligentsia only in artistic adaptations (the tales of Lev Tolstoy, Kvitka-Osnov'ianenko, Aleksei Storozhenko), while in their simple form they are found in the lower classes of the population, primary among the elderly and the very young]. See Sumtsov, "Skazki," 163.

4. Putilova, "Aleksandra Annenskaia," 166.

5. For instance: "Я снова обращаю ваше внимание, товарищи, на тот факт, что наиболее глубокие и яркие, художественно совершенные типы героев созданы фольклором, устным творчеством трудового народа" [I once again direct your attention, comrades, to the fact that the deepest and most vivid, most artistically perfect types of heroes are created by folklore, the oral creativity of the laboring people]. Gor'kii, *Sovetskaia literatura*, 12; also available online, http://feb-web.ru/feb/litenc/encyclop/leb/leb-7751.htm?cmd=p&istext=1.

6. See, for example, Loiter, *Russkii detskii fol'klor i detskaia mifologiia*.

7. Propp, *Russian Folktale*, 63–64.

8. See the description of the special nature or folklore creativity by Bogatyrëv and Jakobson, "Folklore as a Special Form of Creativity," 32–46.

9. The obscene *Zavetnye skazki*, aimed specifically at adults and privately printed abroad in the nineteenth century, were apparently not reprinted in the Soviet period. "Folktales," like Evgenii Zamyatin's "Tales for Grown-up Children," similarly, did not enter the Soviet literary canon. An exception to the rule of broader attention to folklore "for adults" was the fame of *byliny* singers after the surviving tradition of epic songs in the Russian North was discovered in the nineteenth century. Frank J. Miller traces the decline of *byliny* in the Soviet period in *Folklore for Stalin*.

10. Tolstaya, "Loves Me, Loves Me Not," 3–16.

11. Propp, *Istoricheskie korni volshebnoi skazki*.

12. First published in the *Pionerskaya Pravda* as a standalone piece under the title «Сказка о Военной тайне, Мальчише-Кибальчише и его твердом слове», the tale was then incorporated into Gaidar's novella "Военная тайна" (1935).

13. Bukhina, "The Woman Question," 141–42. Here, she cites Larissa Rudova, "Maskulinnost' v sovetskoi i postsovetskoi detskoi literature: transformatsiia Timura (i ego komandy)," *Detskie chteniia* 6, no. 2 (2014): 85–101.

Baa-baa People's Sheep

On the Adventures of English Children's Poetry in Soviet Literature

Ainsley Morse and Dmitri Manin

English children's poetry—first and foremost, "folk" poetry and nursery rhymes—played a crucial role in the founding and subsequent development of Soviet children's literature. At the same time, domesticating translation practices and the wider context of Soviet aesthetic politics contributed to the development of an "imaginary Englishness," sustained in part through this poetry, which has enjoyed remarkable staying power in Soviet and post-Soviet Russian literary culture.[1]

The Soviet history of English children's poetry in Russian translation began with Kornei Chukovsky (1882–1969) and Samuil Marshak (1887–1964), the pioneers and first authorities on matters related to Soviet children's literature in the Soviet Union. Their translations of children's and folk poetry from the United Kingdom were foundational in their time and are still read to this day; in some ways, they also constituted a laboratory for the poets' own poetic innovations. Together, these translations and original works laid the groundwork for modern Russian-language children's poetry and have influenced generations of Russophone writers. But what exactly did Chukovsky and Marshak learn from reading and translating English (British) verse, primarily folk verse? And what has been the afterlife of their translations, and of other English-inflected work, in the Soviet Russian context? In this chapter we discuss Chukovsky's and Marshak's translation practices, as well as subsequent Soviet era translations and interpretations of English poetry—and the establishment of an imagined Englishness—in the later Soviet period.

Chukovsky and Marshak

While Chukovsky and Marshak were hardly the only writers translating English verse in the early Soviet period, their translations loom particularly large given their stature in the history of Soviet children's literature. Chukovsky's literary wanderings began in Edwardian England, where he lived between 1903 and 1904. Marshak, likewise, had some formative direct contact with life in the United Kingdom when he spent a year as a young man living at an experimental outdoor school in south Wales; he would later cite this as one of the factors setting him on the path toward a life spent in children's literature.[2] Both men experienced England in the peaceful pre-World War I "Gilded Age," a "leisurely time when women wore picture hats and did not vote, when the rich were not ashamed to live conspicuously, and the sun really never set on the British flag."[3] This image of well-heeled imperial Britain would remain remarkably intact despite its obvious points of conflict with Soviet values following the 1917 Revolution.

Russian literary history offers many instructive examples of artistic innovation and canon building through translation.[4] It makes sense that, in addition to satisfying contemporary calls for "literature of the people," the translation of anonymous folk rhymes offered fresh lexical, metrical, and cultural material that could be incorporated into the new genre of Soviet children's literature. Indeed, Marshak points out that some of the fairy tales he encountered in the context of one tradition would pop up in another one, rendering them even more "anonymous" and adaptable.[5]

Most of Chukovsky's and Marshak's translations from English for children were, unsurprisingly, subtitled "from English folk poetry." For both Chukovsky and Marshak, folk poetry (*narodnaia poeziia*) was a real golden ticket. They were sincerely interested in the poetic potential of its fresh, direct use of language; as Chukovsky wrote of Russian folk poetry, "All of Pushkin's fairy-tale poems were peasant poems in their vocabulary and diction. And if we recall that Krylov's fables . . . with unsurpassed perfection re-created folk speech, we will have every right to claim that the [Russian people] dictated the best children's books to its brilliant writers."[6] But part of this interest was, in the Soviet context, undoubtedly compounded by the "safe passage" afforded by anonymous works composed by "the people" and brimming with details to warm the Marxist heart: simple agricultural life, manual labor, cruel noblemen and kings. The blunt division of form and content typical of Soviet aesthetic criticism meant that unusual elements of form, including nonsense and *zaum'*, were permissible given the politically correct valence of folklore.[7] The "folk" label also assuaged concerns about unsavory foreign influences making their way to Soviet children through translated poetry.

Matushka Goose

Many of the best-known translations from English folk poetry come from the *Mother Goose* anthology. Chukovsky translated six Mother Goose rhymes (all dated 1922): "Six Little Mice Sat Down to Spin" (Kotausi i Mausi), "The Tailors and the Snail" (Khrabretsy), "There Was a Crooked Man" (Skriuchennaia pesnia), "Robin the Bobbin" (Barabek), "Gilly Silly Jarter" (Dzhenni), and "The Clever Hen" (Kuritsa). Marshak, for his part, translated several dozen Mother Goose poems over the many decades of his career, along with other folk rhymes and "adult" folk poetry, such as Scottish ballads.

Marshak and Chukovsky applied markedly different approaches to the same material. It's worthwhile to compare one of the Mother Goose rhymes they both translated, "The Tailors and the Snail":

Four and Twenty tailors
Went to kill a snail;
The best man among them
Durst not touch her tail;
She put out her horns
Like a little Kyloe cow.
Run, tailors, run, or
She'll kill you all e'en now.

Chukovsky and Marshak both titled their versions "Khrabretsy" (The brave ones) (Marshak, perhaps, simply follows Chukovsky, whose version predates his by thirty years). Notably, neither Chukovsky's nor Marshak's translation tried to make things sound particularly "English." Both translations are domesticating: except for the amusing snail/thread rhyme (his own addition), Marshak's poem is rather bland and devoid of local specificity; Chukovsky, meanwhile, essentially invents a Russian folk poem based on the original.

Chukovsky's version, from 1922, distinctly "Russianizes" the original through specific details like wolves, bears and a fence gate familiar from Russian folklore; still more noticeable are nonstandard verb forms typical of folkloric language—*ispugalisia*, *razbezhalisia*—without vowel reduction in the reflexive particle. Even the first line domesticates the poem, given the assumption that *our* (*nashi-to*) brave tailors must be Russian ones.

	Literal translation:
Наши-то портные	Our tailors are really
Храбрые какие:	Such brave ones:
«Не боимся мы зверей,	"We're not afraid of beasts
Ни волков, ни медведей!»	Not wolves or bears either!"
А как вышли за калитку	But when they went out past the gate
Да увидели улитку—	And saw a snail—
Испугалися,	They got scared-oh,
Разбежалися!	They ran off-oh!
Вот они какие,	That's how they are,
Храбрые портные![8]	The brave tailors!

Interestingly, even as he creates a poem that seems right at home in a Russian village, written in his trademark paeonic rhythm, Chukovsky reproduces something close to the original meter.[9] His rhyme scheme is meanwhile quite different, with overtly folkloric rhyming couplets. Marshak's version, which was first published in 1955, maintains the original's ABAB/CDCD rhyme scheme but introduces alternating iambic tetrameter and trimeter (different from the original but essentially a variant of the English ballad meter)[10]:

	Literal translation:
Однажды двадцать пять портных	Once twenty-five tailors
Вступили в бой с улиткой.	Went to battle with a snail.
В руках у каждого из них	Each of them held
Была иголка с ниткой!	A needle and thread!
Но еле ноги унесли,	But they barely got away
Спасаясь от врага,	Running from the enemy,
Когда завидели вдали	When they saw off in the distance
Улиткины рога.[11]	The snail's horns.

Characteristically, Marshak hews more closely to the original, making slight practical adjustments like twenty-five rather than twenty-four tailors. He seems to think the tailors' profession requires greater justification, arming them with needles for the battle. Curiously, both translators omit the simile comparing the snail to a cow, let alone to a location-specific breed like Kyloe, as well as the address to the tailors, preferring omniscient narration. The latter omission also eliminates the threatening "she'll kill you all e'en now," perhaps considered too frightening (even in its obvious irony).[12]

Borrowings and Inspirations

One of the appealing contributions of foreign-language poetry is the preponderance of interesting and unusual sound play. Both Marshak and Chukovsky reproduce the standard English place names and proper names from *Mother Goose* ("Dzhenni," "Charli," "Meri," "Dzhek"); these are arguably most memorable when incorporated into the sound framework of the Russian text, as in "Bessi Bell i Meri Grei / zhili v dome bez dverei" (cf. Bessy Bell and Mary Gray, / They were two bonny lasses; / etc.") or "Dzhonni Vetts—udalets!" ("Pretty John Watts / We are troubled with rats / etc."). Sound play in the original can inspire further play in the translation: consider Marshak's "Shaltai-Boltai" for "Humpty-Dumpty," which translates both the funny sounds and the verbal associations of the original. Chukovsky's translation of Robin the Bobbin's name expands it to "Robin-Bobin-Barabek." The nonsense word "Barabek" rhymes with *chelovek* (man), but its phonetic makeup (with its mix of plosive and rhotic consonants) evokes words like *baraban* (drum), which seems appropriate for the strong rhythmic drive of the poem.

Of course, the ultimate form of domestication (or the very freest form of translation) is to simply write one's own poems loosely based on the source. Chukovsky famously borrowed Hugh Lofting's *Dr. Doolittle* (1920) to make his original poems about "Doktor Aibolit";

at the same time, Aibolit is pointedly Russian, even if his parentage is foreign.[13] Chukovsky was a true cosmopolitan of a prerevolutionary vintage; he can insert a British doctor into the Russian woods (inhabited by familiar animals like bears, foxes, hares, and squirrels) and make this insertion seem entirely normal in a way that would be difficult for later Soviet authors who grew up behind the Iron Curtain without any direct experience of life elsewhere. Even in poems that allegedly take place entirely in Russia, Chukovsky's fondness for British models is further evident in his adoption of the colonizing mentality, most evident with African animals and locales eventually becoming central topoi of Soviet children's poetry through his work.

Although an imaginary Africa remained open territory for subsequent generations of Soviet children's writers, the valence of "foreignness" was shifting throughout the Soviet period. In works from the 1920s, the reader is easily carried along to distant locales in a cosmopolitan fashion. Chukovsky's Aibolit travels widely on his healing missions; Marshak's "Mister Twister" (Mister Tvister) shows a Soviet Union casually accustomed to visits by foreign tourists. And his *The Mail* (Pochta; 1927) follows the real children's writer Boris Zhitkov on travels around the globe.

An original work, *The Mail* incorporates small but peppy doses of foreignness from Germany, England, and Brazil. Notably, the poem also features unusual metrical variety, similar to that found in Marshak's *Mother Goose* translations. This evident influence suggests that the mixed meters associated with English folk verse may have taken on a more broadly "foreign" association, evoking foreignness in and of themselves.[14] The English interlude in *The Mail* introduces a stern London postman:

По Бобкин-Стрит, по Бобкин-Стрит	Down Bobkin Street, down Bobkin Street,
Шагает быстро мистер Смит	Go Mister Smith's stern steady feet.
В почтовой синей кепке,	His postman's cap is blue and slick
А сам он вроде щепки.	His body's skinny as a stick.
Идет в четырнадцатый дом,	He heads for number twenty-four
Стучит висячим молотком,	He raps the knocker on the door
И говорит сурово:	And pronounces, quite displeased:
—Для Мистера Житкова.[15]	"For Mister Zhitkov, if you please."[16]

In addition to the unusual foreign words, this passage neatly encapsulates the English "type," a collection of characteristics that surround the idea of Englishness as adopted by Soviet children's literature. The postman "Mr. Smith" is tall and thin, walks at a brisk clip, and speaks in a reserved, stern way. These features are particularly prominent in "archetypically English" characters, from Sherlock Holmes to Mary Poppins, but the paradigm arguably extends to include even the poor Mr. Hopp in Daniil Kharms's 1936 translation of Wilhelm Busch's "Plisch und Plum" (Plikh i Pliukh).

As Dmitri Manin notes, for someone who grew up in the USSR in the 1960s and '70s, this archetype of imaginary, or literary, "Englishness" featured a stable collection of characteristics: quintessentially English characters were tall and lanky, calm and imperturbable, possessing dry rationality, dry humor, and inimitable eccentricity.[17] Importantly, they were also champions of justice and protectors of the weak; for instance, Holmes exposes scheming criminals to help their innocent victims, and Mary Poppins helps the Banks children in dire situations. This quest for justice was perhaps sufficiently aligned with the overall Soviet narrative to compensate for these characters being decidedly noncollectivist loners and eccentrics (as well as citizens of an imperialist empire and, usually, representatives of the middle or upper class), although these "English" characteristics were also subject to shifts in Soviet cultural mores.[18] In any event, what unites "archetypically English" characters in the space of Soviet children's literature is their psychological makeup and, to a lesser degree, physique. These characters express emotions in an exaggeratedly reserved fashion.

A later example from the mid-1960s demonstrates the tenacity of this type. In Vadim Levin's poem "A Little-Known and Instructive Story About How Professor John Fooll Chatted with Professor Claude Booll, While the Latter From Time to Time Unexpectedly Appeared on the Surface of the River Ouse,"[19] the first professor is hurrying along when he notices his colleague, Claude Booll, drowning in the river:

—Сэр, видеть вас—большая честь!—	"To see you, sir, is quite an honor!"
профессор Фул воскликнул.	Professor Fooll exclaimed.
—Но что вы делаете здесь	"But tell me what you're doing here
в четвертый день каникул?	with holidays proclaimed?"

And the other professor offers an impartial and thoughtful analysis in response to this respectful inquiry:

Глотая мелкую волну,	Gulping water with a frown,
Буль отвечал:	Booll said, and tipped his hat:
—Сэр Джон, я думаю, что я тону,	"Sir John, it seems that I shall drown,
я в этом убежден.[20]	I'm quite convinced of that."[21]

Levin adheres to the same sprightly ballad-like meter we have seen in Marshak's translations from English and also reproduces the recognizable English type. Just as Americans in the Soviet popular imagination were most often white, tan, smiling, and usually wearing cowboy boots, English people were middle-class (if not nobles or monarchs) and very polite ("SIR"), indeed, to the point of absurdity.[22]

As the exchange between Fooll and Booll indicates, nonsense is another important element translated into Russian from English children's poetry. Both Chukovsky and Marshak comment on the importance of nonsense, although Chukovsky is more insistent on its inherent value, while Marshak only seems to find it charming.[23] Like almost everything in the early Soviet context, nonsense was potentially controversial; it could be perceived as a threat to rational thinking, the driving force behind dialectical materialism. Chukovsky is thus careful to point out that even nonsense rhymes like "eeny-meeny-miney-mo" were meaningful at one point; he gives the example of a child joyfully repeating the seemingly nonsensical word "ekikiki," which can actually be traced to "got this stick [from a guy]" (*eku piku diadia dal*).[24] Still, "the Celts have disappeared, their language has been forgotten, and if a few of the old sounds have been preserved in children's songs, it is precisely because these sounds have *lost their meaning* and become dear to children only in their free-standing melody."[25] English nursery rhymes seem to acknowledge children's natural love of nonsense, which Chukovsky finds in countless spontaneous "ekikiki" neologisms improvised by actual children but not in children's poetry written in Russia before 1917.

On top of its basic phonetic appeal, nonsense poetry in its English guise seems to be particularly appealing because of the apparent contradiction between buttoned-up, exceedingly polite, seemingly humorless and stiff people being pushed time and again into absurd, ridiculous situations. The popularity of limericks as a children's genre—Marshak and many later translators translated many classic ones by Edward Lear—speaks to the lasting appeal of this specifically English brand of nonsense on Russian soil.

Formal Matters

It is already clear that a certain set of ideas about English culture were distinctly present, if not directly influential, from the early days of Soviet children's literature. And it seems likely that some of these notions were quite literally brought home from the United Kingdom by Marshak and Chukovsky following their youthful visits there. To what extent, however, can we talk about direct formal influence? Do these early translations reproduce the form, as well as the sounds and realia, of the *Mother Goose* rhymes?

Chukovsky's "Khrabretsy" (The brave ones) showcases his tendency to "translate" *Mother Goose* rhymes into the forms of Russian folk poetry, in line with his programmatic advice to Soviet children's poets urging them to "learn from the people" (uchit'sia u naroda).[26] His verse tales are written in a similar idiosyncratic meter, which the author continued to employ consistently throughout his writing life, from his 1916 "Krokodil" to his 1956 "Bibigon." A hallmark of Chukovsky's style is paeonic rhythms, decidedly unrelated to anything in English poetry.

Marshak's metric approaches are more of a mixed bag. Let's begin with the widely known nursery rhyme "Baa, Baa, Black Sheep":

Baa, baa, black sheep,
Have you any wool?
Yes, sir, yes, sir
Three bags full;
One for my master,
And one for my dame,
And one for the little boy
Who lives down the lane.

For someone who knows nothing about the poem, the pattern of stresses (rhythm) is ambiguous in the beginning. For example, line 1 can be scanned with all four words stressed, or three, or only two. However, the second half of the poem establishes a pattern of two stresses per line, which can be extended back to the first half—and, of course, that's the way it is sung, as any Anglophone child knows. Meanwhile, the number of syllables varies from only three in line 4 to seven in line 7, and stress positions vary from line to line. In other words, it's an example of purely accentual verse.

The rhythm of Marshak's translation is quite different:

	Literal translation:
—Ты скажи, барашек наш,	"Tell us, our little sheep,
Сколько шерсти ты нам дашь?	How much wool will you give us?"
—Не стриги меня пока.	"Don't shear me yet.
Дам я шерсти три мешка:	I'll give you three bags of wool:
Один мешок—хозяину,	One bag to the master,
Другой мешок—хозяйке,	Another bag to the mistress,
А третий—детям маленьким	And the third to the little children
На тёплые фуфайки![27]	For warm jackets!"

The first four lines are in regular trochaic tetrameter with masculine endings and the rest in iambic trimeter with alternating feminine and dactylic endings. There are, however, correspondences. If we combine lines 3 and 4 of the original, they scan as trochaic tetrameter: "Yes, sir, yes, sir, three bags full." That's the pattern for Marshak's lines 1 through 4. On the other hand, lines 7 and 8 are very close to the iambic trimeter Marshak used in the second half of his translation. Inserting an auxiliary verb makes the meter perfect: "And one *is* for my dame, / And one *is* for the little boy"—the last line even has the dactylic ending of two final unstressed syllables, which is quite rare in English poetry but fairly common in Russian.

It is not that the rhythm of the English original can't work in Russian. In fact, traditional Russian epic songs (*bylina*) used an accentual meter, albeit with much longer lines. In the early twentieth century, accentual verse took off again in Russian literary poetry, as evidenced in work by poets Vladimir Mayakovsky and Ilya Selvinsky.[28] As a proof of concept, here is a nearly equirhythmical translation of "Baa, baa . . ." into Russian—it seems to work fine:

	Literal translation:
Бяша, бяша,	"Sheepy, sheepy,
Черные бока,	Black sides,
Сколько дашь нам шерсти?	How much wool will you give us?"
Три мешка!	"Three bags!
Хозяину—мешок,	A bag to the master,
Да хозяйке—мешок,	And a bag to the mistress,
А третий получит	While the third goes to
Соседский паренек.[29]	The little neighbor guy."

It is likely that Marshak's solution came from a desire to reproduce some of the rhythmic variability of the English original, without veering too far away from the common accentual-syllabic paradigm.

It's worth noting that approximating the meter of the original was not, apparently, a priority for Marshak. For example, "There Was a Crooked Man" is written in regular iambic trimeter, which would have posed no difficulties for Russophone readers. Marshak's translation, though, is in amphibrachic tetrameter with lines twice as long as the original, and in this space he fits many details that are not found in the original. For example, the crooked man lives *on a bridge* (which rhymes with *verst*, the Russian mile), the crooked coin is *dull*, the characters live in the crooked house *until it comes down*, and so on. Perhaps Marshak felt that many nursery rhymes were too ascetic and wanted to embellish them with vivid details; the aforementioned needles with which the poet arms the brave tailors in their attack on the snail is only one such detail.

Chukovsky's translation of "There Was a Crooked Man" shows a different approach to details but is similar in essence. He keeps the cheerful trochaic rhythm, though making it slightly roomier, expanding to four feet. He also makes the poem twice as long, riffing freely on the semantic mileposts of the original—the crooked man, path, house, mouse, and cat—beating the "crooked" theme to exhaustion (he leaves out the sixpence but adds a crooked river, crooked fir trees and crooked wolves). Much of it is driven by easy, common rhymes like *koshka/okoshko* and *elki* (*yolki*)/*volki*, the kind a small child can gleefully fill in as a playful adult reading aloud leaves space for them to complete the aural blanks. Unsurprisingly, Chukovsky's version enjoyed much greater popularity than Marshak's.

Marshak's tendency to hew more closely to the original did yield some notable triumphs, however. His fairly late translation of A. A. Milne's "The King's Breakfast" (Ballada o korolevskom buterbrode)[30] is a marvel of aural and rhythmic fidelity, even as it displays an admirable flexibility of diction:

The King asked	Король,
The Queen, and	Его величество,
The Queen asked	Просил ее величество,
The Dairymaid:	Чтобы ее величество
"Could we have some butter for	Спросила у молочницы:
The Royal slice of bread?"	Нельзя ль доставить масла
	На завтрак королю.

Marshak's translation is not a word-for-word match, but his play with the word for "Her/His Majesty" allows him to replicate the funny formal repetitions of the original as well as provide the delightful half rhyme *velichestvo/molochnitsy*. Even though Marshak's translation adds quite a few more syllables to each line, the resulting rhythm is very true to the original and propels the poem forward with such elegant force that the expansion seems entirely justified. It's also worth noting that Marshak's longer lines are partly an effect of layout; in the passage reproduced below, the Russian lines "Pridvornaia molochnitsa / Skazala: 'Vy podumaite!'" (eight syllables each) are twice as long as the English "The Dairymaid / Said, 'Fancy!'" (four and three syllables). But the subsequent Russian text begins compressing two lines into one, with "I tut zhe koroleve," encompassing two lines of the English ("And went to / Her Majesty"), and so on. Especially when read out loud, the poem and translation demonstrate a striking similarity of rhythm, rhyme, register, and tone.

The Dairymaid
Said, "Fancy!"
And went to
Her Majesty.
She curtsied to the Queen, and
She turned a little red:
"Excuse me,
Your Majesty,
For taking of
The liberty,
But marmalade is tasty, if
It's very
thickly
spread."

Придворная молочница
Сказала: "Вы подумайте!"
И тут же королеве
Представила доклад:
"Сто раз прошу прощения
За это предложение,
Но если вы намажете
На тонкий ломтик хлеба
Фруктовый мармелад,
Король, его величество,
Наверно, будет рад!"

English in Later Soviet Children's Poetry

Marshak continued translating for the rest of his life (he died in 1964, aged seventy-six); as mentioned, he translated "The King's Breakfast" in the mid-1950s. Many of his influential translations from English children's poetry were widely published only in his final years (late 1950s to 1960s); these include translations of other texts by Milne as well as works by Rudyard Kipling, Edward Lear, and Lewis Carroll. Indeed, we can point to a clearly delineated Soviet canon of English children's literature established fairly early in the Soviet period: in addition to folk poetry (*Mother Goose* etc.) and the writings of the aforementioned authors, it includes classic works of prose such as J. M. Barrie's *Peter Pan*, Arthur Conan Doyle's *Stories of Sherlock Holmes*, and Robert Louis Stevenson's *Treasure Island*.[31] It's no accident that most of these authors belong to the nineteenth century; as Ben Hellman notes of Soviet children's literature, "Foreign literature, which had been a vital part of children's reading in Russia right up until 1917, had gradually been reduced to a few old classics. Contact with living children's literature outside the Soviet Union was cut on the pretext that this literature was ideologically foreign or even harmful and, as such, incomprehensible to Soviet children."[32]

A second generation of Soviet children's writers both hewed to and perpetuated this canon, while simultaneously taking an ironically distanced approach to it. For instance, Boris Zakhoder (1918–2000) translated widely from English beginning in the 1950s, creating new versions of classic characters, including *Mary Poppins* (1968), *Peter Pan* (1971), *Alice in Wonderland* (1972), and *Winnie-the-Pooh* (1960).[33] At the same time, Zakhoder's Pooh has been widely recognized as demonstrating distinctly *Soviet* characteristics—a new level of domestication.[34] Still, later children's poets, such as Irina Tokmakova and Renata Mukha, continued to translate the same, primarily folkloric, English poems for young Soviet readers. Even more astonishingly, a 2018 edition of poems translated by Grigori Kruzhkov presents nearly the exact same canon, featuring translations from *Mother Goose Rhymes*, Charles Dickens, Edward Lear, Robert Louis Stevenson, Lewis Carroll, Rudyard Kipling, G. K. Chesterton, and A. A. Milne.[35]

Imagined, vaguely Victorian Englishness—exotic by way of the hypercivilized—seems to have been the most lasting effect of Russian translations of English children's poetry. Two generations after Chukovsky and Marshak, the children's poet Vadim Levin (b. 1933) took the process of domesticating translation to the next logical step by eliminating the original text altogether. In 1969, he published the collection *Glupaia loshad'* (The silly horse) prefaced with the following disclosure:

> Beginning in childhood, I dreamed of translating old-fashioned poems and stories from English. But I was too late: while I was still growing up, Kornei Chukovsky, S. Marshak, and Boris Zakhoder had already translated everything. I was very upset by this. So upset that if I had known any English words, I would have used them to compose my own new old-fashioned English folk ballads or songs. And I would have translated them right away into Russian before other translators

> could find out. And then I thought: "But why, really, should the English-to-Russian translator have to wait for someone to write the English originals in English? Why not do it the other way around: first do the PRE-original translation into Russian, and then let the Brits translate it back? And if they don't want to translate it, so much the worse for them: then we'll have more English poems and stories than the English themselves!"

The Silly Horse is, true to Levin's word, full to bursting with English-seeming poems and stories. Unlike Chukovsky's Russianizing translations or Marshak's more neutral approach, Levin's invented "English ballads" use pointedly non-Russian, "Englishesque" sounds to create an impression of exaggerated imaginary Englishness. For instance, one poem, "Uiki-Veki-Voki," evokes the sound play of "Wee Willie Winkie" (translated earlier by Irina Tokmakova as "Kroshka Villi-Vinki"), while being entirely made up and therefore not traceable to an authentic English original, which, if it existed, could be conceivably reconstituted as "Weeky-Wecky-Wockey." Levin's collection was tremendously popular in its time and was recently reissued under the title *Jim and Billy Once Upon a Time* (Zhili-byli Dzhim i Billi).[36]

Chukovsky's and Marshak's groundbreaking translations of English children's poetry, particularly the *Mother Goose Rhymes*, seem to have simultaneously established a standard and broken the mold. Although the Soviet children's canon, especially that of the later Soviet period, is rich in translated literature, the proportion of translated poetry in it is small.[37] Despite the ups and downs of their respective fates in public life, Marshak and Chukovsky were towering literary authorities for most of their remarkably long professional lives; their early advocacy of English children's poetry seems to have guaranteed its long-term legitimacy. Then, because of its staying power, English—and "English"—children's poems essentially became part of the canon of Russian classics: beloved, idealized, often imitated, occasionally subject to fond parody, and largely unhitched from any "real" historical context.

Notes

1. For a magisterial treatment of Englishness in Russian literature, imaginary and otherwise, see the monograph by Goodwin, *Translating England into Russian*. See especially her detailed discussion of the distinctive Russian image of "Englishness" (2–4, 7–19).

2. "Pis'mo M. Gor'komu (9 marta 1927)" in Marshak, *Sobranie sochinenii*, 8:94.

3. Hynes, *Edwardian Turn of Mind*, 4.

4. See, for instance, Baer, *Translation*, 1–16.

5. Marshak, *Sobranie sochinenii*, 2:566. Marshak makes this remark in correspondence in the late 1950s with A. N. Avakova, who was researching Marshak's work as a translator.

6. *Ot dvukh do piati* in Chukovskii, *Sobranie sochinenii*, 2:337. Chukovsky cites an essay by Marshak titled "O plokhikh i khoroshikh rifmakh" in *O pisatel'skom trude* (Moscow: Sovetskii pisatel', 1953), 122–23.

7. *Zaum'* (literally: beyond sense) was an abstract sound language invented by futurists Velimir Khlebnikov and Aleksei Kruchonykh.

8. Chukovskii, *Sobranie sochinenii*, 1:169.

9. Two lines in the first paeon, four lines in the third paeon (all dimeters); then, two lines with nominally a single stress but with a dactylic ending that somehow invites drawing out and stressing the last two syllables—"is-pu-GA . . . -LI . . . -SYA"—and, finally, a return to the first paeon of the beginning.

10. Marshak's *Mother Goose* translations consistently feature greater metrical variation than his original children's poems (of the 1920s). For instance, his well-known *Detki v kletke* (first published 1923) is mostly written in the standard "children's" meter (trochaic tetrameter), evident in scores of canonical children's poems. Marshak's *Mother Goose* translations substitute metrical variety for the largely unregulated meter of the English originals, which would have sounded sloppy in Russian.

11. Marshak, *Sobranie sochinenii*, 2:122.

12. The history of "difficult topics" or "adult themes" (e.g., death, violence, sex) in Soviet children's literature is quite variable. While books for very young readers (*doshkolnyi vozrast*) would generally avoid frightening themes, young adult literature could be quite frank in addressing difficult issues. See, for instance, comments by scholar Ilya Bernstein on Thaw era YA fiction: https://lenta.ru/articles/2015/10/17/bernstein/.

13. Further important examples of major adaptations include the sanitized versions of the Brothers Grimm fairy tales, Alexander Volkov's *Wizard of the Emerald City*, and so on. For the latter, see Erika Haber, *Oz Behind the Iron Curtain: Aleksandr Volkov and His Magic Land Series* (Jackson: University Press of Mississippi, 2017).

14. "Mister Tvister" (1933) is another metrical outlier, written in dactylic tetrameter that deviates periodically into trimeter or, with unstressed syllables omitted, into *dolnik*.

15. Marshak, *Pochta*, 6.

16. Translation by Ainsley Morse.

17. Compare the physiques of the actors who portray, respectively, Sherlock Holmes (Vasily Livanov in "Sherlok Kholms i Doktor Vatson," 1979) and Mary Poppins (Natalia Andreichenko in "Meri Poppins, do svidaniia," 1983) in very popular films of the period.

18. On eccentrics in Soviet children's literature, see Morse, *Word Play*, 94–98.

19. See Marshak's translation from *Mother Goose*: "Dzhon Bull, Dzhon Bull, Dzhon Bull" in Marshak, *Sobranie sochinenii*, 2:180.

20. Levin, *Zhili-byli Dzhim i Billi*, 10. Characteristically, Spartak Kalachev's illustrations in Levin's book equip everyone (even cats and dogs) with extremely tall top hats.

21. Translated by Ainsley Morse.

22. See also another poem in Levin's collection, "Odin anglichanin tolknul drugogo anglichanina," in which the two Englishmen rudely vie with one another over whose behavior is more correct.

23. For instance, Samuil Marshak remarks to Chukovsky, having sent him some new *Mother Goose* translations, "After all, you love these sweet ingenious silly things [*milye genial'nye gluposti*] as much as I do." "Pis'mo K. Chukovskomu (7 fevralia 1963)," quoted in Marshak, *Sobranie sochinenii*, 2:579.

24. Chukovskii, *Sobranie sochinenii*, 2:282.

25. Chukovskii, *Sobranie sochinenii*, 2:284.

26. Chukovskii, *Sobranie sochinenii*, 2:334. This phrase is the title of the section.

27. Marshak, *Sobranie sochinenii*, 2:104.

28. For example, see Mayakovsky's "Me" [Ia] (1913) or Selvinsky's "Henri de Rousseau" [Anri de Russo] (1935).

29. Translated by Dmitri Manin.

30. Goodwin, in *Translating England into Russian*, identifies this poem as one of the most translated, most published, and best-known works of English literature (77). See also her chapter on Milne (113–26).

31. The most-read Russian translation of *Treasure Island* was published in 1930 by Nikolai Chukovsky (under his father Kornei Chukovsky's editorship). Note the contrast between this Russian take on the American canon and the standard Soviet image of the United States (including associations with both the Wild West and racism/injustice/unbridled capitalism and consumerism). Also see Goodwin's list of the translated works most frequently published and thus representative of "Englishness": J. M. Barrie's *Peter and Wendy*, Kenneth Grahame's *The Wind in*

the Willows, Rudyard Kipling's *Puck* and *Rewards and Fairies*, A. A. Milne's *When We Were Very Young* and *Now We Are Six*, and P. L. Travers's *Mary Poppins* series (*Translating England into Russian*, 76–77).

32. Hellman, *Fairy Tales and True Stories*, 364.

33. The later 1960s and 1970s also saw a revival of translations of English folk songs in a new medium of "bard songs" (this genre corresponds roughly to "singer-songwriter"). The popular Nikitin duo and the singer Viktor Berkovsky both set translations of British folk songs and poems, including "The King's Breakfast," to their own music (usually guitar). See, for instance, http://www.bards.ru/archives/part.php?id=10167.

34. See the articles in Kukulin, Lipvetskii, and Maiofis, *Veselye chelovechki*; and Fishzon, "Queer Legacies of Late Socialism," 440–73.

35. See Kruzhkov, *Vyshel lev iz-za gory*. The only semicontemporary author on his list is Spike Mulligan. See also "Appendix 3" (186–90) in Goodwin, *Translating England into Russian* for a list of British texts translated during different periods (Soviet, pre- and post-).

36. Levin, *Zhili-byli Dzhim i Billi*. This book came out in the Merry Albion series [Veselyi Al'bion], which also features translations of work by Lewis Carroll and Hilaire Belloc as well as original work by Grigori Kruzhkov and Ekaterina Filippova.

37. The translated canon was largely composed of prose by Hans Christian Andersen, the Brothers Grimm, Astrid Lindgren, Selma Lagerlöf, etc. Poetry translated during the Soviet period usually came from Slavic languages (see translations of the Polish poets Jan Bzechwa and Julian Tuwim) as well as other languages of the countries of the former Soviet bloc.

Bibliography

Abramovich, H. "Detskii mir i voprosy obshchevennosti." *Detskie chteniia*, no. 1 (2020): 34–40.

"Anketa DCh." *Detskie chteniia* 14, no. 2 (2018): 6–22.

Attridge, Derek D. "An Enduring Form: The English Dolnik." In *Moving Words: Forms of English Poetry*, 147–87. Oxford: Oxford University Press, 2013.

Baer, Brian. *Translation and the Making of Modern Russian Literature*. New York: Bloomsbury, 2015.

Barto, A. *Sobranie sochinenii v 3-kh tomakh*. Vol. 1, *Stikhi i poemy*. Moscow: Detskaia literatura, 1970.

Barto, A. *Za tsvetami v zimnii les*. Moscow: Detskaia literatura, 1970.

Barto, A. *Prosto stikhi*. Moscow: Malysh, 1974.

Barto, A. *Zapiski detskogo poeta*. Moscow: Sovetskii pisatel', 1976.

Barto, A. *Sobranie sochinenii v 4-kh tomakh*. 4 vols. Moscow: Khudozhestvennaia literatura, 1981–84.

Bazhov, Pyotr. "The Malachite Casket." In *Politicizing Magic: An Anthology of Russian and Soviet Fairy Tales*, edited by Marina Balina, Helena Goscilo, and Mark Lipovetsky, 197–221. Evanston, IL: Northwestern University Press, 2005.

Begak, B. "Kornei Chukovskii." *Literaturnaia gazeta*, April 6, 1934.

Bernshtein, I. "Detskaia literatura sovetskoi epokhi: problemy kommentirovaniia." *Detskie chteniia* 14, no. 2 (2016): 105–24.

Bogatyrëv, Peter, and Roman Jakobson. "Folklore as a Special Form of Creativity," translated by Manfred Jacobson. In *The Prague School: Selected Writings, 1929–1946*, edited by Peter Steiner, 32–46. Austin: University of Texas Press, 1982.

Bolotin, S. "Knizhka, o kotoroi ne sporiat (A. Barto 'Bratishki')." *Detskaia i iunosheskaia literatura*, no. 8 (c. 1933): 16–18.

Bolotin, S. "Tvorchestvo S. Marshka." *Detskaia i iunosheskaia literatura*, no. 8 (1934): 1–5.

&&&Brik, O. "Ritm i sintaksis (materialy k izycheniiu stikhotvornoi rechi) [1927]." In *Formal'nyi metod: Antologiia russkogo modernizma*, edited by S. Oushakine, 823–52. Vol. 3. Moscow: Kabinetnyi uchenyi, 2016.

Brik, O. "Maiakovskii—detiam." *Knigi molodezhi*, no. 9 (1931): 50–52.

Bukhina, Olga. "The Woman Question in Russian Children's Literature." *Russian Studies in Literature* 55, nos. 3–4 (2019): 140–46.

Bukhshtab, B. "Poeziia Marshaka." *Kniga detiam*, no. 1 (1930): 16–20.

Bukhshtab, B. "Stikhi dlia detei." In *Detskaia literatura. Kriticheskii sbornik*, edited by A. V. Lunacharskii, 103–30. Moscow: Izd. khud. literatura, 1931.

Chukovskii, K. "Trinadtsat' zapovedei dlia detskikh poetov." *Kniga detiam*, no. 1 (1929): 3–19.

Chukovskii, K. *Dnevnik 1901–1969*. Vol. 1, *Dnevnik 1901–1929*. Moscow: OLMA-PRESS, 2003.

Chukovskii, K. *Sobranie sochinenii v 15 tomakh*. 15 vols. Moscow: Agentstvo FTM, 2012.

Chumachenko, A. "Veselaia knizhka." Review of *Mal'chik naoborot*, by A. Barto, with drawings and cover design by M. Kanevskii and L. Detgiz. *Detskaia i iunosheskaia literatura*, no. 6 (1934): 17–18.

Darr, Yael. *The Nation and the Child: Nation Building in Hebrew Children's Literature, 1930–1970*. Amsterdam: John Benjamins, 2018.

Domanskii, Iu. "Povrezhdennaia igrushka v stikhotvornykh tsiklakh dlia samykh malen'kikh Agnii Barto i Ivana Nekhody." *Detskie chteniia*, no. 2. (2012): 179–96.

Dragunskii, V. *Rytsari i eshche 60 istorii. Sobranie Deniskinykh rasskazov*. With commentary by Olga Mikhailova, Denis Dragunskii, and Il'ia Bernshtein. Moscow: Izdatel'skii proekt "A i B," 2017.

Dudko, E. "Problemy vospriiatiia tekstov detskoi literatury mladshimi shkol'nikami." In *Aktual'nye aspekty formirovaniia i sovershenstvovaniia lingvometodicheskoi kompetentsii uchitelia 1–4 klassov sovremennoi shkoly*, 125–30. Saint Petersburg: Saga, 2007.

Eikhenbaum, B. "Vmesto 'rezkoi kritiki' [1927]." In *Moi Vremennik: Slovesnost'. Nauka. Kritika. Smes'*, 167–71. Ekaterinburg–M.: Kabinetnyi uchenyi, 2020.

Eikhenbaum, B. "Poet-zhurnalist [1928]." In *Formal'nyi metod: Antologiia russkogo modernizma*, edited by S. Oushakine, 579–81. Vol. 2. Moscow: Kabinetnyi uchenyi, 2016.

Fishzon, Anna. "The Queer Legacies of Late Socialism, or What Cheburashka and Gary Shteyngart Have in Common." In *A Companion to Soviet Children's Literature and Film*, edited by Olga Voronina, 440–73. Leiden: Brill, 2020.

Frost, Robert. *The Poetry of Robert Frost: The Collected Poems, Complete and Unabridged*. New York: Henry Holt, 1979.

Gaidar, Arkadii. *Skazka o Voennoi taine, O Mal'chishe-Kibal'chishe i ego tverdom slove*. With illustrations by V. M. Konashevich. Moscow-Leningrad: OGIZ Molodaia gvardiia, 1933.

Gelfond, M. *Trilogiia A. Ia. Brushteina "Doroga ukhodit v dal'": Kommentarii*. Moscow: Izdatel'skii proekt "A i B," 2017.

Golovin, V. "Zhurnal 'Galchonok' (1911–1913) kak literaturnyi eksperiment." *Detskie chteniia*, no. 2 (2014): 23–27.

Goncharova, D. "Istoriia izdaniia skazochnoi povesti A. M. Volkova 'Volshebnik izumrudnogo goroda' (1939–2012)." PhD diss. Saint Petersburg State Institute of Culture, 2014.

Goodwin, Elena. *Translating England into Russian: The Politics of Children's Literature in the Soviet Union and Modern Russia*. London: Bloomsbury, 2020.

Gor'kii, M. *Sovetskaia literatura, doklad na I Vsesiuznom c"ezde sovetskikh pisatelei*. Moscow: 1935. http://feb-web.ru/feb/litenc/encyclop/leb/leb-7751.htm?cmd=p&istext=1.

Greene, Roland, Stephen Cushman, Clare Cavanagh, et al., eds. *The Princeton Encyclopedia of Poetry and Poetics*. 4th ed. Princeton, NJ: Princeton University Press, 2012.

Grinberg, A. Review of *Skazka o Pete tolstom rebenke i o Sime, kotoryi tonkii*, by V. Maiakovskii, with illustrations by N. Kupreianov. *Pechat' i revoliutsiia* 8 (December 1925): 256–58.

Hellman, Ben. *Fairy Tales and True Stories: The History of Russian Literature for Children and Young People, 1574–2010*. Leiden: Brill, 2013.

Hynes, Samuel. *The Edwardian Turn of Mind*. Princeton, NJ: Princeton University Press, 1968.

Iakobson, R. "Noveishaia russkaia poeziia. Nabrosok pervyi [1921]." In *Formal'nyi metod: Antologiia russkogo modernizma*, edited by S. Oushakine, 246–304. Vol. 3. Moscow: Kabinetnyi uchenyi, 2016.h

Jones, Roy G., *Language and Prosody of the Russian Folk Epic*. Berlin: De Gruyter Mouton, 1972.

Kal'm, D. "'Kuda nos ego vedet . . .' [Protiv khaltury v detskoi literature. O stikhakh K. Chukovskogo i S. Marshaka]." *Literaturnaia gazeta*, December 16, 1929.

Keats, John. *The Complete Poems of John Keats*. Hertfordshire, UK: Wordsworth Poetry Library, 1994.

Kon, L. Review of *Devochka chumazaia*, by A. Barto and P. Barto, with illustrations by B. Redlikh. *Detskaia i iunosheskaia literatura*, no. 12 (1931): 12–13.

Kostiukhina, M. *Igrushka v detskoi literature*. Saint Petersburg: Aleteiia, 2008.

Koval', Iu. *Prikliucheniia Vasi Kurolesova; Promakh grazhdanina Loshakova; Piat' pokhishchennykh monakhov: trilogiia o Vase Kurolesove s kommentariami Olega Lekmanova, Romana Leibova i Il'i Bernshteina*. Moscow: Izdatel'skii proekt "A i B," 2016.

Kruzhkov, G. *Vyshel lev iz-za gory*. With illustrations by Tat'iana Kormer. Moscow: Albus korvus, 2018.

Kukulin, I., M. Lipvetskii, and M. Maiofis, eds. *Veselye chelovechki: kul'turnye geroi sovetskogo detstva*. Moscow: Novoe literaturnoe obozrenie, 2008.

Kümmerling-Meibauer, Bettina, and Anja Müller, eds. *Canon Constitution and Canon Change in Children's Literature*. New York: Routledge, 2017.

Levin, V. *Zhili-byli Dzhim i Billi*. Moscow: Nigma, 2019.

Litovskaia, M. "Kliuchevye teksti russkoi literaturoi v programme prepodavaniia russkogo iazyka kak nerodnogo." *Filologiia i kul'tura* 28, no. 2 (2012): 68–71.

Liubarskaia, A., and L. Chukovskaia. "O klassikakh i ikh kommentatorakh." *Literaturnyi kritik*, no. 2 (1940): 165–72.

Loiter, S. M. *Russkii detskii fol'klor i detskaia mifologiia: Issledovaniia i teksty*. Petrozavodsk: KGPU, 2001.

Loshchilov, I. "Detskaia poema Petra Potemkina 'Vova Skvozniakov v derevne.'" *Detskie chteniia*, no. 2 (2012): 146–56.

Maiakovskii, V. V. *Sobranie sochinenii v vos'mi tomakh*. 8 vols. Moscow: Pravda, 1968.

Malishevskii, M. *Metronika. Kratkoe izlozhenie osnov metricheskoi mezhduiazykovoi stikhologii (po lektsiiam, chitannym v 1921–1925 gg. v Vysshem Literaturno-khudozhestvennom Institute Valeriia Briusova, v Moskovskom institute Deklamatsii prof. V. K. Serezhnikova i v Literaturnoi Studii pri Vserossiiskom Soiuze Poetov)*. Moscow: Izdanie avtora, 1925.

Malishevskii, M. "O poezii dlia detei." *Detskaia literatura*, no. 2 (1935): 7–15.

Mallan, K. "Empathy: Narrative Empathy and Children's literature." In *(Re)imagining the World: Children's Literature's Responses to Changing Time*, edited by Yan Wu, Kerry Mallan, and Roderick McGillis, 106–14. Berlin: Springer, 2013.

Markasova, E. "'Deniskiny rasskazy' i 'Dva kapitana': znaem li my, o chem ne znaiut deti?" *Detskie chteniia* 5, no. 1 (2014): 138–47.

Marshak, S. *Pochta*. Leningrad: Raduga, 1927.

Marshak, S. "Literatura—detiam." *Literaturnyi sovremennik*, no. 12 (1933): 180–203.

Marshak, S. "Sodoklad o detskoi literature." In *Pervyi Vsesoiuznyi c"ezd sovetskikh pisatelei. Stenograficheskii otchet*, 20–37. Moscow: Izd. khud. literatura, 1934.

Marshak, S. *Sobranie sochinenii v vos'mi tomakh*. 8 vols. Moscow: Khudozhestvennaia literatura, 1972.

Miller, Frank J. *Folklore for Stalin: Russian Folklore and Pseudofolklore of the Stalin Era*. Armonk, NY: M. E. Sharpe, 1990.

Morse, Ainsley. *Word Play: Experimental Poetry and Soviet Children's Literature*. Evanston, IL: Northwestern University Press, 2021.

Motiashov, I. *Zhizn' i tvorchestvo Agnii Barto*. Moscow: Detskaia literatura, 1989.

Nekrasov, A. *Prikliucheniia kapitana Vrungelia*. With commentary by Il'ia Bernshteina, Roman Leibov, and Oleg Lekmanov. Moscow: Izdatel'skii proekt "A i B," 2017.

Nikolajeva, Maria. "Guilt, Empathy and the Ethical Potential of Children's Literature." *Barnbroken* 35, no. 1 (2012). http://doi.org/10.14811/clr.v35i0.139.

Nussbaum, M. *Cultivating Humanity: A Classical Defense of Reform in Liberal Education*. Cambridge, MA: Harvard University Press, 1997.

Oushakine, S. "My v gorod izumrudnyi idem dorogoi trudnoi. Malen'kie radosti veselykh chelovekov." In *Veselye chelovechki. Kul'turnye geroi sovetskogo detstva. Sbnornik statei*, edited by I. Kukulin, M. Lipovetsky, and M. Maiofis. Moscow: Novoe literaturnoe obozrenie, 2008.

Oushakine, S., ed. *Formal'nyi metod: Antologiia russkogo modernizma*. 3 vols. Moscow: Kabinetnyi uchenyi, 2016.

Petrovskii, M. *Kniga nashego detstva*. Saint Petersburg: Ivan Limbach Publishers, 2006.

Pokrovskaia, A. "Maiakovskii kak detskii pisatel." *Kniga detiam*, nos. 2/3 (1930): 16–20.

Propp, Vladimir. *Morphology of the Folktale*. Translated by Lawrence Scott. Edited by Louis Wagner. 2nd ed. Austin: University of Texas Press, 1968.

Propp, Vladimir. *Istoricheskie korni volshebnoi skazki*. Moscow: Labirint, 2005.

Propp, Vladimir. *The Russian Folktale*. Translated by Sibelan Forrester. Detroit: Wayne State University Press, 2012.

Pushkin, A. S. *Izbrannye sochineniia*. Edited by S. S. Averintsev and I. M. Makarov. Moscow: Academia, 1992.

Putilova, Evgeniia, ed. *Chetyre veka russkoi poezii detiam*, vol. 2. Saint Petersburg: Liki Rossii, 2013.

Putilova, Evgeniia. "Aleksandra Annenskaia, Mariia Pozharova, and Lidiia Charskaia." Translated by Nora S. Favorov. In *Women Writers and Girl Characters in Russian Children's Reading*, edited by Olga Bukhina. Special issue, *Russian Studies in Literature* 55, nos. 3–4 (2019): 156–69.

Razova, V. *Fol'klornye istoki sovetskoi poezii dlia detei*. Leningrad: Prosveshchenie, 1976.

Sergienko, I. "Detskie knigi—'plokhie' i 'khoroshie': diskussii kritikov 1890–1920-kh gg." *Detskie chteniia*, no. 1 (2020): 11–19.

Shklovskii, V. "O poezii i zaumnom iazyke [1925]." In *Formal'nyi metod: Antologiia russkogo modernizma*, edited by S. Oushakine, 131–46. Vol. 1. Moscow: Kabinetnyi uchenyi, 2016.

Shklovskii, V. "Revoliutsiia i front [1921]." In *Sobranie sochinenii*. Vol. 1, *Revoliutsiia*, edited by I. Kalinin, 25–149. Moscow: Novoe literaturnoe obozrenie, 2018.

Smirnova, V. "A. Barto." *Kniga detiam*, nos. 2–3 (1930): 20–22.

Sumtsov, N. "Skazki." In *Entsiklopedicheskii slovar' Brokgausa-Efrona*, vol. 30, 163. Saint Petersburg: I. A. Èfron, 1890–1907.

Tikheeva, E. "O spetsial'nykh sbornikakh stikhotvorenii dlia detei." *Vospitanie i obuchenie*, no. 8 (1898): 289–316.

Timofeev, L. "O stikhakh dlia detei." *Detskaia i iunosheskaia literatura*, no. 12 (1931): 10–12.

Tolstaya, Tatyana N. "Loves Me, Loves Me Not." In *On the Golden Porch*, translated by Antonina W. Bouis, 3–16. New York: Vintage International/Random House, 1989.

Tsvetaeva, Marina. "The Devil." In *A Captive Spirit: Selected Prose*, translated and edited by J. Marin King, 188–203. Ann Arbor, MI: Ardis, 1980.

Tynianov, Iu. *Problema stikhotvornogo iazyka*. Leningrad: Akademiia, 1924.

Tynianov, Iu. "Promezhutok (1924)." In *Formal'nyi metod: Antologiia russkogo modernizma*, edited by S. Oushakine, 632–62. Vol. 1. Moscow: Kabinetnyi uchenyi, 2016.

Tynianov, Iu. *Permanent Evolution: Selected Essays on Literature, Theory and Film*. Translated and edited by Ainsley Morse and Philip Redko. Boston: Academic Studies Press, 2019.

Vaage, Margrethe Bruun. "Fiction Film and the Varieties of Empathic Engagement." *Midwest Studies in Philosophy* 34 (2010): 158–79.

Venuti, Lawrence. *The Translator's Invisibility*. New York: Routledge, 1995.

Wordsworth, William. *Wordsworth: Poems*. Edited by Peter Washington. New York: Knopf Doubleday, 2014.

Zharkov, I. *Tekhnologiia redaktsionno-izdatel'skogo dela: Konspekt lektsii*. Moscow: MGUP Publishers, 2002.

Žirmunskij, V. M. *Introduction to Metrics: The Theory of Verse*. Berlin: De Gruyter, 2016.

Biographies

Editors

Anna Krushelnitskaya is a translator, writer, and language teacher. Her articles on foreign language pedagogy appeared in *Modern English Teacher* and *ESL Magazine*, as well as in scholarly journals in Russia. Anna's translations have been featured in *Poems from the Front* (Moscow, 2020); *Disbelief: 100 Russian Anti-War Poems* (Smokestack, 2022), and a variety of print and online magazines and literary journals. Her most recent work includes *Dislocation: An Anthology of Poetic Response to Russia's War in Ukraine* (as translator and coeditor; Three String Books/Slavica, Indiana University, 2024) and *Babi Yar and Other Poems by Ilya Ehrenburg* (Smokestack, 2024). Anna's favorite project is the 2019 *Cold War Casual*, a bilingual collection of transcribed oral testimony translated from Russian into English and from English into Russian, which delves into the effect of the events and the government propaganda of the Cold War era on regular citizens of countries on both sides of the Iron Curtain.

Dmitri Manin is a physicist, programmer, and award-winning translator of poetry both from and into Russian. His translations of J. M. Hopkins, Robert Burns, Leconte de Lisle, Stéphane Mallarmé, and others from French and English to Russian are published in multiple book collections. Poetry translations into English have been published in various journals, in Maria Stepanova's book *Voice*

Over (Columbia University Press, 2021), and in *Disbelief: 100 Russian Anti-War Poems* (Smokestack, 2022). His translations of Ted Hughes and Allen Ginsberg into Russian were published as separate books (Jaromír Hladík Press, Saint Petersburg, 2020; Podpisnye Izdania, Saint Petersburg, 2021). Dmitri's most recent book-length translation is *Columns* by Nikolai Zabolotsky, translated into English (Arc Publications, 2023).

Contributors

Marina Balina is Isaac Funk Professor Emerita and professor of Russian studies at Illinois Wesleyan University. Her scholarship focuses on historical and theoretical aspects of twentieth-century Russian children's literature. She is the author of numerous articles on this subject and editor and coeditor of twelve volumes, among them, *Politicizing Magic: Russian and Soviet Fairy Tales* (2005); *Russian Children's Literature and Culture* (2008), *Petrified Utopia: Happiness Soviet Style* (2009); *To Kill Charskaia: Politics and Aesthetics in Soviet Children's Literature of the 1920s and 1930s* (2014), *Hans Christian Andersen and Russia* (University of Southern Denmark Press, 2020), and *The Pedagogy of Images: Depicting Communism for Children* (University of Toronto Press, 2021). Her most recent edited volume is *Historical and Cultural Transformations of Russian Childhood* (Routledge, 2023).

Sibelan Forrester is Susan W. Lippincott Professor of Modern and Classical Languages and Russian at Swarthmore College in Pennsylvania, where she teaches language, literature, and the theory and practice of translation. Most of her scholarly writing concerns poetry, folklore, and women's and gender studies, as well as issues of translation of folklore. She has translated fiction, folktales, poetry, and scholarly prose from Croatian, Russian, Serbian, and Ukrainian, including Vladimir Propp's *Russian Folktale* (Wayne State University Press, 2012).

Svetlana Maslinskaya, PhD, is a research fellow at the Research Center for Russian Children's Literature at the Institute of Russian Literature (Pushkinsky Dom) of the Russian Academy of Sciences in Saint Petersburg and the co–editor-in-chief of the journal *Children's Readings: Studies in Children's Literature* (Detskie Chtenia). She is at the helm of the creation of the Corpus of Criticism of Russian Children's Literature, a full-text database of literary criticism written in the 1840s–1940s. Svetlana has an extensive publishing record in literary theory, sociology of children's reading, normative poetics, history of the criticism of children's literature, cultural recycling of the Soviet past, corpus-based methods, and history of Russian-German contacts in the field of literature for children. She has been awarded a fellowship from the PAUSE program at the Center for Contemporary Slavic Studies at the University Grenoble Alpes for the project Children and War: the Past in the Present (2023–24).

Ainsley Morse teaches in the Literature Department at the University of California, San Diego and translates from Russian, Ukrainian, and the languages of former Yugoslavia. Her research focuses on the literature and culture of the postwar Soviet period, particularly unofficial or "underground" poetry, as well as the avant-garde, children's literature, and contemporary poetry. Recent publications include the monograph *Word Play: Experimental Poetry and Soviet Children's Literature* (Northwestern University Press, 2021), as well as translated work by unofficial writers and children's poets Igor Kholin (*Kholin 66: Diaries and Poems*, Ugly Duckling Press, 2017) and Vsevolod Nekrasov (*I Live I See*, Ugly Duckling Press, 2013), both with Bela Shayevich. She is currently working on the startlingly innovative Soviet era unofficial poet Yan Satunovsky, who also wrote poetry for children.

Serguei Alex. Oushakine is professor of anthropology and Slavic languages and literatures at Princeton University. His interests include early Soviet visual culture, formalist and constructivist movements, and late Soviet debates about aesthetics and space. Recently, he published a two-volume Russian-language edition of crucial texts of such Soviet practitioners of the formal method as Boris Arvatov, Aleksei Gastev, Moisei Ginzburg, Lev Kuleshov, and Evgeny Polivanov (*The Formal Method: An Anthology of Russian Modernism*. Vol. 4: Functions [Ekaterinburg-Moscow: Kabinetnyi uchenyi, 2023]). In 2022, together with Marina Balina, he coedited the volume *The Pedagogy of Images: Depicting Communism for Children* (Toronto: University of Toronto Press, 2022), which received the best edited volume award from the American Association of Teachers of Slavic and Eastern European Languages in 2024.

Soviet Writers

Zinaida Nikolaevna Aleksandrova (1907–1983) was a Soviet children's poet and translator. Her first two books of adult poetry were published in 1928; subsequently, she wrote only for children. Many of her poems were set to music, and her 1935 poem about New Year's trees (the Soviet equivalent of the Christmas trees) became an immensely popular song. Aleksandrova worked as a children's literature editor in magazines and translated children's poetry from Ukrainian, Georgian, Lithuanian, and Yiddish.

Agniia L'vovna Barto (1901–1981) was a children's poet and writer, screenwriter, and radio host. She began her work life as a ballet dancer but was soon encouraged to dedicate her efforts to writing poetry by the People's Commissar of Education Anatoly Lunacharsky, who happened to attend a recital at which Barto read her original work. Barto was a war correspondent during WWII and in the 1960s hosted a radio show uniting children with their families who were separated during the war. A lifelong promoter of writing for children, Barto served on the jury for the Hans Christian Andersen Award for many years. Her poetry for the very young has had immense publishing success through the Soviet years and beyond.

Valentin Dmitrievich Berestov (1928–1998) was a prolific writer of poetry and prose for children, ethnographer, archaeologist, and Pushkin scholar. He translated children's texts from French, Romanian, and Moldovan. As a poet, Berestov benefited from Kornei Chukovsky's mentorship early in his literary career; his memoirs reflect on his experiences with Chukovsky, Samuil Marshak, Anna Akhmatova, Aleksey Tolstoy, and other prominent Soviet authors.

Elena Aleksandrovna Blaginina (1903–1989) was a children's poet; translator of children's literature from Ukrainian, Moldovan, and Yiddish; scriptwriter for radio plays and animated films; and editor of the major Soviet children's magazines *Murzilka* and *Zateinik.*

Kornei Ivanovich Chukovsky (born Nikolai Korneichukov, 1888–1969) was a children's poet, journalist, essayist, literary critic, scholar, theorist, and translator. The most published children's writer in Russia to date, Chukovsky influenced the Soviet children's writing and literary scene immensely. Throughout Chukovsky's career, his work fell in and out of favor with the Communist Party. His idea that writing for children should be informed by the creative way children use language stood the test of time and was implemented in the work of many Soviet children's authors.

Viktor Yuzefovich Dragunsky (1913–1972) was born in New York in a Jewish Russian family who moved back to Russia in 1914. He worked as a theater and movie actor, did a brief stint in the circus, and wrote short stories, plays, sketches, and songs. He is best known for the series *Deniska Stories*, which he started writing in 1959, a cycle of short stories with a common narrator, a boy named Denis Korablev. His two adult novels, *He Fell on the Grass* (On upal na travu, 1961) and *Today and Daily* (Segodnya i ezhednevno, 1964), also remain in print.

Arkady Petrovich Gaidar (born Golikov, 1904–1941) was a children's writer, newspaper reporter, and Red Army commander. His military career was as full and eventful as his literary career. Gaidar's most famous work, *Timur and His Squad* (Timur i ego komanda, 1940), gave rise to the so-called Timur movement within the Soviet Young Pioneer organization—a movement of youth volunteerism. Gaidar was killed in combat by Nazi troops while serving as a machine gunner.

Valentin Petrovich Kataev (1897–1986) was a prominent Soviet writer and playwright. He wrote for adults, young adults, and children. Between 1923 and 1986 he authored over two dozen novels, multiple plays, screenplays, and short stories. His adventure novel for young adults *Lonely White Sail* (Beleet parus odinokij, 1936), based on the events of his own childhood, was reprinted in the USSR over one hundred times and translated into thirty-four languages.

Daniil Ivanovich Kharms (1905–1942), born Daniil Yuvachev, was a key figure of Russian modernism, the cofounder, along with N. Zabolotsky, of the avant-garde OBERIU group. His absurdist short prose, plays, and poetry were never published during his life; they were preserved by friends and rediscovered in the 1960s. Kharms's poetry for children, published in the 1930s in magazines, had enduring success. In 1941 he was accused of belonging to "a group of anti-Soviet children's writers" and arrested. To avoid execution, he simulated insanity. In 1942 Kharms died of starvation in the besieged Leningrad.

Samuil Yakovlevich Marshak (1887–1964) was a prominent Russian-Soviet poet, translator, and children's writer. He studied philosophy at the University of London from 1912 to 1914. At that time he published his first translations of English poetry. In the 1920s Marshak published his first children's poems and headed the children's literature branch of the state publishing house Gosizdat. In this capacity he encouraged many talented writers to write for children. He continued advocating children's literature even without occupying official positions after the publishing organization he created was dismantled in 1937. Besides children's poetry, Marshak is renowned for his memorable translations of English poetry, notably Mother Goose rhymes. He was also a lyrical poet in his own right.

Vladimir Mayakovsky (1893–1930) was a Russian poet, playwright, artist, and actor. A prominent figure in the Russian futurist movement and a signature voice of the early Soviet poetic avant-garde, Mayakovsky wrote mostly for adults. His children's poems, modest in number but not in quality, were written with the same originality and verve as the poet's "serious" work; several such poems enjoyed enduring popularity with the Soviet readership and were included in the secondary school curricula for decades. Mayakovsky's relationship with the Soviet government and censorship was tumultuous throughout his writing career. In 1930, the poet died by suicide.

Sergei Vladimirovich Mikhalkov (1913–2009) was an author of children's books, satirical verse, plays, and the lyrics for both the Soviet and the Russian state anthems. The poem that launched his fame, "Uncle Styopa" (Diadia Stiopa, 1935), remains popular to this day. Recipient of numerous government awards, Mikhalkov was chairman of the Union of Writers of the Republic of Russia between 1970 and 1990. Having enjoyed official success and influence on the literary establishment during the Soviet years, after the fall of the Soviet Union Mikhalkov was criticized by many for following the party line unwaveringly.

L. Panteleev was the pen name of the children's writer Aleksey Ivanovich Eremeev (1908–1987). One of the street kids of the Russian

Revolution, Eremeev spent his teen years in vagrancy, menial labor, and petty crime before being sent to a reformatory boarding school for incorrigible youth. In coauthorship with Grigorii Belykh, in 1925 the very young Eremeev wrote a novella about the school titled *The Republic of ShKID* (Respublika SHKID). The novella was republished dozens of times during the Soviet years, translated into many languages, and made into a popular film. Panteleev-Eremeev was saved from political arrest in the 1930s by Chukovsky and Marshak, who rated his work highly.

Index

www.ingramcontent.com/pod-product-compliance
Lightning Source LLC
Chambersburg PA
CBHW020749240525
27078CB00006B/26

* 9 7 8 1 4 9 6 8 5 6 5 8 6 *